I0653575

ANDROCIDE

INTEL 1, BOOK 5

EREC STEBBINS

TWICE PI PRESS

"STEBBINS IS THE MASTER OF THE THINKING READER'S TECHNO-THRILLER."
—Internet Review of Books

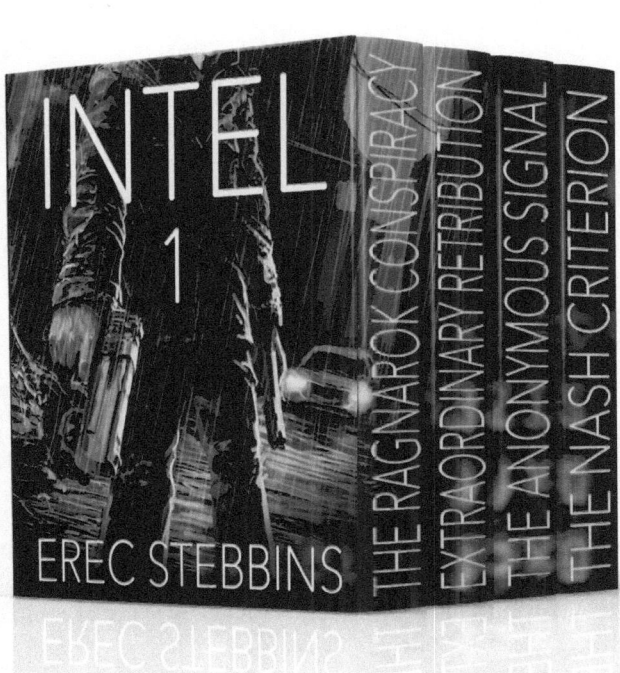

Four Action Packed Political Thrillers. Three End of the World Scenarios. Two Unusual Love Stories. One Secretive Intelligence Branch.

The *Intel 1* Global Thrillers

"A MONSTER NEW TALENT IN THE THRILLER GENRE."
—Allan Leverone,
author of *Final Vector*

Only one thing is impossible for God: to find any sense in any copyright law on the planet.
—Mark Twain

This book is a work of fiction. Any references to historical events, real people, or real locales are used fictitiously. Other names, characters, places, and incidents are the product of the author's imagination, and any resemblance to actual events or locales or persons, living or dead, is entirely coincidental.

Androcide. Copyright © 2017 Erec Stebbins

Published 2017 by Twice Pi Press, erecstebbinsbooks.com

Unless otherwise indicated, all materials on these pages are copyrighted by Erec Stebbins. All rights reserved. No part of these pages, either text or image, may be used for any purpose other than personal use. Therefore, reproduction, modification, storage in a retrieval system or retransmission, in any form or by any means, electronic, mechanical or otherwise, for reasons other than personal use, is strictly prohibited without prior written permission.

Cover design by Erec Stebbins © 2017.

Paperback ISBN-13: 978-1-942360-32-2

Kindle ISBN-13: 978-1-942360-31-5

ePUB ISNB-13: 978-1-942360-33-9

Content Guide

This novel contains depictions and references to events and ideas that some will find disturbing, including, but not limited to, sexual assault, battery, murder, imprisonment, captivity, severe illness, pain, fear, medical procedures, torture, and war. There is also profanity and strong language, the challenging of some accepted norms, and the questioning of different kinds of authority, religious and secular. It could be rated PG-13, R, or even NC-17 in the Motion Picture Association of America film rating system. The book also contains religion, partisan politics, Oxford commas, and an unnecessary number of tpyos and, grammer misteaks. Readers are asked to prepare accordingly.

To Mark Ward

for fond high school memories
of vigorously debating
the relative merits of the genders

also for taking turns
drop-kicking copies of "Great Expectations"
into our lockers after class

"An evolutionary arms race is a struggle between competing sets of co-evolving genes that develop adaptations and counter-adaptations against each other. The co-evolving gene sets may be in different species, as between a predator species and its prey, or a parasite and its host. One example of an evolutionary arms race is in the conflict between the sexes. Sexual antagonism represents an evolutionary conflict at a single or multiple [genetic] locus that contribute differentially to male and female fitness."

— FROM THE MARCH 11, 2013 WIKIPEDIA ENTRIES
"EVOLUTIONARY ARMS RACE" AND "SEXUAL CONFLICT"

PART I

DEAD AND GONE

"*And Dinah the daughter of Leah, which she bare unto Jacob, went out to see the daughters of the land. And when Shechem the son of Hamor the Hivite, prince of the country, saw her, he took her, and lay with her, and defiled her. The sons of Jacob came out of the field when they heard it: and the men were grieved, and they were very wroth. They took each man his sword, and came upon the city boldly, and slew all the males.*"

—Genesis 34

1

REAPER

The whore by the 7-Eleven was perfect.

Too perfect, really. Wetback cunt with long black hair. Seventeen maybe unless that bucket of makeup lied. Goddamned chest nearly exploded out of the tight, zippered jumpsuit. And those round hips—he felt them under him while she screamed for help.

Jack Reaper stepped out of the shadows. His hand reached casually into his pocket and he palmed the bills. Sadly, there would be no cries for help tonight.

Can't believe I have to pay these sluts now.

He sure hated the bitches. They deserved what came to them. But after Attica, well, he wasn't going back behind bars. He had to be smarter. He'd do her hard, get a little fun in. *Maybe.* But not too much. And he'd fucking pay.

The whore sized him up across the street. Arcing her exposed breasts in his direction, she sauntered toward him, wisps of fog escaping her painted lips. He felt an erection stirring, and a burning need to grasp her throat, see the fear in her eyes.

Too perfect.

"You wanna party tonight?"

Where did they get these lines? Whore school? Reaper licked his lips.

She smiled. It was fake. "I know a nice place, 'round the corner." She slid her arm around his waist and rested her hand in his pocket, long fingernails clawing near his groin. His breath deepened. "We'll have a *good* time."

The pair left the wan radiance of the streetlights and walked along shuttered businesses. Reaper watched drug pushers distributing product and other whores dancing for their Johns on the street. They approached the doorway of a neglected apartment building, the señorita pressing her hips against his. He scowled. It burned that she toyed with his body, flicked switches, pushed buttons and what could he do?

Fucking pay.

Once, I took what I wanted. I had control.

He taught them lessons. Lessons they never, ever forgot.

You get what you can now.

She led him into the building, stopping at a ground-floor room. A filthy window overlooked trash and grime in the alley. The little whore rocked her hips side-to-side and smiled, her tongue to her teeth. Well, he would at least drive this car.

"Unzip that. To your waist."

She dragged the zipper out and down. He throbbed, aroused from the teeth pops, her magnificent breasts a revelation erupting from the tight fabric. His mouth was a desert.

"On your knees," he managed.

She complied, placing her purse on the ground beside her as she sank to the stained carpet. Gazing up at him, her big brown eyes and fake eyelashes and bounding breasts, it was utterly, completely, *perfect.*

He remembered the blade.

You still took it tonight, Jack.

He approached. "Eat me, *bitch.* Slowly."

She grinned and unfastened his belt, dropping his pants to his ankles. She gasped as he yanked her hair back.

I'm in charge.

Reaper pulled harder. Like some little girl, she grabbed her purse for security. Her muscles tensed. The fear response blossoming. A thrill raced through him.

It's going to be a beautiful night.

A sharp sting burned his left thigh.

"Fuck!"

He grabbed the leg, squeezing with both hands to stop the pain. The whore leapt backward, a miniaturized jet injector in her hand.

What the hell?

He gaped at the muscle, an inflamed circle bursting from his skin.

"You bitch!" *I'm really going to hurt this one.* He stepped toward her.

And fell on his face. His leg didn't respond. He tried to stand, but couldn't coordinate his motions. He slurred his words.

"What'd th'you gib me?"

She backed further away. Icy rivers ran up his leg through his body. He couldn't speak. His hands twitched, refusing commands, muscles paralyzed. Only his thoughts flowed.

Time dragged and stumbled. Words spilled toward him in waves.

"Gave him the shot. Yeah, just like you said. He ain't moved. Yeah, he's breathin'. No, still awake. He's lookin' right at me. Now? Sure, yeah, unlocked."

What's happening!

Her zipper ripped across his consciousness. Heels clicked as she strutted past him, the disturbed air burning hypersensitive skin, the rough carpet on his face an agony. Drool dripped from his mouth, his leg a fire of a thousand needle pricks. His body twitched, helpless and alone.

The door opened with a sound of heavy steps. Powerful hands lifted and tossed him on the bed like a postal package. *My eyes are screwy.* He couldn't focus on the blurred giant. *Her pimp?* What was this thug doing here?

He couldn't ask. Couldn't bargain for his life or whatever they wanted from him. He gazed helplessly as the shadowed figure removed several tools from a dark and heavy bag.

Oh, God.

But the tools weren't for him. The shape turned to the window and disengaged the two sashes, a foul breeze pouring into the room. A long zippering sound tore at his ears. His vision darkened, a synthetic surface raked over his face. Hands shoved his body into a bag face first. A tightening of fabric and pressure on his back muffled the sounds outside.

He was entombed.

Reaper screamed, but nothing came out. He strained madly, but nothing moved. The strong arms raised him off the bed and onto a solid shoulder. He struggled to breathe. A dizzying lurch, and he was airborne, falling several feet to a painful landing on the trash in the alley.

Someone landed heavily to his left, and jerked him upward like a sack of cement. An angry hinge screamed as doors opened, and the giant flung him to a hard floor. The doors slammed, rending the air.

I'm going to die.

His bones tingled, a fateful certainty like poison inside. How did this happen? His life crashed so terribly off course? He didn't deserve this!

Someone help me!

A final hour remained for Jack Reaper to contemplate these mysteries. The vehicle coughed and started, lurching forward, disappearing into the night.

2

TEHRAN

Sara Houston adjusted the folds of her custom abaya in the
failing light of the Tehran sunset. *Custom* was a kind word.
Her garment simulated Arabic tradition, not Persian, but
function did not follow form. Combat ready, she'd designed it to give
her complete flexibility and range of motion, the fabric a microfiber
turning most bladed weapons. Hidden pockets lined the interior,
storing unladylike contents.

Like my Browning.

A matching black niqab left only her eyes in view. The formal
Islamic garb singled her out as conservative in comparison to more
modern women sporting a manteau and stylish roosaris. But it
covered her face and skin, hiding her Western appearance, and the
full black fabric suggested men gaze elsewhere. For the new INTEL 1,
secrecy was everything in this mission.

So what else is new?

Deception and concealment—Houston was well acquainted.
Years of running, a fugitive plastered at the top of the FBI's most
wanted list, framed for terrorism and the assassination of the former
VP of the United States, she was hardened to it all.

At least the Iranians are clueless.

Her lover and partner in crime, the former priest Francisco Lopez, walked beside her more openly in a rundown corner of Tehran's District 14. The ramshackle neighborhood was isolated, a long walk from the metro lines.

And state security cameras.

His muscular frame strode through streets built by rural immigrants decades ago, his salt-and-pepper beard thick and trimmed like a cleric's. His Central American bronze stood out even in former Persia, giving him the look of an Imam who worked construction on the side.

A pace in front shuffled Nader Zaringhalam, a bookish and bent computer scientist who was their contact in Tehran. Zaringhalam worked in the covert Revolutionary Guards Corps with an elite collection of hackers who had targeted US banks, water, and power companies. A double agent, he sympathized with the West. Following a long tradition of Iranian revolutionaries, he resisted the ruling powers, funneling information to the CIA and other agencies. Rumors tagged him as instrumental to the Israeli malware destroying hundreds of uranium centrifuges a decade ago.

INTEL 1 now had access to such assets. After the crippling cyber-attack of the Anonymous hacker Fawkes, after his revelation of a global ruling conspiracy INTEL 1 helped bring down, President Elaine York had taken control of the decimated FBI special division. York buried INTEL 1 and resurrected it, creating a shadow corps of some of the most unorthodox and talented counterterrorism and espionage agents in the United States government.

And not of the government.

Houston smiled. What a scandal! Hunted terrorists, part of covert intelligence forces, answering only to the President. Their newfound power thrilled her. Lopez, the priest in him remaining despite excommunication, mulled the darker undercurrents. But Houston saw the *possibilities*. She liked to get things done.

"This city never sleeps," mumbled Lopez as vehicles raced along larger roadways surrounding them. "And it's like every block is a new socio-economic sector."

Zaringhalam chuckled. "Yes, we have Rolexes and minarets. Drug addicts, prostitutes, and the Holy Qur'an. Much oil, no rivers, deserts, and a giant sea." He gestured around them. "This neighborhood used to be called Beseem-E Najafabad. Peasants moved in for decades in the millions. Then the state decided it was too much and moved them out. Capitalism and socialism. Mountains and plateaus. Shahs, revolutions, rich and poor, building up and earthquakes taking down." He shook his head. "Only a fool tries to understand Tehran."

Headlights flashed as a van rounded the corner in front of them. Zaringhalam held up his hand.

"Wait," he hissed, ushering them off the road to the broken sidewalk. The lights bounced and flickered through the windows of parked cars. "Something isn't right."

"What?" asked Houston.

Zaringhalam eyed the approaching vehicle. "I'm not sure. See the antenna they tried to hide in the back? Not civilian."

Wonderful.

Houston ground her teeth behind the abaya. Her eyes, blue turned dark brown from colored contacts, squinted down the road.

We're almost at the safe house!

Zaringhalam read her thoughts. "We shouldn't go to the house. Not until this clears."

"We need to contact New York," she said. "We've got the arms dealer. He's one step from Mirnateghi herself!" Houston removed her Browning from an inside holster.

Lopez put his hand on her shoulder, his firm grip calming.

"We're blind here, Sara. Isolated. Let's be careful before we start shooting. Okay, hothead?"

The corner of her mouth ticked upward. She holstered the weapon.

"Yes," whispered Zaringhalam, eyes darting between them and the approaching van. "Walk normally. Make no eye contact. They'll pass by. We're nobody."

They walked forward, the headlights blinding, Houston glancing away not to lose her night vision.

The van did not pass by.

"I don't understand," said Zaringhalam as the vehicle stopped, the brake engaged. Two men stepped out of the van in worn police uniforms. He dropped his voice. "Scammers? At night, here?"

The men shouted in Farsi. Zaringhalam took the lead, walking toward them as Houston and Lopez hung back. Lopez spoke under his breath.

"Like we practiced. I'm a foreign imam, you're my wife, Nader is our host. We say nothing. If we're engaged, we sterilize."

She nodded, adrenaline flowing like cold water to her extremities, sweat building under the fabric even in the chilly October night. The pitch of the discussion rose, Zaringhalam gesturing with both hands. The policemen stared over his head at them.

"Okay, Francisco, the needle's in the red. Get ready."

The men brushed aside the computer scientist and marched toward Lopez and Houston. They reached down.

For weapons.

Instinct took over and two raptors pounced. Their aggression startled the policemen, weapons kicked from their hands and clattering against the stones. Then the chaos flared in earnest.

These can fight.

Professionals, not random Iranian beat cops. The initial surprise gone, Houston's target thrust her into a defensive mode, the man's size and strength hard to counter. The move to disarm weakened her position, and her attacker pressed the opening. Vibrations from a battle beside her resonated, thundering impacts suggesting someone getting the upper hand.

She fought for leverage, using her greater speed and flexibility, never giving the man a hard target.

Just one slip, friend. I'll give you a surprise.

Bone cracked, splintered with an expulsion of air to her right. She ignored it, ignored the fate of her lover, and maintained her focus. But her foe wavered, his eyes darting toward the sound.

Slip.

Her Ka-Bar knife whistled as it cut the air. The man raised an arm in defense, but too late. The knife slashed his throat, major arteries severed. Blood burst from the wound and he fell to one knee, hands at his neck, gasping wide-eyed at a red river flowing down his arm. He collapsed. Houston tasted copper in the mist around them.

Francisco.

Her chest tightened as she spun in the direction of Lopez. She lowered the knife, exhaling. He clenched and unclenched his fist, knuckles red and inflamed. At his feet lay the unconscious form of the other policeman. His lower jaw jutted to the side of his face.

Zaringhalam sprinted over, his eyes wide. He stared at them and the downed forms of the policemen. Kneeling, he examined the bodies, avoiding the growing pool of blood.

"Mary and Gabriel. God be praised. Your reputations are deserved." He grimaced. "This one's dead, of course. I think the other's jaw is shattered." He stared at Lopez. "You're a strong man." Turning back to the bodies, he ripped the tattered shirts open, revealing body armor underneath. "Shākh dar āvordam!"

Houston knelt beside him, the energy rushing from her body, her voice hoarse. "Okay, Nader, who the hell are these guys? And don't tell me police."

"No, not the police. But they were meant to seem so. The black kevlar underneath, their skills? They're NOPO." He looked back to her and held her gaze. "You've been compromised."

Lopez's bass reverberated over them. "The NOPO?"

"Yes!" he said. "Iranian special forces. Under the NAJA, the special police units. Such men do not patrol run-down sections of Tehran. They are put on missions. They take out serious targets. Someone powerful is looking for you."

Houston stood and wiped the knife on the dead man's shirt. "*Mirnateghi.* Iran's her home base. She's like an octopus here, tentacles in everything."

Zaringhalam also stood, clouds of air puffing between clattering teeth. "So you say. Until tonight, I admit I was skeptical. But if she can control the NOPO, well, she controls Iran."

Lopez grunted. "She used to control a lot more than that."

The Iranian glanced up and down the street. "You were wise to stop them without shots fired, but we'll have to move to the other safe house. This neighborhood's dead to us now."

Houston pointed. "Pull them inside, off the streets. Tie this one up. Search them and the van for GPS devices. We move to the second location, tonight. But first we contact New York." She glanced toward the idling van. "Things are moving fast now."

3

MAN PARTS

Detective Tyrell Sacker pulled the dilapidated Crown Victoria to the curb and sighed.

Yellow police tape was all over the picturesque Upper East Side brownstones near Central Park. The flashing lights of police cruisers blinded him in the early morning darkness. Pedestrians strained from a distance to glimpse the victim. Flashes burst from windows above, the upper crust Manhattanites documenting the grisly scene at their doorstep. They were likely tweeting them already.

And pictures of the lanky black dude at the crime scene.

He'd lost count of how many times he'd been mistaken for a suspect.

Sacker grunted as he eased his six-two frame out of the vehicle. At thirty-five, telltale signs of age simmered in his muscles and joints. Two tours in Iraq, shrapnel wound in the thigh—easier to take at twenty-two than yesterday's workout. His younger self took a personal oath to stay in fighting shape, not understanding the future struggle.

The alcohol isn't helping either, Tyrell.

He grabbed his vintage Bailey Ice Topper hat, slammed the door, and marched toward a man and woman shivering beside the tape.

Two assistant detectives he'd been saddled with. Their young faces were slack, blank. Shock flooded them. The pair weren't ready for this.

I need to take charge.

He fitted the hat on his head.

"Morning, detectives," he said, rubbing a hand across his smooth cheek. Sacker rarely needed to shave. "Got the boss up early for this one. What we got?"

The two parted, saying nothing, allowing him to peer into the center of yellow tape. The crime scene did enough talking for the both of them, a corpse staged as some spectacle of street art. Naked, propped up on stacked bags of garbage, the victim rested with his back to the plastic, arms and legs splayed out. Bruises covered the skin from head to foot like some purple Rorschach test. But it was what was absent that focused all attention.

"Well, *damn*." Sacker turned a piercing gaze toward his trainees.

"Garbage crew found him this morning," said one of the pale detectives.

"Just like this?"

The young man swallowed, his blond hair disheveled in the wind. "Ah, yeah. No clothes. Someone beat the shit out of him. And, um, missing, well, you know, his man-parts."

Sacker grimaced. *I need a smoke.* "Man-parts? New jargon they teaching you at the Academy?"

The pair squirmed.

He turned to the male. "Snyder, right?"

"Ah, yes, sir." The kid looked seasick. Nothing like a mutilated body at dawn to get those stomach juices churning.

Sacker eyed the woman. "Hill?"

"Kathy Hill, sir, yes."

"Ladner wants me to babysit you two. That's fine. But my case load isn't always pretty. You're gonna see scenes like this," he gestured toward the body. "You gotta be able to handle it or ask for a transfer. Am I clear?"

They nodded.

"So let's game up. Act professional. Look on the hard things." He smiled. "You're detectives for some reason, I assume. I trust your reports will have real medical terms?"

"Yes, sir," they stammered.

"Right." Sacker shook his head, donning nitrile gloves and coverings over his shoes. He exhaled soft clouds in the late October chill, stepping over the tape. "Where's the medical examiner?"

"En route," said Hill

"This one's sure gonna break the monotony." He crouched beside the body, his head inches from the gaping wound in the groin. "There's no blood here at all," he muttered, voice monotone. "Those man-parts—yeah, looks like they were cut out." The young detectives struggled to look at the body. "Damn. Just a big, clotted hole."

Snyder coughed. "No clothes. No ID. Nothing."

"Witnesses?"

"Just the garbage guys," Hill noted. Her voice was a mellow alto. "Body was already here. No one saw the murder."

"Hmmm." Sacker straightened. "John Doe was certainly murdered, but not here. Our killer worked the poor bastard over something fierce. Mutilated him, then dumped him in one of the wealthiest neighborhoods in Manhattan."

Hill frowned. "Doesn't make any sense, sir. Why leave the body where it's certain to be found?"

Sacker removed his gloves and stepped outside the tape. First day of criminology 101. He needed another coffee.

And a damn smoke.

"Why indeed? Unless you *want* it to be found."

Hill furrowed her brows. "Why would the killer want the body to be found?"

"Look at the crime scene. Most bodies I've come across are in dumpsters, the river, or some alley or room where the perp capped them. Crimes of passion are in random places. More careful killers use the trash. Usually, that's as clever and far as they go. Here the vic's propped like porn. Sure to catch everyone's attention, especially considering the whole missing man-parts problem."

"Killer's making a statement," said Hill. Snyder glanced at Sacker for confirmation.

"Why else? Our killer wanted the world to know about this murder and to utterly humiliate the victim. One *nasty* piece of work. I'm going to call the captain."

The two young detectives scribbled on notepads as Sacker took out his cell phone. He tapped the screen to make a call. A reddening sky signaled the creeping dawn.

"Yeah, Ladner? It's Sacker at the 92nd crime scene." Sacker listened. "Yes, Sutherland's on his way. He's going to have a party over this one—not that his ass ever saw a party." Again the silence. "Right. Well, it's pretty bad. I'd say *newsworthy*, if you get my drift. Every damn phone's popping like Christmas. It'll be everywhere in a few hours."

Several police vehicles approached and additional officers got out. With them strutted a tall, older man in a lab coat, issuing orders with gentle points of his finger.

Sacker frowned. "Speak of the devil. Sutherland's here. Full *I'm-a-doc* mode. I'll let you go and brief you at the precinct." Sacker kept the phone to his ear as the tall doctor approached him. "What do I think?" He smirked at Hill and Snyder, who hung on his words. "No disrespect intended to any man-parts involved, looks like we've got a Bobbitt on 'roids."

He winced at the first arrival of news vans.

4

GONE TO THE OFFICE

Grace Gone pulled the rusting Jetta to a stop in front of a run-down block in Astoria, Queens. The car sputtered to silence and she glanced at the bent sign beside the curb: two-hour parking after nine. She'd leave it the whole day. The traffic cops only cared about Manhattan and other upscale locations. Where the fines got paid. Where you wouldn't get shot.

She yanked down the sun visor and slid the mirror cover to the side. *Passable.* Bordering on graduate student, but it would have to do. Besides, without clients, what did it matter?

She flipped the visor up, gathering the river of black from her shoulders and stuffing it into a ponytail. She tried to suppress the afterimage. Vietnamese features on a Chinese girl brought school-yard bullying in Shanghai. Photos populated with pale skin and a mouth forever assuming a pensive pout. Gone couldn't abide makeup, but longed for more color. She always looked tired.

You always are tired, Gracie.

The hinges groaned harshly as she opened the door. Her left leg stumbled and jerked from the floorboard and she swung the right leg over, planting it on the ground as an anchor. Falling was losing its novelty, and she wasn't going to test the strength of the poor limb again. Grasping the steering wheel in her right hand and the seat in her left, she propelled herself upward.

Steady as she goes.

Gone closed the door, prayed for a desperate car thief to pass by, and limped from the curb to her office door. A bright, new sign hung over the entrance, black lettering on a white background: *Gone Investigating, LLC.*

She unlocked the door and eased her way inside. Spartan, musty, and creaky, her office was the converted husk of a family home. She intended the living room for the queue of clients yet to queue up. Dust covered the secondhand furniture—a couch and several chairs —and danced in the morning sunbeams. To the right a door led to her office. Half a century ago, it had served as a kitchen for a growing family. Stripped of counters and ovens, only the sealed gas lines revealed its origins. A small, round carpet of faded brown rested in front of an uneven IKEA desk of matching color.

Damn, this is getting harder.

She limped toward the desk, dropped her keys and mail, and fell backward into the chair with a sigh. Nine in the morning and she wanted to quit. Forget the fatigue, she couldn't get a serious client or case into her docket. She knew starting out was hard. She knew it took time to build a reputation. But, she had to start *somewhere.*

And how much time do I really have?

A few missing animal cases. A jealous pervert who wanted to hire her to take porn videos of his ex-girlfriend and her new lover. And her personal favorite, a man who offered real money to investigate whether he'd been cloned by aliens and determine if he occupied his original body.

"Should have taken the clone case," she muttered, tilting the chair forward and flipping through her mail. He at least had *money.*

Instead, she had bills. Licensing fees for her agency. Oh, God, *rent.* Car insurance she stopped paying. *Not much use for that anymore, I think.* Coupons (she set those to the side). Three or four useless catalogs. One by one she chucked them into the garbage.

She stopped, staring at one aimed at upwardly mobile yuppies who swarmed Brooklyn and Queens. The clothes were fashionable yet reserved, attractive without being provocative, practical rather than designed to uncomfortably accentuate body parts. She liked this catalog. She liked the clothes. She wanted to order several boxes of things.

Gone tossed it into the garbage and opened her laptop.

A series of scripts ran, automatically culling news and headlines from the online universe. World politics, gang violence, another political sex scandal. She flew through the articles of interest at lightspeed. Using a pirated version of a speed-reading app, she focused on one region of the screen. Words flashed like machine-gun rounds. Her eyes stationary, she halved the time to process printed language. Gone digested four thousand words a minute, racing through the day's information in a fraction of the time anyone else would spend.

Her hand hovered over the trackpad as she stared forward. A large and bold headline covered the top of the screen: *Junk Male: Killer Castrates Manhattan Man.* Grisly photos accompanied the New York Post article. Gone leaned back in the chair and pressed her fingertips together.

I need this.

A game-changer. Something loud and big and interesting to plant her flag as a PI. She didn't care if it came from the garish Post or sounded like a bad summer slasher. *Something big.* Something forever linked to her name, ensuring a steady flood of customers for her unique services. Of course, the point was to bring in other interesting cases, spread her reputation, increase her earnings.

Survive.

Her head crashed on the desk. *I'll never change.* One dream after another to secure her now dwindling future. A desperate need to contribute, to make up for so much, to use her talents for good.

Meanwhile, I'm about to be evicted.

Gone's soft brown eyes peered above the fold of her arm and stared at the Post headline.

"So who's the lucky bastard who got this case?"

5

PHONE HOME

Two forms slumped in a closet, one pale as snow, a large and clotted gash across his throat, the front of his shirt a giant blood stain. The other bound with wire, his shattered jaw roped with one of Houston's black hijabs.

It was a good thing the safe house was close. That it was late. That no one was out this hour in this section of Tehran. Somehow, they managed to drag the bodies in without being seen.

We were just lucky.

Lopez closed the prayer book and made the sign of the cross over the body of the dead man.

"In your mercy and love, blot out the sins he has committed through human weakness. In this world he has died; let him live with you forever. We ask this through Christ our Lord."

Zaringhalam whispered to Lopez. "He's a Muslim. Why do you offer this Christian prayer?"

Lopez stared at the corpse. "For souls to find peace. I don't give a damn how they find it." He shut the door of the closet and turned to the center of the cramped apartment. "He's not going to wake for a few hours. Besides, I don't think he'll be saying much."

"Ceremony's over," barked Houston. "Peace sounds nice, but I'm not ready for my soul to find it quite yet."

She crouched in the middle of the dim space, windows covered with cloth, a large and battered briefcase opened to reveal computer hardware. A collapsible antenna rose a foot and a half over the table, connected to the case. For Lopez, the sight of her lithe form sprawled over the computer in a cramped hideout triggered memories of a dark time. Hotel rooms and car chases. Murder and mayhem. A time of desperate flight from authorities trying to stop a toxic CIA program run out of control. A time when he'd lost everything—his brother, his church, his former life. *When I found her.*

Zaringhalam slapped him on the shoulder. The Iranian hacker gesticulated, talking shop.

"You're using a nested series of key encryptions to connect. Fairly secure, but not perfect. We've broken a lot of them at the IRGC."

"We do use better, but that's Angel's department," Houston answered. "She set up all the secret digital handshakes that fly through the satellites."

"Who is Angel?" He glanced at Lopez. "You? You're called Gabriel."

"I'm not Angel. I'm just called one." His face was expressionless.

Houston smiled as she typed. "Who *is* Angel? Now that's a question. Right now, let's just say she's a contingency."

"Angel, Gabriel, and Mary." The Iranian shook his head. "I never knew dealing with the Great Satan would be such a religious experience. Anyway, for your short communications bursts, your setup is secure enough."

"There's also organic," said Houston.

"Organic?"

She frowned at him. "Pretty standard for field work in hostile settings. Memorized lists of phrases and facts. Code words to indicate status. Nothing proceeds until the right combination of codes and status information is received on both ends. Code lists are rotated."

He grinned. "Paranoid. I like it."

"Life and secret saving."

Lopez leaned over, staring at the screen. "And about to be implemented." *Knock, knock, New York.*

The monitor flickered and transitioned from random static to a man's rasterized face.

"Captain Overlord, sir," said Houston, smirking.

Former FBI agent John Savas frowned on the screen. "Seriously, Mary, Angel is bad enough with that crap. I assume Gabriel is there."

"All the hosts of heaven."

Zaringhalam whispered to Lopez. "Is this the *organic* part?"

Lopez held his finger to his lips.

"Protocol, Fearless Leader," said Houston.

Savas cursed under his breath. "It's all Greek to me. Broadcasting from under a very rotten apple. I'm with the Jew and the gun-toting CEO. We're flatlined."

"Mary and Gabriel here. FUBAR as normal. Area 51, but we're hoping ET."

Savas nodded. "All clear. So, you've got company."

"Boss's CIA liaison," said Houston.

"CEO's following this closely in the command room," said Savas.

"Tell her he's been instrumental."

An older woman's voice sounded over the video feed.

"I read you loud and clear," said President York. "He came highly recommended. Do you trust him?"

"We have to. We're deaf and mute here. He's our only way to Mirnateghi."

Savas cut in. "We *know* she's there. We lost good agents tracking her after Bilderberg. She's the last, and a hell of a chase she's given us. That monster leaves a trail of bodies wherever she goes."

Lopez spoke up. "Her operation is more extensive than we thought. She controls elite forces in the country. Her reach is to the highest levels in the Iranian government."

A younger woman's face appeared on the monitor.

"Jew speaking," said Rebecca Cohen. "Your contact okay with that?" Her eyes burned.

Zaringhalam stared at the intense face and swallowed. "Yes, of course. We have Jews in Iran, you know."

"Less than ten thousand left," said Cohen. "Your oil money went to Hezbollah. They blew up a bus killing half my extended family."

He swallowed again. "Not my oil money."

"But moving on. You said you've got an in."

Houston spoke. "Reza Zanjani."

"The executive?" asked Cohen.

"He's much more," said Zaringhalam, eyes darting to the screen. "His black market business includes arms and tech smuggling. Spyware. State secrets."

York spoke. "There were rumors. But links to Bilderberg? How deep did that damn organization go?"

"We'll never find out everything," said Cohen. "Tell us about Zanjani."

Lopez spoke. "Your contact hacked a list of connections out of some deep web cache. Looks like he's been on Mirnateghi's books for some time. She aimed to rival Bilderberg itself."

"Nemesis had ambitions," said Houston.

Zaringhalam furrowed his brows. "Nemesis?"

"Her code name within Bilderberg," said Lopez. "She tends to extract vengeance on anyone who messes with her." He turned back to the monitor. "We've arranged through Zaringhalam's contacts to meet for a potential sale of highly classified NSA equipment."

"How'd you get him to agree to do that?" asked Savas. "You're nobodies. No history."

Lopez laughed. "You'd be surprised what US gear the Iranian government already has in its lockers. Our hacker here picked out some choice equipment for a sample and knows the lingo and needs. Sounds like Zanjani was practically salivating."

"Sounds like Nemesis is getting a little desperate," said Cohen.

Houston shrugged. "Bilderberg's collapsed. So has their infrastructure. She's isolated. We have to get to her before she can regroup and rebuild."

"We'll bag him at the meeting," said Lopez. "Your contact was skeptical at first," he said, glancing toward the Iranian, "but I think we've convinced him we can do the job."

York replied. "The special forces team we smuggled in place might help a little."

Zaringhalam's eyebrows twitched upwards. "Special forces? How did you do that?"

Lopez ignored him. "Angel's with them and will coordinate. Now we just need to get our man."

York leaned forward, her expression stern. "And what do you plan to do with him?"

Lopez set his jaw. "Nothing a CEO need know about."

"Not sure that's the kind of leader I want to be, whatever this monster's crimes. But the way things are going with this election, you might just get a very different one come January. We might all need to think about that and about what we are leaving behind."

"If we don't stop Nemesis, Bilderberg might return," Houston said. "Whatever the campaign rhetoric, that's what we have to fear the most."

York sighed. "Maybe. Regardless, Mirnateghi's on our watch. Stop her."

"We will," said Lopez. "We have to."

EYE FOR AN EYE

"Jack the Reaper," said Hill, dropping a folder on Sacker's desk. Snyder frowned at her as she beamed at the two men. "Prints are a lock."

Sacker sighed. "Why have the gods so favored me?"

He'd resigned himself to the new operational structure Captain Ladner had imposed. *Mentor* Hill and Snyder, two young cops who just made detective. Sacker hoped Ladner might balk at this murder case and bench them. Instead, his chief declared it the perfect learning environment. Get them up to speed.

And slow me down.

He studied the trainees. The brunette Hill attracted his interest. *Little Latina in that one.* Tall, athletic, Bronx Science and CUNY graduate, she was bright. She was good-looking. She had charisma to spare, a sense of humor and a wholesome look putting many at ease. Rick Snyder was another story. The blond kid wasn't the sharpest tool in the shed. He tended to get under the skin with stupid questions.

Sacker turned to the desk and opened the folder. He double-checked Hill's work, scanning through the forensics summary. But there wasn't any doubt.

"Good ol' Jack," he said with a laugh. "I'm not going to say he didn't have it coming, but, *damn!* That had to hurt."

"Wait," said Snyder, forever two steps behind. "You mean the Bronx rapist?"

"Mmmm-hmmm," Sacker unwrapped his nicotine gum and popped it like candy. "Who else?" he mumbled, tossing the wrapper into a wastebasket. "Terrorized the city for three damn years. We'll never know how many women he raped."

"Did *you* catch him?" asked Snyder. Hill rolled her eyes.

"No, not my case. Hell, not my generation—I'm not *that* old. I'd just joined the force. But it was a public relations disaster for the department. Then he started hitting high society types. Forget about that. The commissioner was asked to resign. The mayor nearly lost the election. All because of old Jack." Sacker exhaled. "But that's how they got him. Dim alleys and poor prostitutes are one thing. Park Avenue debutantes are a whole different hornet's nest."

A booming voice cut in behind them. "Seems like something else did him in, Detective."

Sacker rose. "Captain."

The stout form of Mike Ladner stood before them, hands on his hips, his bald head gleaming under the fluorescent lighting. He spit out his phrases like gunfire.

"Damn press is having a field day with this. Sacker, I want this investigated quickly, quietly, with no bones to the press. Snyder, Hill —best to watch detective Sacker closely, do whatever the hell he tells you to do. All we need is more fuel for this fire. *Understood?* Good! With any luck, this will quiet down and you can conduct an actual investigation."

"We're still waiting for the forensics, sir," said Sacker. He held Ladner's gaze.

Ladner rolled his eyes and turned toward his office. "I'll call Sutherland. Every damn thing's got to be drama with him."

"Sutherland?" asked Snyder.

"The Medical Examiner," Hill responded. "Tall old guy. Practically acted like we didn't exist on the elevator."

"That's Sutherland," said Sacker, easing back into his chair at Lander's departure. "He's good enough at his job to keep it, but not to be parading around the damn precinct like he's Albert Einstein. But we've got to talk with him about the autopsy." *Back to criminology 101.* "In any murder case, the victim's body is usually a key part of the evidence, both in identifying the killer and cause of death, also in the trial. In this case, it's all we have. Reaper was killed somewhere else and we might never have access to the crime scene. The body may be all we have to go on."

"What do you think happened, sir?" asked Snyder. "What's your theory?"

Sacker sighed and leaned back in his chair. "It's way too early to speculate seriously. Dangerous to get too involved with a pet hypothesis with little data. But if I had to guess, I'd bet on a revenge killing. How many women did this perp violate? Gotta be at least one who's thought about hitting back."

"He served time," said Snyder.

"Sometimes that isn't enough for a vic. But there are other possibilities."

"Like what?" asked Hill.

"Boyfriend or husband of a vic. Some men have a caveman response to their wife or daughter being raped. I've seen it before. Usually they just grab a gun and do something stupid that gets them hurt or locked up. But maybe we had a more careful crazy here."

Hill nodded. "The mutilation seems more than just coincidence for Jack the Reaper."

"Exactly," said Sacker. "Serial rapist murdered with his junk removed. You don't exactly have many ways to make a stronger statement than that." He crossed his legs. "At least I hope there aren't."

FLASH AND BANG

S ara Houston strapped several magazines full of ammunition to the inner pockets of her black abaya. She fastened a layer of dark fabric over them and adjusted the body armor beneath.

She glared at the Iranian hacker. "If Nemesis knows we're here, this could be a trap."

Zaringhalam tried not to stare as the two lined up weapons and devices on the small table between them.

"Of course. I am not stupid," he muttered. But joining this pair in whatever they planned? He was indeed beginning to question his intelligence.

Lopez swept to the side two flash-bang grenades to make room for firearms. He scowled. "What are the odds that Nemesis spills secrets to someone so far down in her pipeline? An arms dealer?"

Houston fitted knives and throwing stars into slots in black boots. She stood straight, the fringes of her abaya flowing down to cover everything but the toes. Her brown-tinted eyes flashed.

"Trap is definitely a possibility," emphasized the former priest.

She pressed her body against Lopez and grabbed his head with both hands, bringing his mouth to hers.

Zaringhalam couldn't look away, not sure what was more disconcerting. Was it the cold lethality in their actions or its juxtaposition with such a passionate disregard for proper norms? Embracing like the world was about to end?

Maybe for them, it's always near.

"No way to know," she said, pulling away breathless. "So, the usual. Prep for the worst. Hope for the best."

"Lord hear our prayer." He stashed the grenades and grabbed two handguns from the table.

"You both have enough weapons to arm a squad," mumbled Zaringhalam.

Lopez scanned the street from a small window. He nodded to Houston. She sighed and moved to the door, grasping the handle.

"He's wise to us or not, one thing's for sure: he won't go quietly." She opened the door. "Let's move."

Houston vanished into the misty October evening. Lopez strode forward and past the Iranian without a glance. Zaringhalam stared ahead and wiped sweat from his forehead. He exhaled and followed the pair outside.

Madness.

～

THERE WERE no formal introductions outside the abandoned warehouse on the outskirts of Tehran. No names spoken, no checks for weapons. Security for the arms dealers was found in the overwhelming show of force: men with automatic weapons in a semicircle around a thin executive in an Armani suit.

Three enigmas faced the thugs across a span of ten feet. The broad shape of Lopez on the far left, his mass palpable even at a distance. The lanky form of Zaringhalam trembled in the middle. And on the right, the strangest sight of all: *a woman.* Houston's garments blended with the darkness, the tension of her body coiling outward like an electric field.

Breaths danced in the chilled air. The moon ducked behind an encroaching cold front, the main light the beams of the BMW idling behind the dealer.

"That him?" Houston whispered, eyes focused on the killers.

Zaringhalam swallowed. "Yes. Reza Zanjani. CEO of the MW Group."

"Chief supplier to Nemesis," said Lopez.

"Not a man to be crossed idly," hissed Zaringhalam. His teeth chattered.

"Six guards, closely spaced. Perfect orientation and distance." She flicked her head toward Zaringhalam. "Clock's running. You're on, cowboy."

Zaringhalam felt his stomach drop. He longed for religion, the warm comfort of eternal certainty. *What did grandmother use to say to us at night?* Now was the time for a prayer to come to mind, *anything* to calm his nerves.

Instead, he cleared his throat and stepped forward, pulling a wheeled suitcase. Houston and Lopez remained motionless as he approached Zanjani. The men with weapons aimed in his direction. Zaringhalam paused, holding his arms up, forcing a smile that hurt his face.

"*Salam. Asr bekheyr,*" he opened in Farsi.

Zanjani did not move. He replied in the same language. "Who are those two? You never mentioned others! What's a *woman* doing here?"

"Americans," he said, his attempted shrug a short spasm. "*Bebakhshid.* No sense of propriety. But they have access to the tech. We cannot always choose our suppliers." He held the face-splitting grin. His bladder ached.

"They look like assassins."

"They live dangerous lives."

The CEO muttered to the guards, who trained their weapons on Lopez and Houston, ignoring the hacker.

"Show me the merchandise."

Zaringhalam froze, his smile failing.

And now it plays.

A forgotten fragment of prayer returned. He begged to God these insane Americans knew what they were doing. The area's most ruthless dealer didn't show mercy.

He bent down and opened the suitcase, the contents facing the dealer. He stepped behind the case and tried to make himself as small as possible.

The CEO twitched toward the case. A henchman approached, his eyes darting between the contents and the dark forms behind Zaringhalam. The man looked inside, turned to Zanjani, and nodded.

Zanjani stepped forward, his entourage of guards shadowing him, weapons at the ready, their forms tense and prepared for any assault. Lopez and Houston remained statues. Only Zaringhalam moved, shivering in the cold breeze, one hand after another reaching up to an ear, pressing, and repeating.

Crouching, Zanjani reached into the case, removing a fist-sized bundle of circuit boards. He studied the devices, turning them over in his hands. The guards around leaned in to glimpse the prize sought. Zanjani smiled.

Now, damn it! Zaringhalam spun away from the suitcase.

A dark shadow of his form materialized as he crouched, the ground around lit like a lightning strike. Even with the earplugs, the blast stunned the hacker, knocking him to his knees. He looked back toward the Americans.

But now they sprinted forward, blurred, cats-eyes rushing past him with weapons in their hands. Time slowed. He tracked them rocketing past, metallic glints from Houston whistling through the mist, slow-motion explosions of gunfire from Lopez. Before Zaringhalam turned, stumbled to his feet, and focused his spinning head, it was over.

The guards were down. Four motionless, two thrashing on the ground. One gurgled with a razored star in his jugular. CEO Zanjani screamed on his knees, hands over his eyes. Powder burns darkened his fingers.

The flash-bangs.

Houston had embedded them in the suitcase, linked them wirelessly to a controller in her hand. How many he didn't know.

But enough.

The explosions of light and sound had incapacitated Zanjani's bodyguards. As he'd seen on the streets of Tehran, these American killers required only one moment. *A moment is death.*

"Vâysâ!" Zanjani stumbled, trying to push away from Lopez.

Lopez wrenched the Iranian's arms behind his back, forcing another scream from his lips. The scream was cut short as Houston stuffed gauze into his mouth and sealed it with duct tape. Eyes wide, the arms dealer breathed in spurts through his nose.

"He'll hyperventilate. Or worse, vomit and choke on it," said Houston to Zaringhalam. "Tell him!"

The hacker pleaded with Zanjani as Lopez lashed the dealer's wrists with wire. The man panicked.

"Fuck it," said Houston. "He's going under." She plunged a hypodermic needle into the man's thigh. He collapsed in Lopez's arms.

"And I suppose I get to carry him?" said Lopez, positioning himself underneath Zanjani's chest.

"Sorry," said Houston, turning from the lights of the vehicle and scanning around them through night-vision goggles. "Had to make the call. All's clear. They didn't have backup."

Zaringhalam startled. "You said you scouted!"

Lopez inhaled and lifted Zanjani over his shoulder. He gasped. "We did. But the smart move would be to bring them in after a delay. Their tactics were poor." He trudged away from the warehouse.

"Tactics?"

"No way we should have won this, hacker man," said Houston. "They had all the advantages. They screwed up."

"No way they should have won this." *Unbelievable.* "You put me in a death trap." *Who were these people?*

Houston smiled. "That's our calling card. Death traps." She yanked his jacket, tipping him toward the ground as she followed Lopez.

"Close your jaw and move."

8

ONE SMALL STEP

The 12th precinct morgue spanned a city block. Dedicated rooms kept corpses chilled in rows of refrigerated storage lockers. Crime labs buzzed with forensic scientists sampling DNA, running ballistics, and examining the most minute gunshot residues with an electron microscope. The autopsy suites adjoined the cryogenic storage rooms.

In one such room, fog and stink rose from a gray corpse atop a stainless-steel examination table. A long, Y-shaped incision split the corpse shoulder to shoulder, meeting at the sternum and extending to the pelvis. Scalpels, saws, and other stained paraphernalia glinted on a tray. The medical examiner had closed the body after inspection, but for the peep-hole in the pelvis opening to the internal organs.

The three detectives waited by the corpse of Jack Reaper. In front, a thin, older man in a white lab coat gesticulated, highlighting anatomy of the cadaver, the younger detectives writing as he spoke.

"As you can see, there is extensive bruising across the entire body," said Sutherland, his eyebrows raised as he moved his index finger lengthwise. "I've never seen anything quite like it, actually—the patterns, blood vessel bursting. In fact, there is evidence of deep trauma to internal organs and other tissue, massive internal bleeding.

I might not know how to interpret it except for the rather obvious other signs of torture and the cause of death."

"Which was, what?" asked Sacker, tiring of the old man's theater.

"I'm getting to that," Sutherland responded. "But as for the bruising, while I can't say for sure, it is obviously from some kind of blunt-force trauma, perhaps a special torture devised by the perpetrator before killing the victim." The examiner moved toward the pelvis. "Now, there is no more obvious sign of physical damage to this body than the removal of the genitalia. The clotting and vesicle patterning here clearly indicates that the victim was likely dead when it happened."

"Thank God," whispered Snyder. He swallowed.

"I said *likely*. There are other anomalies that complicate interpretation and analysis, but I'll get to those. The cuts are surgically precise—whoever did this had a very steady hand. It would be required of course that the victim not move for such precision, and indeed we find evidence of harsh restraints on the body, although those may have only been in place for the torture." Hill shuddered as Sutherland pointed out bruised and raw skin around the wrists, ankles, thighs, midsection, and throat. "Looks like the head was also directly restrained with bolts—there are pressure wounds on the skull. Not invasive, but terribly tight and painful, I am afraid."

"He was strapped down and they did all this to him?" Snyder said, a look of horror on his face.

"Indeed, indeed, yes," said Sutherland, smiling. "Quite the setup, isn't it? Our victim seems to have been put out of his considerable misery by asphyxiation." The doctor walked them around the table to the victim's head. "Notice the marks around the mouth? A hard-edged object was affixed around the mouth and nose with considerable pressure. This blocked oxygen intake and smothered the victim. Normally, I would look for standard signs of asphyxiation, but the global bruising from the trauma makes it hard to be sure what caused what damage. But the facial marks are continuous, and there is clear cyanosis in the lips and fingers."

"What's cyanosis?" Snyder asked.

"Dark pigmenting—blue and purple—of certain extremities upon prolonged oxygen deprivation.

"Why kill someone like that?"

"Motive is your job, detective, not mine. But the complete helplessness of the victim rendered such a procedure quite feasible."

"Anything else?" asked Sacker.

"Only the lack of other things arises as evidence."

Oh, good God. "What does that mean?"

"Standard procedure is to also check fingernails, teeth, and so forth for skin and other tissue that might belong to the murderer. Usually obtained from struggling with the perpetrator."

Pompous asshole. "Yes, something we don't know?"

Sutherland sighed. "Usually from these studies we get genome data from the victim, which of course must be filtered from the large background of data from microorganisms. If we are lucky, we also get other human DNA not matching the victim. Sometimes even traces of compounds that help us ID the location."

"Microorganisms?" asked Hill.

"Yes, bacteria, virus, fungi. We're pretty filthy creatures, you must understand." He sneered at Hill as if she might be contaminated. "Except in this case, well, *nothing.* No signs of microbes in sequencing or in culture. No other DNA but that of the victim."

"How is that possible?" asked Sacker.

"To be honest with you, detective, I'm not sure." Sutherland pursed his lips "Only some kind of extreme sterilization procedure could have achieved this. There is in addition evidence that the body was refrigerated for some time prior to being left on the street. All samples and efforts to date the time of death run into the problem that the biochemistry of decay seemed to have begun in earnest on the evening before the body was discovered. The complete lack of a crime scene, the evidence of sophisticated tampering with the body... We may never know exactly when or where the victim died. At best I can say that it wasn't more than several months ago."

"More questions than answers," said Sacker.

Sutherland straightened and looped his fingers together. "Quite a straightforward case for me, actually, requiring no further or more in-depth examination. The cause of death is obvious, with evidence of extreme trauma, mutilation, and death by smothering. There will be no further evidence from this body to link the death to the killer, I am afraid. The challenge in this case, I assume, will be to determine why such extreme measures were taken and obtain other evidence. That, I am afraid, is squarely in your domain, and not mine."

The doctor wheeled away. He halted and spun back.

"You nearly had me forgetting. The killer left a calling card." The physician raised a plastic sample bag with a strip of paper inside. Faded letters ran along the ragged surface. "Stuffed in his mouth."

"Jesus. What does it say?" asked Sacker, taking the bag and squinting at the paper.

"One small death of a man; one giant leap for womankind." Sutherland retrieved the bag from Sacker and returned it to the tray.

"Now, if you will excuse me, we do have other unfortunate victims to examine today."

~

SACKER SHUFFLED out of the morgue, his mind racing. The case continued to grow stranger and more unsettling as facts rolled in. Hill and Snyder shadowed his steps as they made their way back from the basement to their fourth-floor offices.

"Does this hurt the theory of a revenge killing?" asked Hill.

Sacker ran his hand over his close-cropped hair. "I don't know. Sure doesn't seem to fit with your average payback. Who would have the expertise for this? Who would go to these lengths, even for revenge? But everything about this case is extreme—the killing, the torture, the public exhibition. I'm starting to think that we aren't dealing with your average angry Joe or Jane."

Hill agreed. "Yeah, it seems like Jack the Reaper tangled with the wrong person."

"A real psycho." He glared at his assistants. "See that none of this gets out of this department. Outside of Ladner, *no one* is to hear a word until we've got a better handle on things. Remember—no one keeps secrets. *No one.* If you break that firewall once, it's over. The press is already foaming at the mouth for leaks."

They both nodded as the elevator door opened. The three got inside.

"Meanwhile," he said, pressing a button, "we need to get a list of all of Reaper's known victims. Their family members, too. Let's hope that it was one of them."

"But you said we don't know many of his victims," said Snyder.

"That's right, and the killer could be one of those we don't. But there's nothing else to work with. The revenge killing is still the most viable theory we have. It leads us to names and follow-up police work. We need names, locations, and professions of the victims and their family. Any doctors or nurses in the group—anyone with medical training—they are priority one from what Sutherland revealed. Psych profiles, criminal records. Patterns. Anything that might give someone a means beyond their obvious motives."

"On it, sir," said Hill as they exited the elevator.

Sacker gazed across the busy floor, the image of a corpse lodged in his mind. "Let's hope we find something soon. I've got a bad feeling about this case."

9

OUT OF CHAMPAGNE

The Crown Victoria's suspension was shot. The car rocked over busted New York City streets, rattling bones on a big pothole and churning stomachs as they surfed warped roads resembling solidified lava. Riding shotgun, Snyder held his hand to his mouth.

Hill spoke from behind. "With no clear time of death, month of death even, we're screwed. We can't narrow any suspects' locations, test alibis. And now that some jerk's leaked Reaper's name to the press, it's that much harder to operate."

A horn blared. Sacker refused to let a shouting cabbie cut him off.

"Right. We're at a huge disadvantage, so we're moving fast. That's why we're on the road today. But we do know something about the killing. There's a damn good chance our killer has medical expertise. Hard to imagine he or she doesn't. That narrows the list substantially. Now we pray for a miracle, a reveal in the mannerisms, poorly concealed evidence we can glean without a warrant. *Anything.*"

"Mannerisms?" asked Hill.

"Yeah, they don't teach you that in the academy," said Sacker. "I've broken open as many cases with intuition as I have with evidence.

Partly experience. Partly a sensitivity. It's all about paying attention to what's in front of you and getting out of your own head."

"*You have arrived at your destination,*" came the soulless voice of his GPS navigator. Sacker switched off his cell phone. Cursed with a terrible sense of direction, even the New York grids confused him. GPS might be embarrassing, but it was required.

They pulled up to a brick and mortar, World War I-era apartment complex. Scaffolding obscured the facade, workers pummeling the old brick to a fine silt. Sacker imagined the dust worming into the apartments facing the orange cloud. Near New York Hospital, several medical institutions cooperatively owned the building to house staff. Their trauma surgeon lived on the second floor.

As they approached, Sacker pulled his detectives aside. "Remember, this guy lost his wife six months ago. Suicide. He's got all kinds of motive, but let's try to move slowly."

THE DOOR OPENED to reveal a disheveled figure in his forties. His eyes were sunken, his face unshaved. Receding, curly hair danced around his head. His features drew tight at the sight of the detectives.

Sacker removed his hat. "Dr. Russo? Detectives Sacker, Hill, and Snyder. We called earlier."

The doctor put his hand on the back of his neck. "Yeah. Right. Look, sorry for all this, but I was in the ER late last night."

"May we come in?"

Russo opened the door and shuffled into his small apartment. He motioned toward a couch and set of chairs. Hill and Snyder sat on opposite sides of Sacker, wide-eyed, scanning the room.

The apartment mimicked a museum piece, a space once occupied and tended, now frozen in place. Only the layering of dust testified to the passage of time. Sacker spied a narrow kitchen with piles of unwashed dishes. However useful Russo may or may not be in the clinic, he'd let his life go.

One thing stood out clearly in the disorder: yesterday's New York

Times, front page spread open on the coffee table before them, complete with a mugshot of Jack Reaper.

Everything in place for one hell of a conversation.

The doctor returned with a stained coffee mug and dropped into a wicker chair across from the detectives. He spoke over the steam.

"So, what can I do for you?"

"We're here about the Reaper murder."

Russo choked back a laugh. "Sorry, I'm out of champagne."

Sacker smiled. *Might like this guy.* "I understand how you could feel that way Dr. Russo. I trust you understand we have an investigation to conduct."

"Well, if you find the guy, I'll buy him dinner. Pin a fucking medal on him."

"What we're trying to ascertain, Dr. Russo—"

"I'll save you the tap dance. I didn't kill the son-of-a-bitch. Search my place; you won't find anything. I'm logged constantly at the hospital. Working until I drop is my way of avoiding more therapy. I wouldn't have the energy to chase that monster down."

Snyder cut in. "Revenge can often bring a lot of energy."

Russo drank from his cup and shook his head. "Not in my nature, I'm sad to say. When I saw Linda in that hospital room—God, her face was a horror show. Swollen-up so bad I could hardly tell it was her. You bet I wanted to hurt someone. But that only lasted so long. I could burn up with it. Or I could take care of my wife. She was never the same. She needed me. I put my energies in healing, detective. That's my whole life. And it wasn't enough."

"Was your wife in therapy after the assault?" asked Hill.

"She was raped and tortured for *three days*. Left to die on the side of the road. What do you think?" He scowled at Hill, who squirmed under his gaze. "We saw individual therapists, did couples counseling. It failed. *I* failed. Something primitive snapped when my wife became the plaything of an animal like that. I hated myself for it. I tried. We worked hard in therapy. But I didn't step up, and Linda had a history with depression. She just couldn't get out of this hole. You can't imagine the pain she was in."

Get this back on track.

"The reason we're here, Dr. Russo," said Sacker, "is that we believe the killer possesses considerable medical training."

Russo squinted. "The mutilation?"

"Yes. It's not the cutting of an amateur."

"More like an artist," said Russo. "But I see where you're going. You're rounding up the folks in Reaper's wreckage zone and picking out those like me."

"That's right."

"And that means you're in real trouble."

Sacker winced. *It's always harder with the smart ones.*

Russo waved his hand. "It's all over your faces. You're desperate, knocking on doors hoping for a bloody scalpel to fall out of someone's pocket."

Dammit.

Hill and Snyder glanced between the doctor and Sacker, who put on his best smile.

Russo laughed. "Well, good luck, detectives. But I don't think you're going to find anyone in this little group who's at all interested in helping you track down Jack Reaper's killer. He's our new hero."

SERIAL KILLER

Sacker eased the car into traffic and watched the towers of New York Hospital recede in his rearview. His trainees didn't speak, their enthusiasm dashed on the heartbreak of a victim's husband. He decided to break the funk with some analysis.

"Okay, detectives, pop quiz: your assessment of Russo. Rick?"

Snyder's eyes darted between Sacker and Hill. "I dunno. Seemed pretty combative to me, didn't show you much respect. Maybe he's hiding something."

"What makes you say that?"

"He clearly had motive. He was practically cheering on the murder."

Hill interrupted. "And why wouldn't he? You heard what happened to his wife."

"What's your take, Kathy?" asked Sacker.

"Objectively, there was no evidence. Not that we searched or anything. But his hate for Reaper—too raw, too open to come from a killer hiding his crime. It just didn't feel right."

Sacker nodded. "I think we're going to see more Fred Russo's as we go down the list. He stays on it, but for now, there's just not much for followup."

"We still should search his place," said Snyder. "He was willing. We won't even need a warrant."

"Time's finite, Rick," said Sacker. "We have ten more names on this list, which is going to take us I don't know how long. Meanwhile we need to keep the press at bay with something. Departmental resources are stretched pretty thin."

"So we don't search it?"

"No. That's my call. I think it'll slow us down, put us off track. And it'll end up in the papers, which means when we find nothing, we look like idiots. Publicly."

Sacker's phone buzzed. "It's Ladner. This can't be good." He tapped the screen and dropped it into the cup holder. "Hey, Mike. Driving back with Snyder and Hill. You're on speaker."

A distorted voice crackled through the device. "Change of plans, Tyrell. Everything's changed. We've got a second body."

"A *second*?"

"That's right. From initial reports, it sounds like the same killer. Same MO, down to the below-the-belt trimming. Body's on 3rd and sixty-eighth."

Oh, shit. "That's right next to Canid."

"Exactly. Get your asses over there now and take control of the situation. Expect the cameras."

"Hang onto your badges." Sacker hit the sirens and pulled a U-turn. "This is going to get ugly."

THE CAMERAS WERE INDEED OUT in full force. A half-dozen lenses locked on them as they exited the car. They fought their way through the throngs. Shutters assaulted them like a cicada swarm. Reporters dogged them, shouting out questions and demands for answers. The word summoned to Sacker's mind was *bedlam*. He focused like a laser beam on the NYPD presence at the corner of the block.

Sutherland had beat them there.

"Ah, detective Sacker," he said, ignoring Hill and Snyder. "Still sporting that antiquated head covering, I see."

"It's *vintage*. Cotton Club era."

"No doubt," he said, the smile mocking. "It looks like your case has now been complicated exponentially."

His smile infuriated Sacker. "What do we have?" He popped another nicotine strip.

The body was splayed in front of the Food Emporium, mounted like a trophy on bursting garbage bags. One quick glance told the story.

"The sanitation crews once again won this lottery," chirped Sutherland, his eyes twinkling. "Their truck ran behind schedule, explaining the relatively late hour of discovery as compared to the first corpse. But no doubt this killing is related to Reaper's."

Hill covered her mouth. "This one stinks more."

"A near carbon copy of the first murder." The doctor led the detectives under the police tape. "The positioning of the body is very similar to Reaper. Naked, no ID. The horrific bruising even worse in this case. And, of course, the removal of all external male genitalia." He stopped gesturing and turned to the detectives. "No blood. No other evidence."

Sacker rubbed his temples. A whopper of a headache gestated. He turned to several of the uniformed officers around him. "Let's get this body covered and that crowd pushed back!"

"My team will get the body to the lab," said Sutherland, "but I do not anticipate any surprises." He removed and tossed his gloves into an evidence bag, walking away from the crime scene. Several assistants from the morgue began to cover the body.

"There goes the damn list of suspects," said Hill, hands on her hips.

"Wait, why?" asked Snyder.

She puffed brown strands out of her eyes. "Well, it's unlikely any of them did this. Reaper's dead, right?"

Snyder furrowed his brows. "Well, there might be a second killer. Maybe a copycat killer?"

Sacker sighed and waved him silent. "No, Rick. We're not looking at multiple killers. We're looking at one killer, same MO, multiple vics. Please tell me you know what that means."

Snyder glanced to the right. "A serial killer?"

"Bingo. Two might not technically qualify, but that's what we have."

Puffing out his chest, Snyder smiled. "A serial killer! So now what? Why did he kill this guy? What's the relationship?"

"I have no idea," said Sacker. "We need to ID this vic and then we can begin to try and find out." Sacker scanned the sea of faces and cameras aimed in their direction.

Hill followed his gaze. "This is going to turn into a circus, isn't it?"

"Mmmm-hmmm. Two dickless vics? They're gonna Son of Sam this till the ratings come home."

Hill squinted. "Two murders in less than a week. One busy killer."

"Maybe," said Sacker, watching the body placed into a bag. "But remember what Sutherland said. Time of death, possible cold storage. All the dirty work might have been done weeks ago. The last five days could just be drop offs."

"Drop-offs." Hill grimaced. "How many more *deliveries* do you think are in the queue?"

Sacker's lip curled. "That's what I'm afraid of, Kathy. That's exactly what I'm afraid of."

GONE SHOOTING

Grace Gone focused and steadied her aim, holding the weapon one-handed in her right because the left had begun to tremble too much. Her weight rested mostly on the right leg as well, the other side of her body relentless in its determined progression to fail her. The target sighted, she exhaled and pulled the trigger.

Dust popped from the innermost scoring ring of the LE Silhouette, the bullet hole obliterating the "X" in the chest cavity. Her mouth formed an impatient pout as she aimed again.

Her Glock 42 wasn't very intimidating, and the .380 ACP rounds not the cannon loaders many of the larger men around her liked to fire, but Gone knew that big rounds meant little if they didn't strike true. Her gun was compact, light, and the recoil manageable for a small woman.

Shot placement is everything.

She'd read the studies and analyzed police reports. Shootouts where men blasted each other in the legs, arms, and shoulders, missing the vital organs even at close range, criminals refusing to fall. Psychological stopping power in some cases. But pain and mild blood loss often only angered the truly determined. If Gone came under attack, she had resolved to damage key life-support—heart, lungs, brain. She fired again, a hole rupturing the forehead of her paper assailant. Her aim was true.

Until the right side goes to hell.

The thought demoralized her and she lowered her weapon, forcing her mind to shunt to another topic. She closed her eyes and removed the protective earmuffs. The arms fire around her in the underground Long Island range echoed. On her right came the artillery blasts of a massive weapon and the shouts and back slaps of young men. Gone rifled through the firearms she had observed and studied, their sounds and mechanisms memorized.

Desert Eagle. .50 AE barrel. No muzzle brake.

"My turn, Henry!" came a cry.

Gone frowned. *Inexperienced group, three men with local accents.* The gun owner was showing off, bringing his buddies and his biggest weapon. *Moderate probability of mishap.*

"Easy, partner! Whoa! Point the fucker down-range! Look, this isn't for pussies. I said wait! First—"

Again the powerful blast. Then a cry and bursts of laughter.

"My nose!"

The men were hooting and hollering. Gone opened her eyes, stepped back, and looked over. A muscular man in a tight T-shirt held his face in both hands, a massive handgun dropped at his feet. The white cotton rippling under his bulging pecs was stained red as blood gushed between his fingers. His friends rushed to get him towels as they tried to contain their laughter.

Inexperienced shooter. Recoil uncompensated.

"All right boys," came a curt baritone. Swooping in from the far side of the booth, an older safety officer scowled. "You're outta here. I don't know who the hell let you in with that, but anything fifty and over is a no-go. Session's over."

She turned her attention to a quick succession of small calibre shots on her left. *Very small calibre.* 22s in a revolver from the mechanism sounds. Her call was a Ruger LCR, purse gun, small woman like herself practicing for self-defense. She peeked around the wall's edge.

A diminutive Latina with a fierce expression removed eye guards and popped the six-shooter open. She glared up at Gone.

Gone nodded and looked away. Images from the cable news program on the television behind the observation glass caught her eye. A reporter shouted over flashing emergency lights and the bustle of a crowd.

Gone stiffened. As she stared at the video feed, her head barely moving, she removed the ammunition magazine without glancing down, checked the chamber with a quick look, and put the weapon in a carrying case. She walked to a hook on the wall and grabbed her purse, marched to the door, and entered the observation room. The television blared with sirens, crowd noises, and the giddy words of the local reporter.

"New York First here at the headquarters of Canid News on the Upper East Side of Manhattan. The initial footage appears to show a second, I repeat a *second* mutilated murder victim. Mutilated, I mean, like before, like Jack Reaper. Ah, castrated." He laughed nervously.

As the reporter continued in voiceover, the camera left his face and zoomed to a chaotic scene of police and emergency responders. Every few seconds, the scurrying bodies parted enough to see into their midst, glimpse momentarily a pile of garbage bags, a gray and naked form compressing them from the top.

"Hey, Grace," came a older woman's voice behind a counter. "Gonna have to ask for that license next time. Get it renewed, honey, okay?"

"Yeah. Will do, Darlene," she said, eyes still at the screen.

Gone turned from the video and headed to the exit. In those few moments, everything had changed.

JUST A TASTE

Sacker stared across the table. *My how we've grown.*

Along with Snyder and Hill, Ladner assigned him three junior detectives for the case. They'd run searches, do background checks, interface with other agencies. Make the damn morning coffee. Maybe even follow down leads.

Whenever we have some.

The *ad hoc* group sat around a conference table on the 12th Precinct 4th floor. Sacker walked them through a multimedia presentation he'd thrown together. Ladner presided over the proceedings, a brooding presence in the back of the dark room. The mood was anxious and grim. The projector beam cast a gray hue over their faces.

"The second vic's been IDed as Anton Tarakovsky," said Sacker, showing a photo of a bearded white male. "Former adjunct professor, serial rapist convicted in California in the nineties of six counts of sexual assault, two against minors. He served fifteen years and was paroled for good behavior with an agreement to wear a GPS ankle bracelet. Three years ago he moved to New York, taking odd jobs in construction and the like."

"Any connection to Reaper?" asked Ladner.

"None we can find. We're still looking, but they seemed to have lived entirely separate lives on different coasts."

"No DNA? No prints? Anything?"

"Strike out. The forensics report might as well have been Reaper's. Evidence of prolonged and severe bodily trauma. Nearly head to toe bruising and damage to internal organs, internal bleeding. Death came from asphyxia from an object placed over the mouth and nose. No identifying samples on the body to connect to the killer. The body was sterilized, same as Reaper. Sutherland says we won't find anything there."

"Damn." Ladner threw his pen down and pushed a notepad away. "This guy's good. *Too* fucking good."

"And the killer cut off his dick and balls, again?" It was the voice of one of the assistants assigned to the case. He sounded amused.

"Surgically removed," finished Sacker. "More than that. The entire reproductive plumbing. Body parts never recovered."

"I wonder what he's doing with those hot dogs and meatballs? Grilling 'em? Maybe he's a Lector with a fetish."

"Enough, Jones." Sacker stared the young detective down. "We've got enough of that online." He addressed the rest of the group. "While the corpse likely won't yield any clues, there is one more piece of evidence from the autopsy. Something we were meant to find— another note left by the killer."

An image of a wrinkled piece of paper appeared on the screen.

"Where was that found?" boomed Ladner in a deep bass. "Not in his pockets, obviously."

"In his mouth," said Sacker. "Folded in a ziplock bag, shoved into the throat. No prints, no fibers except for the paper, nothing. The message is typed, likely printed from a desktop instrument. Let me zoom in."

Sacker advanced the slide. Ladner read the words slowly. "*A taste of things to come.*" People stirred in their chairs, murmuring.

Sacker spoke over them. "Doesn't leave much to the imagination. We were focused on a revenge killing of Jack the Reaper, but this second murder—of a convicted rapist—changes our model." He switched off the projector and flicked the lights on. "We're dealing with a serial killer. Probably a psychopath. And this note suggests the bodies aren't done dropping."

"Profiling? Calls into the Feds?" asked Ladner.

Sacker motioned to Hill. She turned to the captain. "I'm on it, sir. We have contacts at the FBI itching to get involved in this case. They're friendlies and won't snatch the case. All they want is acknowledgment for any collars."

Sacker shook his head. "Better to defuse a full federal take-over. Throw them some bones. Hopefully they help but leave us alone."

"We're also listing convicted rapists and pedophiles in the tristate area," continued Hill. "I'm prioritizing those with multiple convictions, especially if they had any press coverage."

Sacker nodded. "If this pattern holds, the next target will be on that list."

"We can't shadow all of them," said Ladner.

"No, but have any disappeared in the last few months? Forensics suggests refrigerated storage. The killer might have multiple bodies stashed in coolers to drop on us." He smirked. "Hell, for all we know, all the killings are done already."

"At least monitor the top, press-worthy members of your list."

"That's the plan, Mike. We're getting the list together."

"What about the bruising?"

Sacker exhaled, flipping back several slides to find an image of both bodies. "Here are photos side-by-side. Washed out in this light. But the discoloration is similar. Supports the idea of a single killer."

"No, I meant any idea on what the hell did that? I've never seen anything like it."

"Neither had Sutherland. He thinks it's some kind of custom torture the killer devised to make the victims last moments especially horrible. It'd take a special kind of beating to do that damage. Across the entire body. It's as brutal as it comes."

Ladner stood. "Alright, I've got other business to run, but this case is getting top departmental priority. I've already gotten a call from the Mayor's office. We've got the PR team working overtime to smother this, limit the damage. But there's only so much they can do. Less than twenty-four hours and the tabloids are blasting away already."

"We've got ten separate confessions," said Hill. "Wasting our time in following them up."

"Always the case, Kathy, but we have to," said Sacker. "The real problems come from the amateur sleuths, PIs who stick their noses into these investigations. More time spent on them, their interviews with the press, critiquing our efforts than the false confessions."

"You've got that right," said Ladner. He scowled. "The press is *not* your friend. We've already had someone break protocol. Leak information. This is unacceptable, and I am confident it's no one in this room. But keep the lid tight on this investigation. Don't give any of those vultures any meat. Now, get your asses out there and find our killer." Ladner turned around and stormed out of the conference room.

"Yeah," mumbled Hill, "before the next eunuch shows up."

13

DAILY NEWS

D EAD DICK AND HARRY: BALLSY SERIAL KILLER
UNMANS VICTIMS
City in shock, police flummoxed as second gruesome mutila-
tion dumped in Manhattan.
By Alex Goldstein New York Daily News

I T BEGAN *with the murder of the infamous "Jack the Reaper", serial rapist and abuser John Richard Reaper who once left the city quaking when the sun set. But Reaper was found last week sitting on a pile of garbage in front of an Upper East Side apartment, naked and castrated. The death sent shockwaves and spawned impromptu celebrations, across the city. The NYPD had few comments on their investigation, but speculation has run rampant that a former victim was behind the killing.*

Until yesterday, when a second mutilated corpse made its grisly appearance in front of a grocery store in a nearby neighborhood. Once again, the victim turned out to be a rapist convicted of numerous sexual assaults: Anton Tarakovsky. This perp hailed from California, gracing New York City streets as of several years ago. Once again, the killer had left his prey naked and castrated for all the world to see. Photos of both killings have made quick trips around the internet and been redacted for cable news.

The police department has scrambled to put together an investigatory team. The News has learned that senior detective Tyrell Sacker is heading the investigation from the NYPD's 12th Precinct, headed by Captain Michael Ladner. Reporters swamped Mr. Sacker as he left the precinct this evening, but the detective brushed away their questions (and microphones), refusing to issue a statement. Michael Ladner stood with Commissioner Bravel at a tightly controlled press conference later that evening, providing no new information and declining to take questions.

Concerns have been raised about the ability of the NYPD to handle the investigation. The example of Jack Reaper himself was raised, a rapist who terrorized women and their families for years before he was finally caught with the late intervention of the FBI.

Jennifer Riley, the presumed challenger to the mayor in next year's election, voiced her concerns at a separate press conference, accusing the mayor and former police officer of "appointing cronies" to high-level positions at NYPD.

"We can expect the same level of incompetence from this investigation of these horrible crimes as we have seen from Mayor Johnson's other debacles. His cronies and lobbyist friends have corrupted our city governance for too long, and it's time for a change, for a new face to come in and clean house."

However, not everyone was so disturbed by the killings. Sanitation worker Fredo Labriola was all smiles. "So what? This dude's rubbing out rapists? Cry me a river. The killer's doing us a favor. I hope we keep finding them with the other trash."

14

ZANJANI

Reza Zanjani screamed.

Houston tossed the duct tape to the ground in the dank Tehran basement. Small patches of skin stuck to the adhesive. She angled the bright light into his eyes. The businessman-turned-arms-dealer squinted and turned away.

"We're going to ask some questions, Reza. And you're going to answer them truthfully," she said, straddling a rickety chair behind the bright light, her features a blurred shadow.

"Motevajjeh nemisham," he croaked, squinting at Houston. His eyes darted in several directions, avoiding her glare and the light.

Zaringhalam spoke from the back of the room, his voice strained. "He says he does not understand."

A knife whistled through the air and embedded itself in the wood of Zanjani's chair between his legs. Again he screamed, eyes wide, his arms struggling against the restraints behind him.

"Yes, you do," whispered Houston. "We don't have time for dancing, so let's get to the point: *Mirnateghi*."

Zanjani gasped.

"We need her location. And you're going to give it to us. Or else." She glanced at the knife.

Sweat flowed from the gelled curls above Zanjani's raised brows.

"No. *I can't*," he hissed. "I'll be a dead man!"

Lopez's deep voice rolled out of the darkness. "You already are, Reza. She knows we're here. Soon she'll know we have you. That's a death sentence. Your only hope now is to get out of Iran. We can help you with that."

Zanjani squinted but could not see the source of the deep voice. Only Houston's darkened face danced behind the blinding light.

"But there's a price," she said. "*Mirnateghi*. We know she's here. Tell us where. Who knows, maybe we'll remove your problem. Do you a favor."

"You fools! She is powerful beyond your small minds."

Houston laughed, startling the dealer. "Don't you know why we're here? You don't think we drove her back to Iran, destroyed her global organization, only to leave her time to regroup? We've come to finish the job."

"You're mad."

"This is your last chance." She reached over and yanked the knife from the wood. The metal glinted in the spotlight. Zanjani looked away. "Die here now, by our hand or hers, or tell us what we want. Run to live another day."

Zanjani's body slumped, his will broken. He whispered, staring at the ground.

"Azadi Tower."

Zaringhalam exclaimed behind Houston.

"Nemeeshe! Impossible."

Zanjani said nothing.

"The giant monument?" asked Houston. "At the entrance to the city?"

"Yes. Beneath the tower are structures, underground buildings and tunnels. The government is ignorant." He exhaled. "She is there. Her base of operations."

Lopez spoke again from the darkness. "You've been there? Underground?"

"Once only. I was blindfolded. But not even Sonbol imagined that I carried a hidden GPS. They never found it."

"Sonbol?" asked Lopez.

"A flower," offered Zaringhalam from the back. "You call it hyacinth."

"My God!" said Houston. "The flowers on the dead agents. All hyacinths." She cocked her head at Zanjani. "Why do you call her Sonbol?"

"She gives us the name."

Lopez grumbled. "Lady has a lot of names. Why flowers at kills? A softer side to Nemesis? Why am I skeptical?"

The corner of Houston's mouth twitched to a half-smile. "Trust your instincts. Hyacinths are beautiful. They're also poisonous."

"As is our Sonbol," said Zanjani.

Houston leaned back and spoke to Lopez. "Azadi Tower? That's like Times Square. How the hell are we supposed to pull that off?"

"You can't," said Zanjani. "As I have told you. Only fools would try."

Houston turned back to the arms dealer, her brow furrowed.

"We need to phone home. Infrared sat scans, verify what he's saying." She rose from the chair, staring down at Zanjani. "But if there is a lair under Azadi Tower, we'll find its weak points. And we'll hit it hard. She's within striking distance."

Zanjani shook his head. "Khodā margam bede."

Lopez and Houston turned to Zaringhalam.

"He ridicules your plans," he said. "And asks God for death."

15

GONE FISHING

G race Gone blew over her tea before sipping. Her left arm trembled holding the white china cup to her mouth, her eyes gazing forward at the slew of online articles about the new serial killer in New York. The aroma of lemon and spices danced around her face. She placed the cup down without drinking.

I'm doing this.

The general press ran with the Post's headline: the *Eunuch Maker*. She coded scripts for web searches related to the killings, culling thousands of photos from news sites, crime and sexual forums, the major social media sites, piping the data flood into a homemade image processing program. She tweaked the parameters, filtering images by the GPS coordinates of the photos and dead bodies, trashing those with signs of digital manipulation, low resolution, or dates outside the last week.

Tens of thousands of snapshots from the cell phones of bystanders and reporters piled up in a folder. The program sorted them into unique angles and distances through a pattern recognition algorithm. She was left with fifty unique shots of the victims at moderate to high resolution.

Hours passed as she scanned through the photos manually, organizing them based on certain attributes and clarity. She developed three special categories of images. The first highlighted the unusual purple and black patterns across the skin of the corpses. Not tattoos or birthmarks, to her they resembled blood vessel trauma, bruising and hemorrhaging, with no location on the bodies free of them. The second was the crotch where the genitals were removed. The third was the mouth. In several photos, she noticed extensive bruising or blueness near the mouth and lips. Examining related views, she saw evidence of trauma to the same area, fitting the shape of an edged object placed over the victim's face.

Typing on a dual-alphabet keyboard, she recorded her notes in Mandarin. Paranoia perhaps, or a comforting reminder of a life lost, the Chinese characters marched across the screen along with embedded images and videos of the police and crime scenes.

Her face darkened, her body bent in half over the screen, the hated pout asserting itself. Dashing across medical websites, she blasted through pages of criminal autopsies. Cases upon cases of physical abuse, torture, mechanical trauma. Her searches led her farther and farther afield, scanning multiple medical reports from the FBI, CDC, and the WHO. Phrases like subcutaneous hemorrhaging, carbonic anhydrases, and multiple organ dysfunction recurring in her scans.

She straightened into the backrest of the chair, hair whipping backward. Her eyes blazed into the distance.

I need to see those bodies.

But how? To see the bodies required a miracle, break through the wall between police and PI. It almost never happened. It certainly wasn't going to happen with a nobody gumshoe from Queens. Might as well buy a lottery ticket.

Gone switched the keyboard back to English and brought her browser to the NYPD home page. She scrolled through page after page, cross checking with numerous articles about the case. She queried online forums and search engines. After several minutes of searching, she pounded her keyboard.

Damn, they aren't making this easy. Time for my black hat.

It wasn't impossible to hack the NYPD. The deep web hoarded reams of data. She navigated through encrypted tunnels, scouring sites listing governmental emails, logins, and passwords. All illegally obtained.

And here we go.

A handful of entries were logged over the last few years for the 12th Precinct. All targeted jobs, not low hanging fruit from the security breaches of large companies like Adobe and Yahoo. And someone had put these up without a price tag. *Hackers bragging. Mounting heads like trophies.*

Several entries matched names on public records. There was little need for anything more than some moderate extraction work to get the addresses.

"Okay, let's see—Ladner, Sacker, and the medical examiner Dr. Sutherland." She opened her agency email and typed in addresses for the three men. The cursor dropped to the subject line and she typed, "Eunuch Maker Killings". The department was likely getting hundreds of emails about this, but she doubted many were addressed to the cops involved in the case. Not to their internal email accounts. The cursor blinked in the body field of the program, waiting for her to begin the message.

What would she say? *"Hi Cops, need a look at your morgue. Sincerely, nobody PI."* She couldn't open the message asking for anything. She had to dangle something *they* wanted. Ideas or deductions they might not be making. Judging from the lack of any noise on the bruising, she doubted her worst suspicions had been considered.

Short, to the point, carrot.

That was the what she would write. The question now was, *who?*

Gone considered the faces and comments, positions and body language of the people involved gleaned from her media searches. Ladner—a hard ass, aggressive to the point of harassing, likely territorial. *Bull dog.* Sutherland—too remote, self-absorbed, and arrogant. *Asshole.* No, it had to be Sacker, the detective. He looked troubled, concerned, bright enough for deductive work, maybe open to crazy ideas. Of course, none of them would be easy, her bad leg squashed in the door.

But I have to try.

She had to hook them with something. This case could be her breakthrough.

Her fingers sped over the keyboard.

"Dear Detective Sacker...."

16

GONE POSTAL

The criminal psychologist droned on.

"So, in my assessment, you have a ritualistic serial killer. And I say ritualistic because he repeatedly kills in the same way, with great precision, displaying signs of a serious obsessive compulsive disorder and a need to reenact the same crime again and again. This almost certainly stems from a long-suppressed trauma, likely sexual abuse, which dovetails nicely with the sexual mutilation observed and the choice of sexual predators as victims."

"You keep saying 'he,' doc," said Hill. "What about a woman?"

Tall and thin, the psychologist stooped, rectangular eyeglasses framing an angular face. His hands jerked and he avoided eye contact, acting more neurotic than many mental patients Sacker had known.

"Yes, well, it might seem that a female would be a likely suspect. These were rapists who targeted women. But you must understand that statistically, men are the predominant multiple count killers. Indeed, men are more likely by very large margins to commit any violent crime. Therefore, the odds are that it was a man."

Hill shook her head. "Those are general stats not looking at any particulars. We have a very specific set of particulars. I think we should keep both genders in play as suspects."

Enough already.

Two hours of psychobabble was his limit. "Let's thank Dr. Monroe for his time. We've got a lot to chew on. Let's regroup and look at the data with fresh eyes."

His team shuffled out of the conference room. Sacker engaged in the expected pleasantries with their criminologist consultant. But it was a sham. There wasn't much to chew on. No new data needing *fresh eyes* illuminated by the noble doctor.

Empty words.

They had zero leads, only an MO, and a developing PR nightmare. Meanwhile, Ladner continued to demand a speedy resolution to the case. Each summoning to the chief's office more browbeating than the next.

Sacker got it. Jobs and careers were at stake.

Not to mention lives.

He fell into his desk chair with a grunt and slid another nicotine strip between his gum and cheek. *Whoever banned smoking should be shot.* He clicked on his desktop, entered a password, and checked his email.

"Well, hello."

Clever lady. He wasn't sure how she did it, but whoever this Grace Gone was, she'd gotten his protected email address. He might have been intrigued by her finesse if she hadn't blown it with the subject line: "Eunuch Maker Killings." Crass, but it did get his attention. Sacker sighed. *Another gumshoe looking to cash in.* His finger hovered over the delete key, eyes roaming the body of the email.

Interesting. He sat up in his chair. *Check for internal organ hemorrhaging?* How the hell had she suspected that? He read the email in earnest.

> *Dear Detective Sacker,*
>
> *You don't know me and I don't know you but I can help you solve this case. I'm one of hundreds writing and offering services right now. I can't*

show you a list of cases I've worked on, unless you want to count the recent spate of alien abduction inquiries.

Clever *smartass*. He continued.

So let's see if this gets you interested. I recommend that your forensics coroner makes a careful and biosafe study of the internal organs of the victims. Look for internal hemorrhaging beyond the skin bruising. Also, check the mouth pH. Perhaps it's more acidic than you might have expected, above even death-related acidosis.
    Sincerely,
    Grace Gone
    Gone Investigating, LLC

Sacker scratched his head. *Mouth pH? Biosafe?* What was the woman talking about? He pushed it to the side and turned his mind to the organ bleeding. Sutherland hadn't explained *that* to Sacker's satisfaction. Had the trauma that caused the skin bruising also damaged tissues deep in the body? He couldn't imagine how the vic could have survived such an ordeal. *Baseball bat to the entire body?* The killer had to be the damn Hulk. No one would ever have suspected the kind of internal damage they found. It was the stuff of traffic accidents and high-rise suicides.

So how'd you guess, Ms. Gone?

He leaned back in his chair, shaking his head. A very wild guess, no doubt. How many wacko theories would pour in over the next few weeks? If one in a thousand had a bit of luck, that'd explain it. And the craziness with mouth pH—who'd ever heard of something like that? The woman was likely unbalanced.

Still....

He opened his web browser and looked up the agency. Gone Investigating. Little play on her name. Well-designed webpage, looked professional, attractive photo of perky Asian chick right under the banner. *Grace Gone.* Sounded like a piece of noir fiction. Queens office, bit of a run-down neighborhood if he remembered correctly.

Nothing else on search engines. No consulting for big agencies or on any important cases. He tapped into the business databases. *Jesus.* Her license wasn't a year old. A complete rookie.

Still....

He rose and walked across the buzzing floor to Ladner's office. The captain banged a phone receiver down and waved him in.

"What's up, Sacker? Make it quick. I've got Internal Affairs coming by in fifteen."

Broad and insulated, Ladner's office dwarfed the space allotted to his detectives. The room visually connected to the floor by a set of large windows. Ladner brought an old-fashioned sensibility with lots of wood and brass, his wrestling trophies displayed, his hunting photos prominent. Sacker dropped into one of the two leather chairs facing the captain's desk.

"You check your email? See this one from some PI named Gone?"

Ladner cocked his head to the side. "You here to waste my time with some PI? Hell, Tyrell, I don't even check my email anymore. Diminishing returns in my position."

"Look, Mike, this should be a quick delete issue, but something's nagging me. First, she got our work emails, which means she's serious and able."

"Hackers do this stuff for minimum wage, these days."

"Point taken. But she also tells us to check for internal organ damage. As far as I know, that hasn't gotten anywhere beyond the confines of the forensics report."

Ladner ground his teeth. "*Dammit!* I'm going to personally shit-kick the leakers. Once these IA folks finish the yearly sermon, I'll check down with the morgue. They better be keeping things tight."

"It's Sutherland, Mike. Things are as tight-assed as is humanly possible."

"And?" asked his boss.

"So, just hypothetically, what if the report hasn't gotten out? What if she knows something that we don't?"

"Like what? What's there to know? The perps got worked-over

like we've never seen at the hands of some whack-job killer. Stuff broke. Stuff bled. End of story."

"When did you ever see that kind of damage, Mike? Even in a bad beating? I never have. Not like that, all over the body. That's been bugging the hell out of me. So here comes Ms. Private Eye and drops the observation like she'd figured it from something."

"Just got a lucky guess."

Sacker nodded. "My opinion, too. She also told us to check the mouth pH."

Ladner squinted. "The mouth what?"

"pH. I'm not sure what it is, but has something to do with chemistry. Acids, bases, salts and things."

"You ever heard of anyone checking the mouth pH as part of a homicide investigation, Tyrell?" Sacker shook his head. "Yeah, me neither. She's a hack. Don't waste any more time on this Gone. Okay?"

"Right, Chief. Thanks."

Doubts appropriately vindicated.

He stood and left the office. It didn't make any sense to bring in a nobody PI. Not on a case like this. Embarrassing he'd bothered his boss, really.

Mouth pH.

He sat down and stared at the email. A random guess on the organ damage, that's all. Gone was a startup looking for a break. Ladner was right; this was a waste of time. He deleted the message.

Still....

17

BEST LAID PLANS

Beneath the frenetic motion of busy civilians on the island of Manhattan, buried seven stories in the bedrock of a resurrected governmental Cold War bunker and accessed only through a hidden and guarded parallel passage to the Holland Tunnel, another kind of activity dominated. Here hundreds of men and women labored, their employment absent from all governmental ledgers, their names scrubbed from official databases. Soldiers and intelligence agents intermingled, weapons and computers side by side, high-tech equipment covering the thick, granite walls throughout a honeycomb of rooms. The hum of electricity and cooling fans hung in the air like an invisible fog.

In the center of this place that did not officially exist, in a cavernous room taking a page out of NORAD command centers, John Savas and Rebecca Cohen stood before a set of enormous monitors displaying false-color, real-time satellite imagery, reconnaissance photographs, and the pixellated faces of INTEL 1 agents Sara Houston and Francisco Lopez. On speaker was the midwestern twang of Elaine York, President of the United States.

"I don't have much time," she said. "Putin is stirring things up again. You folks need to sell me on this mission. Go or no go."

This is moving too fast.

Rebecca Cohen's brunette strands were in disarray, the eyes behind her square-rimmed glasses bloodshot. She sipped from a silver thermos, the coffee pungent in the filtered air. She glanced up at the screen.

"There are so many unknowns, Ms. President," Cohen said. "It's very high risk, very high reward."

"Give me the ground game again."

Cohen looked at Savas who rolled his eyes. *He's reaching his limit.* The quest to hunt down the vestiges of the Bilderberg Group drained them terribly over the last year. Months of little sleep and intense pressure, chasing a deadly quarry, one to become more deadly if they allowed it to escape. Deadly in a way they knew only too well. Lost agents, murdered in foreign lands far from home, tortured, and left as warnings, their broken bodies discovered by INTEL 1 as Nemesis deigned: corpses decorated with a single, purple hyacinth.

Sonbol. Cohen grimaced and returned her eyes to the screen.

She didn't need to look to see the graying of Savas's hair, his olive skin a rich caramel underneath the crown of white. She knew every contour of his form, had felt his exhaustion each night as they lay in each other's arms. This destructive chase had to end soon.

I just hope Nemesis cracks before we do.

"The infrared and microwave imaging from space is definitive, Ms. President," she began. "Zanjani was right—there's an extensive network beneath the monument. The underground buildings are accessed via a central shaft located here." She moved a digital pointer on the satellite imagery. "Likely an elevator. Thermal imaging patterns—heat sources, venting—show occupation. Someone lives underground. Whoever it is, they've gone to a lot of trouble to hide themselves."

"But not the Iranian government?" said York.

Savas cut in, his voice a rasp. "Negative, Ms. President. Of course, there's no way to know for sure, but there's been zero chatter, no data on this hideout from any intelligence source, foreign or domestic. The Iranian government couldn't hide its centrifuges from us, no way they could keep something like this quiet." He squeezed the bridge of his nose. Cohen felt a tension headache radiating toward her. "Nemesis is in Tehran. Everything backs that up. It's logical Bilderberg would have funded this lair for her alone. From all the data we've gathered, she basically controls the Iranian government, anyway."

The voice of Lopez crackled over the distant connection. "The last tentacle of the octopus. No other Bilderberg node exists that controls something so large as a nation-state. She came after us with *governmental* special forces."

"Given this assessment," said Cohen, "and the recent attack on our agents there, we are convinced she is in Tehran, mostly likely in the Azadi Tower bunker. This is a unique opportunity to finally end this."

"Exactly," said Savas. "Our recommendation's the full assault plan outlined in the report. We have a team of special forces with agent Lightfoote undercover in Tehran. They are Farsi-speaking Iranian-Americans, well-recruited, excellent soldiers. They'll accompany Gabriel and Mary, along with our CIA contact in the city, infiltrate the bunker, and neutralize any of Mirnateghi's forces. The intention is to capture her and render her to American-controlled areas."

York exhaled. "What's the old saying about intentions, roads, and hell? This could blow up in our faces. Your forces will be in the center of Tehran conducting an armed invasion of a national monument. What could go wrong?"

Cohen ground her teeth. "A lot could go wrong. It could become an international incident, tarnish your presidency, not to mention getting our agents killed."

"Don't worry about us!" clipped Houston through the static. "We're good to go!"

There was silence on the presidential line. Savas looked at Cohen, who shook her head.

I don't think she's this crazy, John.

And maybe she was right not to be.

"Your fail-safe?" came the President's words.

Cohen swallowed. "Blow the entire location. We have two teams for bugging our people out. But if all fails, her lair has to be taken out. All involved know the stakes."

"*Jesus.*" York was silent another moment. "You know, back when the country was collapsing around us and we were flying down the highway firing shotguns out of a '70s recreational vehicle, I felt I got to know the bunch of you. In a way nothing else in life can equal. But now?"

She paused. "It was some kind of crazy to give INTEL 1 this power, bury you in the irritable bowels of America, black-ops every god damn thing you did. But I *trusted* you misfits after we climbed out of hell together. And we had to do *something* after Bilderberg. Free the world and all that good stuff. But fighting these monsters, we're starting to look too damn much like them. Getting sick to my stomach."

Cohen watched Savas put his hands on the table in front of him, locking eyes with her. He shook his head. The mission was dead before it began.

"Green-lit," came a sharp voice over the speakers. "Keep me in real time when it plays. Don't fuck this up."

The connection was broken.

Cohen let out a long breath. Through the monitor, Lopez's voice broke the silence.

"Be careful what you ask for. You just might get it."

18

LOADSTONE

"Oh, holy hell."

Sacker rued answering the phone this Saturday morning. Two weekends in a row, he'd been hauled out of bed to a crime scene. His personal and social life smoked like the usual wreckage it was, so he was happy to keep distracted. But there had to be limits.

Especially with this case.

"Well, this raises the profile a bit." Hill's eyes were wide.

The yellow police tape clashed with the dark grays and greens of the soaring gothic structure and its pitted stone facade and towering spires. Spectacular crowds gathered for a Saturday sunrise in the city. The atmosphere crackled, New Yorkers boisterous. And why not? It wasn't every day you found a body displayed like butcher's meat in front of the nation's most famous house of worship. The Eunuch Maker had hit celebrity status.

Never take a work call Saturday morning, Tyrell.

He should have been deep in dream, waking later in blissful forgetfulness of the last week's insanities. Then a warm shower, some cool jazz, buttered toast, eggs, *bacon*.

Instead, a body dumped in front of St. Patrick's Cathedral.

He raised his eyes to the glory of the cathedral's main entrance, focusing on a cross-topped spire over concentric stone arches and dropping to an enormous wooden door. He didn't want to look farther than the door. But the monstrous demanded attention.

A naked body, corpulent, purple and bruised, squatted in front of the ornate wood. The cadaver was dismembered, the dissected crotch the focus of jutting hips.

It's just open season on our man-parts.

The corpse sported an unusual decoration: a donut-shaped concrete slab the size of a tire around his neck. Words were painted in red on the stone.

"Who IDed him?"

"A representative from the local bishop," said Hill. "These Catholics have a military grade rapid response team for these PR problems. Want to take a guess about our victim? You're gonna love it."

Sacker frowned. "Please don't tell me he's some defrocked priest that molested little boys."

"Ca-*ching!* Good guess, sir. But not defrocked. Just a forced retirement."

"Oh, Lordy. Eunuch Maker's developing a flare for the theatrical."

He took a deep breath. Time to go up there, examine that corpse, take notes and parse mutilation and death before breakfast. Once again, enter into the diseased mind of a killer.

Sacker squinted toward the body and stalled. "What's the stone say?" He sipped at the lousy deli coffee, uninterested in getting any closer without caffeine.

Snyder answered. '*Better with a millstone.*' No one has any idea what it means."

Sacker laughed. "None of you ever go to Sunday school?" There was an awkward silence. "And Jesus spake unto the disciples: '*It were better for him that a millstone were hanged about his neck, and he cast into the sea, than that he should cause one of these little ones to stumble.*'" Sacker shook his head. "When *I'm* the learned Christian in the world, the apocalypse is nigh."

"Killer's going pretty literal with that," said Hill.

"How'd he get that thing around the poor bastard's neck? Let me guess, no witnesses."

"No living witnesses."

"I didn't mean the priest."

"Me, either," said Hill. "This is St. Patrick's, right next to Rockefeller Center, not some Upper East Side residential. Cameras all over the place."

Sacker cast a withering look in her direction. "And you have leveraged the full weight of the NYPD to get access to the footage, right?"

"Already done, sir," she beamed. "Mentioned the killer could be a terrorist. Opens all the doors."

Real potential in her.

"Good work, detective." He looked back to the sacrilege above them. "He's getting grandiose. And pride cometh before a fall."

Snyder scowled. "I can see the bruising from here. And the mutilation."

"Yeah, same MO. Same general class of targets. It's our guy, all right."

"Or girl," said Hill.

"Or girl," said Sacker. "It might as well be Hercules for how that rock got here. Okay, let's give it a closer once-over and get ready for Sutherland and his team."

"Detective Sacker?" A nasal voice behind him.

He turned to see a suited man accompanied by uniformed officers.

And the lawyers arrive.

"Yeah, that's me."

"The church authority has asked me to arrange for the removal of the body. We just need your permission and a location, and we'll have it delivered."

"Anxious to clean up the Cathedral front door?"

"Yes, of course they are."

Sacker watched as news crews set up around the crime scene. "Well, we've got a little thing ongoing called an *investigation*. You might have heard of those." The man swallowed. "Means we do things our way and at our own pace. Apologies for the coming YouTube videos, tweets, and Facebook posts. But those horses are already out of the barn."

The lawyer's mouth drew into a line and he turned on a heel, storming off.

"You'd think they would care as much about finding the killer as protecting their image," said Hill.

"You'd think we all would, Kathy. Glass houses and stones."

Sacker turned away from the cathedral and popped a nicotine strip. The crowds had grown even larger. He felt another headache coming on.

"I wonder what qualifies for early retirement."

He glanced at the statue of the Virgin Mary and prayed the growing noise wasn't the blades of a news helicopter.

19

HERE TODAY, GONE TOMORROW

"Y ou drivin' home tonight, Chief?"

Sacker's head swam. He tried to place the voice. A shot glass swayed in front of him, the whiskey low.

How many tonight?

He couldn't remember. A bad sign.

Why am I so drunk?

Another bad sign.

"Yo, Chief? You there?"

Oh, yes. *Pat.* The bartender. *Weren't they all named Pat?* Well, he thought it was Pat. The bartender he thought was named Pat blurred in front of him.

I'm at Merry's! That's right. Nice little pub. Few yuppies. Too grungy for them, too many colors and odd people. A place Sacker could get a bit hammered in comfort.

"What's that, Pat?"

"I asked if you was drivin' tonight. I don't think you'll be passin' any breath-tests."

"Right. Yeah. No. Not driving. Gonna walk it off. Lot on my mind."

Pat nodded. "It's that killer sawin' off those guys' junk, ain't it? I seen you on TV. I knew it was you, right off. I told my wife, 'Damn if that ain't Chief Tyrell!'"

"Not a chief, Pat." His stomach heaved. Bile-flavored.

"Yeah, yeah. So, the cops found anything on this guy?"

Don't talk. Walk away, Tyrell.

"No. Not a damn thing. So, whiskey." He waved the glass around.

"Mmmm-hmmm. I get *that*. News can't stop talkin' about it."

Sacker downed the rest of the glass. "See, Pat, my *chief's* pretty upset about it all. 'We're gonna need some answers soon, Tyrell. Somebody's gonna find them, Tyrell. I hope to God it's not the Feds, Tyrell.' We don't catch the guy, we look bad. NYPD looks bad. The *mayor* looks bad. See what I'm saying?" He fought to stop the room from spinning.

"Gotta say, it all looks pretty bad on the TV."

"You oughta see the bodies up close. *That's* bad."

The bartender grimaced and took a step back, shaking his head. "No sir, that's why I pour drinks. Makes people happy." He smiled and stacked glasses.

The blurred lines were solidifying a little. Yes, the name was *Pat.* Irish, supposedly. *Weren't they all?* Seasoned, probably in his sixties. *Or older.* Gap-toothed with a face of Rosacea scars, shock of blazing white hair always in disarray.

Now, what was I gonna say to Pat?

His cell buzzed.

Fumbling with the device, he managed to enter the passcode before it locked him out. A text message. He squinted at the screen. *From Grace Gone.*

"What the hell? Don't these gumshoes ever quit? How'd she get my cell number?"

"Sorry?" asked Pat, as the bartender turned toward Sacker.

"Nothing, Pat. Message."

"From a lady, I hope?" He flashed the gap again.

"As a matter of fact, yes. But business related."

"Can start that way."

"Mmmm." He read through the long message. Same things she

said before. Mentioned the third killing. His mind treaded water with the booze and words. *Internal hemorrhaging. Marks around the mouth and nose; pH.*

"This girl's just crazy."

"Maybe crazy's what you need, Chief."

"Like an amputation," he said, pocketing the phone.

Pat leaned forward, donning his best bartender-therapist expression. "You say business, right? Well, that means police. Right now, that's gotta mean the killings. Am I wrong?" Sacker looked away. "So, that means your lady's got ideas you don't like about the killings? Yeah?"

"She's not my lady. Yes, she has ideas. She wants to meet. She's a private eye."

"Gumshoe! Yeah. Like Mike Hammer. I get it. Do the work you can't 'cause it's too rough, dirty."

"She's a tiny Asian chick with an expired firearms license. There won't be any Mike Hammering going on."

Pat embraced his time as a psychologist. "Yeah, then she's brainy, like Sherlock Holmes. She'll see all the things like a computer you can't. *That's* why she sounds crazy! Just like in the shows and then all the clues will show she's right!" He beamed.

Sacker frowned. He came to the pub to escape the precinct, not debate case procedure.

"Or maybe she's a nobody gumshoe working out of a dump in Queens who hasn't been involved in a single meaningful investigation. Drop it, Pat. We don't outsource work to PIs at NYPD. Not in my precinct, not on this case." The anger sobered him up a little.

Pat tried one more volley. "Okay, Chief, but like you said, things are bad and heads gonna roll soon. Ha! Maybe some more willies gonna roll, too! Ha! Ha!"

"And?"

"Maybe it's time to get desperate. Sometimes, ya gotta throw the Hail Mary." Pat winked and walked off to serve another customer, leaving Sacker to stew in his fermented juices.

The irony.

He'd considered bringing the woman in. But Ladner shot it down. An impossible dilemma. Boss is going to cook you if you don't solve the case pronto, but don't you dare try anything *creative* to get the job done.

But her words were nagging the hell out of him. Sherlock or not, she was either damn lucky or had some insight that might be useful. A whiz at digging up their private and confidential information. Unusually good or unusually lucky. But Sacker didn't think much of luck.

I should talk to her.

There. He'd admitted it. In his head, okay. But that's the first step. And why not? Ladner hadn't forbidden communications with Gone. Nothing wrong with a little chat, right? She'd reveal herself to be the amateur her resume suggested. That would be that. No harm, no foul. Crossed off the list.

Don't drink and sleuth, Tyrell.

He responded to the text.

"Interested to talk. Privately. Your office in Queens. Tomorrow?"

His phone buzzed. *That was fast.*

"My office. Any time that's good for you."

He tapped. "9 am."

He was going to have a hell of a headache. But nothing was moving in New York at that time of day on a Sunday. He might could manage it.

"Perfect. See you then!"

She closed with an emoticon smile.

"Unbelievable."

He punched numbers into his phone. A rough voice answered.

Focus, Sacker. Don't sound drunk.

"Frank? This is Tyrell. Remember that PI, the one who got our emails? Do me a favor. Run her through the system. Under the radar. I *know* what Ladner said. Just *do* it. As a favor. Yeah? Thanks, Frank."

He closed the call and put the phone away.

"Pat, tall glass of water, please."

He pulled out two aspirins from his bag. He'd have to detox as much as possible before tomorrow's meeting. Gulping down the water and pills, he tipped Pat, and turned to exit.

"Chief! Your hat." Pat held up the Ice Topper. "You said it was worth something."

Sacker pivoted back, swaying, and grabbed the hat. "Damn right, it is. Great grandfather's. Had a bar and dance joint in Harlem. During the Renaissance." He slipped it on.

"Well, if the lady made you forget *that*, she must be something special."

God I hope so.

He said nothing and walked into a biting evening breeze. Couples darted about, cars flashed past beyond the tracking capabilities of drugged eyes. He removed a pack of smokes and stared at the plastic covering.

So it's come to this. Two years on the gum and here I am.

"Fuck it." He opened the pack and pulled out a cigarette, lighting it with some matches swiped from the bar. He took a long, slow drag.

"Damn, that's good." If he was going to hell, he might as well enjoy it.

He shuffled down the road toward home, replaying events with staccato interruptions from each inhalation. Images from the PI's website danced in his mind.

"God, she's desperate."

He stopped as a taxi turned in front of him, wheels jumping the curb. He exhaled a cloud of smoke and water vapor into the night sky.

She's desperate? Well, so am I.

20

AZADI TOWER

The colossus of Azadi Tower glowed in the spotlights. Reflected rays from its massive contours illuminated objects around the structure, dooming any covert mission. Houston glared at their whining, international CEO and arms dealer Reza Zanjani.

"You idiots!" he hissed between his teeth, arms tied in front of him. He struggled against a special forces soldier, one of four, chaperoning him on the mission. "You'll be spotted before you get near the tower. *They'll kill us all!*"

Houston frowned. "Tape him."

The soldier yanked a strip of duct tape from his pack and stretched it over the muttering Zanjani. The soldier scowled.

"He shouldn't be here. Him either," he said, his eyes flicking toward Zaringhalam. "They'll compromise the mission."

"Calculated risks. One's our CIA contact. He's deep in Iranian cyberwarfare. Tape Mouth's the only one we have who's been down there, met the target. We might need him. I'm counting on his cowardice."

"It's his clumsiness that worries me more," said the soldier, turning away and surveying their surroundings. "But what *are* we going to do for cover? This mission is too improvised."

"No time. Intel came yesterday and the target might rabbit." She checked the smartwatch around her wrist as it synced with a communications satellite. "We have a plan for the lights. Trick of some old terrorist buddies." Her eyes never left the digital display on the watch. "In three, two, one...."

The bright light evaporated. A section of the electrical grid failed, plunging many blocks into darkness. Zaringhalam gasped and Zanjani wheezed through his nose.

"Our guardian Angel. One for one." She turned to the tower. "We *move*."

The strike team fitted night vision goggles and jogged toward the monument. The Seals fanned out in a fluid pattern, individual soldiers taking the lead in turn and holding a point. The rest followed behind, Lopez shoving the dealer forward with Zaringhalam at his side. Houston covered their backs.

Near the tower they saw the first signs of Nemesis. Shadows materialized by the elevator shaft INTEL 1 imaged from space. The forms gestured to the lights and surrounding city.

Not your normal blackout, boys.

"Hostiles, twelve o'clock," came the voice of the Seal commander.

She whispered into her mic. "Engage. Terminate and secure the entrance."

The soldiers struck like serpents. A single shot fired, the other guards brought down by hand. Lopez and Houston arrived with the Iranian pair as soldiers dragged bodies through a hidden doorway. The commander of the team exited the structure.

"Clear to the elevator," he said, "We should take the upper deck. There's an old-school hatch we can jimmy."

Houston nodded. "Just leave the bodies here. There's no time for more."

They entered the elevator. The team worked the fire-access hatch in the ceiling. It opened. One-by-one, the team boosted others through the opening to the roof of the cab. Safety rails lined the edge. Houston pointed to Zanjani.

"Tie him to the railing or he'll fall off. Nader—hold on."

Two soldiers complied, and Lopez called up from within the cab. "Secured?"

Houston gave him a thumbs up. He pressed the single button in the cabin. The cab jolted and dropped. Lopez leapt and grasped the edges of the hatch, hoisting himself through the opening. Soldiers aimed weapons through the ceiling toward the doorway as they descended several stories beneath the surface of Tehran.

Thirty seconds later, the elevator shuddered to a stop. Houston waited with her Browning in her hands, Lopez beside her with a stun grenade. The soldiers faced the doors as they sighted their weapons.

The doors opened. Lopez and two other soldiers bounced grenades off the floor and into the room. The explosions rattled the elevator car.

"Let them walk into the line of fire," said Houston.

They waited. No one came.

The soldiers looked to Houston and back to the doors.

"Go!" she shouted.

They leapt one after the other, the first wedging the doors open, automatic weapons aimed into the unknown. The troops landed, crouched, and moved out. Behind them Lopez and Houston followed, firearms raised and readied.

They burst into an empty room.

Damn.

Houston gazed around the space. *Definitely a command center.* Monitors displayed the darkened footage from outside. Tables were lined with the detritus of human occupation—papers, food, eyeglasses. Chairs were overturned, doors to other rooms left open.

"They bugged out," said the commander.

"We just missed them," whispered Lopez, his brows furrowed. "Something doesn't make sense."

Houston holstered her weapon. "Too damn easy. They knew we

were coming." She looked back toward the elevator. "Somebody go get Zaringhalam and that asshole down here. Maybe somebody knows something we don't."

Lopez approached a table in the middle of the space, a glass vase set alone in its center. He reached a black glove toward it, grasped something inside, and turned around, holding up his hand. His deep voice rolled through the still space.

"It's a trap."

Sonbol. A beautiful flower was set against the dark fabric of his glove, the many-petaled purple like a royal emblem. The sign of death from Nemesis.

"Iranian forces approaching!" called the commander, staring at the security cameras. The bright beams of a hovering helicopter strobed the ground in front of the tower.

Houston stared at the flower. "She's played us from the start."

"We have to get out!" cried the soldier.

"Not yet!" She glared at the elevator. "Disable the lift—slow them down. If we get out of this, we're not going home empty handed."

"Angel's worm," said Lopez. He pulled out a thumb drive. "Will any of the computers do?"

"If they're networked. Her code should spread and infect them all and start copying. Go!"

Lopez sprinted to the nearest machine and inserted the drive. She turned to the soldiers.

"The elevator. Now!"

The men ran to the lift and darted inside. Seconds later, the two Iranians stumbled into the room.

"Clear!" yelled a soldier.

An explosion rocked the space. Smoke and dust billowed from the mangled elevator, the lift machinery scattered across the floor. The commander approached Houston as his team moved the dealer past them, tying him to a chair.

"There's no going out that way," he said. "Unless we find another exit, we're sitting ducks."

"Sitting for a while," said Houston. "If they don't know another way in, it's going to slow them the hell down. Meanwhile, fan out. Search this place. Find me another exit!"

21

GOING, GOING, GONE

S acker put the mobile phone on speaker with one hand as he steered with the other. His head pounded. His stomach lurched rattling over a road that resembled a carpet bombed and neglected war zone. He glanced forward after dialing.

Oh gentrification, how fickle art thou.

He sped through a desert of ramshackle apartments, abandoned warehouses, and junked cars. The new money sweeping through Brooklyn and Queens snubbed this stretch. No doubt the rent was low. Gone worked on the edge.

"Yeah, Frank. Go ahead. And thanks for pulling weekend duty on this."

A distorted voice crackled out of the tiny speaker. "I owe you more than a few, Tyrell. Anyway, this is a weird one. Interesting."

"How so?"

"Superficially, all looks good. Agency's legit, licensed. She's got college records, birth certificate, no priors. Grace Gone, twenty-five, valedictorian and dancer in high school, first in class at CUNY: Forensic Science, finished in three years. Applied to—get ready for this—NYPD and served two years as a beat cop downtown."

"She was a cop? What the hell? How?"

"Beats me. Sounds like she's a little Einstein so maybe she was being groomed for detective."

"Then what happened?"

"That's one of the weird things. Suddenly, she's gone, no record as to why. A bit later, she opens her little agency."

"Maybe she couldn't hack a cop's life."

"Yeah, maybe. But to the really weird stuff. All the superficials are in neat order. When you dig a little deeper, things get murky."

"What do you mean?" He was nearing the address and began to slow down.

"Look, I couldn't do much, and I won't do more or Ladner will roast my ass. But to start, the parents. They're ciphers. Can't pull anything outside of her documents and some local registrations for marriage."

"Well, they immigrated or something, right?"

"Yeah, except there'd be some sort of record. A lot of records, Tyrell. There's nothing."

"Illegals?"

"Maybe, but Chinese? And they materialize all middle class with a genius daughter? Something smells funny here."

"Like what?"

"I don't know. But I've seen a lot of records, Tyrell, real people and not so real people. She doesn't look real."

"What do you mean 'not real'?"

"If I had to bet, if this were part of something a lot darker, I'd say her paperwork's forged. Her identity's fake."

Fake? What the hell? This was just getting better and better. "Witness protection?"

"Or mafia underworld—who knows? But I'd stay clear of this one. Too many red flags."

Shit. He was right outside her office building. "Thanks, Frank. Strike one off the debt."

"You got it, Tyrell. Good luck."

He stopped the car and shut the engine down. His head was a nail and the world a hammer. Even the damn hat hurt, so he left it in the car. He squeezed his temples and tried to figure out again what he was doing here.

"Okay," he muttered. "I've got a nobody detective I'm not supposed to work with who hacked into our NYPD mail servers. She's likely not who she says she is with a fake life story. I'm about to go in there and talk to her about New York City's most prominent serial murder case in over a century. My job is likely on the line. Now, why am I going to do this?"

He stared at the sad looking building and sign hanging over the door.

"Because I'm a damn idiot, that's why."

He opened the door and exited the Crown Victoria. A short walk brought him to the door of Gone Investigating. He rapped on the wood and pressed the buzzer on the side.

"One minute!" came a strained shout.

A woman's voice, and judging by the pitch, an anxious one. *Two desperate souls.* This had all the ingredients for a disastrous meeting. He heard movement, a confusing rhythm to her gait, but the door burst open before he could process more.

Grace Gone.

Frank had his research right. Chinese ancestry probable. Asian features, dark hair tied back. At five-four, he towered over her. She was thin, but athletic, the records of her dancing in high school making sense. Her dress was modest yet elegant, materials bought on a budget but worked together effectively. She wore no makeup or jewelry. Her eyes were keen—unnervingly bright—offset by their warm brown and a smile radiating from her face.

"Detective Sacker!" she said. "Please come in!"

He grunted and followed her inside.

Holy hell, what a dump.

It was every bit as threadbare as he imagined for the location and Gone's status. He adjusted his step, noticing she lagged with a pronounced limp, and let her lead him into an office. The space had all the appearance of once being a kitchen. She took a seat behind a simple desk and he dropped into an opposing chair. It felt so comfortable he wished he could sleep in it.

"Thank you for coming down here," she offered.

"Well, there was no way I was going to have you come to the precinct."

"I'm not a popular option in your group?" She smiled again.

She's cute. But not my type. Too small. "You could say that."

"Then why are you here?"

"Your emails got me thinking. I wanted to find out more about you. Meeting seemed the logical next step. Consider it a job interview with a very low chance of success."

"I am," she said, holding his gaze.

Sacker returned the stare. "Some things you said dovetailed with certain aspects of our investigations," he began.

"Like the internal organ damage."

He cocked his head. "Yes, exactly."

"But you think my idea to examine the mouth pH a little batty."

Had she bugged the precinct in addition to hacking it? "Lots of us did. That and your, how shall we say—"

"Status as a complete nobody?"

He laughed. *Cute and funny. Like the emails.* But laughter prodded the headache. "Right. Well, that's why I'm here."

"What you want is to be convinced I'm going to be useful to your investigation, that what I got right wasn't just a lucky guess and what I suggest—which could embarrass you if wrong—will be right more than wrong. Basically, you want me to convince you today I'm an investment worth the risk."

"You're an honest one, that's for sure. At least on the surface," he said, mulling the background check. "Since you like taking the lead so much, how are you going to convince me?"

Her jaw set. "Until you trust me, at least a little more, I can't do much for this case. I'd need to view evidence, examine bodies, crime scenes. So, I'm left with what we have here. That means I have to impress you with my skills as a private investigator using nothing more than what we both can access in front of us. Logically, it follows I have to train my deductive powers on you, detective."

"On me?" Sacker grinned.

"Yes! How is this for a deal: I'll tell you what I've figured out about you from our short time together. If you're sufficiently impressed, you put me on this investigation."

Sacker shook his head. "I'm not here to make a deal, Ms. Gone. But nice try."

"A tough negotiator." Her bottom lip pouted. Sacker had an urge to ease it back into her mouth. "Well, I'll do my dog and pony show anyway, and we'll see what you do."

"So you're gonna profile me, break me down? Things you can't look up online or your average Joe wouldn't have guessed by looking at me? And I'll be impressed?"

"We'll see."

Sacker eyed the small woman across from him, one side of his mouth twitching.

"All right, Ms. Gone. Impress me."

22

MISSION FAILURE

"They've rigged a rope-ladder," said Lopez, his face grave before the security footage. "It'll be soon."

Houston rolled a chair up beside him, placing her hand on his shoulder. "The worm?"

He opened another window on the screen. "Bug's fast. 90% coverage of the LAN-connected drives."

"That'll have to do."

"We're shut out here. Hardline's dead, and the place is shielded. No frequencies getting through. All this data's gotta get out the old-fashioned way."

Zaringhalam stood behind them, shaking his head. "Who is this Angel? The code is brilliant. It has spread like fire through their network, copying everything. And many of these drives have been recently erased—my guess is right before we came. They didn't have time for a secure erase, but the worm is resurrecting all the deleted files as well."

"I hope you'll get to meet her someday," said Houston. Lopez brandished the thumb drive. She walked over and grabbed it. "Meanwhile, this little stick might hold all the goods on Nemesis and her worldwide network." Houston removed a short knife from her combat boot and inserted the drive in its place. "We lost her, so it's all we have from this mission, which is going south very fast. Priority one: get this stick out of the country."

"The charges?" asked Lopez.

Houston nodded. "They're set. Proximity trigger on the timers. Nemesis isn't coming back here after today."

The commander of the Seal team jogged into the main room, shaking his head. Sweat and dirt stained his face. "Doesn't look good. They blew the back exit. Debris has us trapped in good. Tried to dig through, but it's half a day's work at least."

"We don't have half an hour," said Houston.

Another soldier slapped his firearm. "Then we give them one hell of a party before we go."

"No," said Lopez. "We've got to be smarter than that. Getting killed doesn't further our mission. The information will die with us."

Houston stepped toward the elevator, the sounds of Iranian troops echoing down the shaft as they descended.

"He's right. We play for time. Engage only if they discover the stick. This is going to be a PR bonanza for them. They're praying they can take us alive, believe me. Let's make it easy for them."

The commander glowered. "We have *very* specific orders, and they are *not* to be taken alive."

"And I'm running this mission," she said. "Those orders assumed a mission failure. We still have a shot to avoid that. We have the data. We're going to do everything in our power to get it out of Iran. Even if it means some personal humiliation. Or worse."

"Fuck that," said the other soldier.

Houston glared at him. "Don't make it personal, Sergeant. There's a bigger goal."

"Then what about the nation?" he asked. "They'll parade us in front of the whole damn world! Talking a lot of damage. Your stick worth it?"

"It likely is," said Lopez.

Heavy impacts came from the elevator cab, boots on metal. Shouts in Farsi burst from the shaft.

"Won't matter," said Houston. "We won't let it get that far. Escape is viable only in the next few hours, during transfer. Before they stick us into separate dungeon cells. Stay alert."

The soldier shook his head. "And how are we going to control the situation once they bag us?"

Houston grimaced. "We aren't out of options yet."

Lopez locked eyes with her. "A little divine intervention wouldn't hurt."

Iranian soldiers leapt into the cab from the opening in the ceiling, their boots slamming steel reverberating through the room. The first exited in combat readiness, aiming weapons at them and shouting. Houston raised her arms into the air and glared at the Seal team. They scowled, placing their weapons on the ground and hands in the air.

She returned her gaze to the onrushing troops. Their eyes were wary, fearful, yet determined. Sweat glistened on their faces. One came to a stop a foot from her, his weapon aimed at her face.

Houston smiled. "Howdy, boys."

～

"HAVE WE RE-ESTABLISHED CONTACT?" The voice of President York was cold and matched her hard expression on the large flatscreen.

"No," said Savas, his fingers scraping through his gray hair. "Not since they entered the bunker." He locked eyes with the image on the screen. "With the satellite data, troop movements around the monument, we've got to assume the mission's compromised."

"Compromised. What does that mean, exactly?"

Rebecca Cohen spoke. "We don't know. Transmissions were interrupted underground. It must be shielded. Maybe scrambled. Protocol demanded contact every hour. Someone would have left the bunker to send a signal. It's been silent. We conclude they couldn't."

The president bowed her head. "Then the chatter on NSA intercepts might be correct. They've been captured."

"The probability's growing, yes," said Savas.

"You understand what this means, John." No one answered. "It's not just the end of INTEL 1, possibly of my presidency. It means Iran and Nemesis will have a new freedom and leverage across the world. Our efforts will be shut down." The president shook her head. "I think Mirnateghi's played us. She's been one step ahead of you since Bilderberg. This whole thing was one long setup."

"I don't think so," said Cohen. "We've made progress. We've damaged her network. She had nowhere else to go. She was trapped!"

"And what do they say about cornered beasts, agent Cohen?"

"We're not abandoning ship yet, Ms. President," said Savas.

"Noise out of Tehran is there's going to be an international example made," said York. "Your people, some of them anyway, must be alive. And they're going to break them, make them confess to the world. It will be a spectacle. We've signed their death warrants, and worse."

Savas looked at Cohen, her face pale and hard. His voice was raw. "Yes, Ms. President. If it gets that far."

"If? What options are left?"

"There's no room for failure in this mission. *You* made that clear. In the event of capture of the strike team, the plan dictates a final secondary team operation."

"Carter rescue mission in the desert, 2.0?"

"Rescue is only one of the options—only when viable."

York's eyes burned on the screen.

"The secondary team is still in play," finished Savas.

"Our entire geopolitical strategy is at risk," said York. "I hope this mission was worth the coming sacrifice."

"They're my people, Elaine. We'll do what we have to."

"I want to know any changes, any updates. Use the red line." He nodded but her dark expression remained unchanged. "We're going to have a lot to answer for."

The connection closed and the screen darkened. The cavernous room was silent but for the hum of the machinery around them.

Cohen didn't look at Savas, staring forward at the cold mug of coffee in front of her. A rainbow from skin oils danced on the surface under the glare of the fluorescent lighting.

"John, you can't—"

"Rebecca! This is bigger than us."

"We've been through too much! I don't care what York or anyone else says, you can't!" She walked up to him and glared. He avoided her stare. "And even if you did, so what? Angel won't! There is no way in hell she's going to order the execution of our team. No way!"

"You're so sure about that?"

"Of course I'm sure! I've known Angel through too much. Fire and blood. You tell her to do that and she'll flip you the damn bird, go in herself and drag them out of the Iranian dungeons!"

Savas smiled. "Yes," he said, opening a secure communications link. "That's exactly what I'm counting on."

23

DEMAGOGUE

Elaine York struggled to compartmentalize. Ten minutes before, she'd left a situation room, briefed remotely on the catastrophic failure of the INTEL 1 mission in Tehran. A failure likely to doom her re-election campaign when the Iranians made it public. Ignoring that ticking bomb, she wrestled her mind to that very campaign in a meeting with her political advisors. Winning was critical. Losing could mean a setback in the broad effort to end the Bilderberg threat. And her opponent—his administration could mean an end to a great many things.

"I just don't understand this polling. It's like the rules of politics, of human behavior are suspended!"

She paced the Oval Office. Her two closest campaign staff, chief Greg Evans and media strategist Nina Raf, sat across from the presidential desk, watching their Chief Executive rant. They could not meet her eye.

"For every minor misstep we make, some less-than-stellar, or, *God forbid,* misspoken phrase, we lose measurable standing. Meanwhile, this...*man* can attack minorities, disparage women, even refuse to play by any norms of financial transparency. With every ignorant and bigoted thing he says, he *gains!* His numbers go up." She whipped around, trying to stare an answer or solution out of her advisors. "Your job is to explain this. Stop this. Defeat this. And you are failing!"

Evans cleared his throat. "Ms. President, we are in unprecedented political times. There is a pent-up resentment against a woman holding power. We've got to call it what it is. Many voted for you four years ago, overcoming biases for a historical moment. But it only made things worse when the usual problems in the nation remained only partly addressed."

"*Usual problems?*" shouted York. Evans shrunk into his chair. "Does this country forget what happened? That the survival of our democracy was up in the air? That Anonymous had crippled the country by sabotaging the digital world? That there was a military coup that nearly led to a civil war? And that it was that *female* in the Oval Office who stood up to that coup? That she *won*?"

Raf shook her head. "Memories are short, but it's worse than that, Elaine. Those were dark days. *Confusing* times. Suite's clever. His white nationalist attack dog Brennem put the blame for the crises at your feet. There's no lie they won't tell. Truth, consistency isn't the point. Pushing buttons is. They make up a reality many are desperate to hear. That's why every lie stains your reputation. Half the nation thinks you started the conflict now, that the military was trying to stop *you*. They've enlisted enough former soldiers who turned on you to give it credibility."

York shook her head. "Documented facts on this corrupt tycoon —fraud, civil rights violations, audio tapes that would have ended *careers*, proof of his monstrosity—nothing hurts him."

"It's hard to understand," said Evans. "But we have to accept this truth: facts, reason, evidence, consistency—none of this matters to his base. They treat Suite like a cult leader. A true, charismatic demagogue."

"He's taking his cues right out of the 1930s playbook," said Raf. "The chaos and economic damage from the crisis has many suffering. You know that. Combined with the deep misogynistic vein running through society—women haven't even been full citizens, able to vote, one hundred years—it's political napalm."

Evans cut in. "Exactly. Then you find a group the nation distrusts, is afraid of, and shape an entire platform around it. Use fear to drum up support. Use fear and blame to create simplistic problems and solutions. It was Jews and Communists once. Now it's Mexicans and Muslims."

"I can't believe this is America." York sat down in her chair behind the Resolute desk, drumming her fingers. "You know this wood came from a boat? British Royal Navy. Frozen in place, trapped in the ice at the North Pole." Her aids glanced between each other. "A challenge like this from some normal politician I could accept. But from this bigoted demagogue, this con man and liar and ignoramus—this is the nastiest political beating I've had in my life."

"We feel a lot of the strategy, the focus, is from Brennem. What he did with the white nationalist supporters—"

"Bigots," said York. "Stop normalizing them with euphemisms."

Evans swallowed. "He took the fringe to mainstream *despite* blatant bigotry—that's a political genius of a very high kind. His documentary films show he believes in a world clash of civilizations between the US, the Islamic world, and Asia. He's a fanatic. But he's organized. Suite doesn't have the discipline for this campaign. He's too much a narcissistic playboy."

"Whoever is shaping this strategy," said Raf, "the bottom line is it's working very, very well."

"We still have a significant lead in the polls," said York. "Most forecast us winning with high confidence."

"There's that, at least," sighed Evans.

Raf leaned forward. "I would like to play devil's advocate, Ms. President."

York glared at her. "You would challenge this narrative?"

"Yes," said Raf, holding up a hand as Evans tried to interrupt. "We're doing well in national polls. State polls are much closer. And some of the best prediction sites have unusually large error margins."

"Why?"

"The sampling is uneven, the results poorly reproducing. Some speculate there is a *shame* factor in admitting support for Suite distorting the polling."

"All purely speculative, Nina," said Evans, his face reddening. "We're very strong—"

"If the vote swings the wrong way," said Raf, "if the error is in the wrong direction in just a handful of states, it'll be close. We'll almost certainly win the popular vote. But the EC is a very different story."

"Another Bush-Gore scenario?" asked York.

"The polling shows you winning a lot more votes. Millions more. So, if Suite takes the College, it'd be worse than Bush-Gore. The raw differential in popular vote might be history making."

Evans shook his head. "Nina, what are you saying? Because it sure sounds like you might be suggesting—"

"She's saying we might lose, Greg," said York, leaning back in her chair. "That the voters of this nation, a minority of them, might just hand the most powerful position in the world to a monster. And God help us if they do."

24

GONE UNDER

S acker suppressed a laugh. *She's got spunk, that's for sure.* This might be fun.

Gone inhaled and fired words out like a machine gun.

"You're a heavy smoker, but have tried to quit for some time, and off the wagon recently because of the stress of this case. You tend to self-medicate stresses like this with different drugs, your personal vices the common ones of nicotine and alcohol. You're left handed, a former soldier, serving sometime before 2007, which likely places you in the Iraq War. You received a military scholarship and attended college, entering the police force as a beat cop but because of your intellectual abilities moved up to detective. You're single, and have never been married for any length of time, although you are very interested in women and date as frequently as your job allows. Currently this case is in big trouble, is going nowhere, and you have no leads to assuage the growing impatience of your bosses and the public. I could tell a lot more about you if I researched social media, public records, hacker databases. But this much I could get from our introduction."

Sacker sat still, his mouth open. "And I'm supposed to believe you just deduced all that? From meeting me this morning?"

"Yes."

"No way. I don't buy it. You've been looking into me. I like my privacy, Ms. Gone. I think this interview is over." Sacker stood to leave.

"I was fairly on target, wasn't I?" He scowled at her. She rose from her seat and steadied herself on the desk. "I haven't investigated you, detective, and I can tell you how I know each of these things. I also know that *you* have begun investigating *me*."

Sacker raised an eyebrow. "How would you know something like that?"

"Credit reports have been called out on my name today, right after you agreed to meet me. I monitor a lot of channels, detective. No doubt you had a colleague begin to look into my background."

Dammit! Okay, sister, I'm intrigued.

He sat down. She followed suit. "All right, let's pretend that you haven't been spying. How the hell did you come up with all that? What makes you think I smoke?"

Gone laughed. "That's an easy one. To a non-smoker with a good sense of smell, the products of burnt tobacco leave a strong, acrid odor easily detected on a person's clothing, skin, and their breath."

"Really?"

"Really. Nothing very impressive there. Look it up online and use mints." She frowned. "As for how I knew that you were a heavy smoker, several things. The first I admit to using a little outside information: the video of you on television at news conferences. You're there, just last week, right behind the mayor. You put a strip of gum in your mouth. But you don't chew it long. You park it in your mouth and stop chewing. You repeat this process of short chewing and then long periods of holding the gum in place. Not regular gum. Nicotine gum. Altogether, it was obvious you were a smoker and failed to quit, indicating heavy dependence on cigarettes."

"You're pretty damn observant."

"Part of my gift for the job, detective. A photographic memory also helps."

"Go on." Intriguing *and* uncomfortable.

"It's the failure to quit—which clearly happened over the last week because of the video date—that leads to the next conclusion. You use pharmacological compounds to self-medicate your psychological needs."

"Really."

"Yes. Why did you fail to quit just this week?"

"Maybe I tried the damn gum last weekend and it sucked. Went back to smokes."

"A military man, detective, assigned a high-profile case lacks the discipline to go more than a week on the gum? Low probability. The much higher probability is the stress of the case drained your willpower, a finite resource of the nervous system. This sent you back to the physical cigarette. Next, add your abuse of alcohol."

"My what?"

"Bloodshot eyes, dehydration evident in your skin and lips, squinting at lights—you have a hangover, detective. You were drunk last night and made a considerable effort to hide it, but all the signs are there. The timing is interesting. Right when you fall off the smoking wagon you also get drunk, yet keep enough control to function as a police officer. All the signs of a high-functioning alcoholic, and more generally someone who hasn't resolved his emotional issues and uses these vices to suppress the problems."

"Well, Ms. Gone, please don't hold anything back." *Definitely more uncomfortable than intriguing.*

"I'm not trying to insult you, detective. You asked for my analysis, and I consider this part of my evaluation in this interview, to show you the value of my services." She grinned innocently, as if she hadn't just picked apart his addictions.

"As for other aspects, your military service is obvious in the sleeve tattoo you try to hide under the shirt but which shows the Marine eagle near your wrist." Sacker looked down and sure enough, the shirt had pulled up. "Sleeve tattoos were banned from the Marines in 2007, so your service likely came before that, which puts you in Afghanistan or Iraq. Many more troops went to Iraq so the most probable assignment statistically for you is there. Detective at such a young age after military service? Indicates higher education, probably law enforcement related, and a sharp mind to promote you from the ranks of the beat cops. Unless you are wealthy, which doesn't match your speech or mannerisms, you went on a scholarship from Uncle Sam."

"*Jesus.*"

Gone smiled. "And you're not very religious, or you'd stop taking the Lord's name in vain."

Sacker shook his head. "And my personal life? I have a wife and kids at home. How about that?"

"Unlikely. First there's the drinking. Second your ability to schedule your time so freely without any concern for a family or its incredible scheduling demands. Now, you could just be an absentee father, but that doesn't fit the personality I see, at least at first glance. To back up that assessment, there's no ring, and no evidence on any finger of a prolonged wearing of a ring. You aren't married or weren't married very long. You don't have children."

"Maybe I'm gay."

"Not the way you continue to check me out."

Sacker sat upright a little more. "Now wait a minute. You've got that all wrong."

"I'm not offended. You don't leer. I'm not judging you." She smiled. "So, you aren't married, have likely never married, yet are interested in women. A detective, former marine—a good catch I would think except for the emotional issues revealed in the drug abuse. Perhaps those are military related or a longer-standing issue, but whatever the cause, it likely explains your lack of settling down, or at least trying to." She bit her lower lip, hesitating. "The longer-standing issue, of course, is the biggest secret you've been hiding."

Sacker stared at Gone, his expression frozen. "What secret?" His mouth went dry.

"It was the bone structure that clued me in. Hips, shoulder width. Of course, there are variations in the population depending on heredity and genotype, so this is a probabilistic analysis. And you were born unusually tall. Growth hormone use can lead to some additional bone development, but after puberty, it's not enough. Then there are the mannerisms. It's hard to lose decades of socialized gender norms." She leaned back in her chair. "And judging from your reaction, I'm now certain I'm correct."

Sacker stood. "This time, the interview really *is* over." His eyes were wide.

"*Please,*" she whispered, color draining from her face. "I'm sorry. Sometimes solving puzzles blinds me. I won't say any more. And I won't say anything to *anyone*. You can trust me. Who'd believe me anyway with your record?"

I'm completely naked here.

This was the strangest conversation he'd ever had. This diminutive woman possessed some sort of oracle-like power to pierce through the thickest armor and disguises. She could in minutes uncover the deepest secrets. Part of him wanted to leave and never return.

Hell, I want to deck her.

Another part drew him in. For no reason he could justify, despite Frank's strange background check and the risk he was taking, Sacker trusted Grace Gone. He worked against it, tried to devil's advocate that feeling into the grave. But it proved indomitable.

"You said the case was going nowhere. How do you know?"

"That's the easiest of all, detective," she said, meeting his gaze. "You're here."

He coughed. "Well, all very impressive. Really." His eyes darted to her and away. "And we're done talking about me, understand?"

The pout. "I have so many questions. There has to be a story about how you got into the armed services."

"There is."

"But I'm not going to hear it."

"No, you're not going to hear it."

She beamed. "Good! Then let's talk about murder, shall we?"

PART II

TOO FAR GONE

"In vine-clad Lemnos, where in far-off days they had abducted women from Athens and raped them producing children, their wives wreaked murderous vengeance on all the men."

—Quintus Smyrnaeus, *Fall of Troy* and the *Byzantine Greek Lexicon* (10th Century A.D.)

25

GONE WRONG

"**A**bsolutely not!"

Sacker fought an eye roll. Ladner's bald head was red, his teeth in full grit, his hands clenching and unclenching. This was not the time to show any impatience with the tantrums of his boss. Now was the time to sit there like a man and take the beating.

"Didn't we have this conversation? Didn't I make my position clear?"

Never answer a rhetorical tantrum question.

"I just got back from the mayor's office. Our fucking jobs are on the line. Do you know what that Cathedral debacle is costing this administration? No, of course you don't. You're too busy wasting all your goddamn time chasing after some crazy chick in Queens! Normally, I'd tell you to do what you want on your own time. But until this case is solved or filed in a vault, you don't have any free time, detective! Do you understand that?"

Okay, maybe it's time to fan the flames.

"She's a damn genius, Mike. A short and pouty Sherlock Holmes. She's free and she's hungry. I want to crack this case as much as you do. That's why I say *bring her in.*"

"What part of *no* is confusing you? All we need's the press to get wind of something like this. Jesus! The next headline is "Floundering NYPD Outsources to Charlene Chan!"

"Grace Gone."

"Whatever. This is the end of this bullshit, do you hear?"

I'm getting nowhere. "All right, Captain."

"I'm serious, Tyrell. We're playing big league ball here. I like you, but don't cross me. My job's on the line. You're known to buck orders."

"You've never complained before."

"You're productive. But this one is different. We're *far removed* from a homicide investigation. This is a glowing ball of radioactive political waste. The rules change. Don't screw with me." Ladner glared at him.

Sacker had never seen the man so hostile. "Or what, Mike?"

"Or I'll have your badge, Tyrell. That's a goddamn promise."

❧

SACKER STORMED BACK to his desk.

"Shit!"

The chair creaked as he fell into it. Snyder and Hill kept their distance, eyeing him from their desks.

Ladner's tying my hands.

They had nothing to go on, only cryptic murders, devoid of incriminating evidence, unlinked to any location or individual. A small army of detectives across the city chasing down one dead end after another. He needed something. Everyone knew they needed something. So why was Ladner being so damn stubborn?

And a voice materialized to answer his question. "He can't risk the exposure."

"So says this ancient relic."

Brad Rosenberg. Supposedly retired a year ago, but he continued to haunt the corridors of the 12th like some ghost that couldn't pass to the next world. His thick Long Island accent gave him away even before Sacker turned around.

The old Jew's eyes still burned behind his glasses, his beard short and hair trimmed. He sat on the corner of the desk, squashing case reports.

"Egos are always the problem. This case sounds bad. You'll need all the help you can get. Wherever it comes from. Even if others don't approve."

"I'll be out on my ass."

"He said that?" Rosenberg sighed. "Too much fire in Ladner. Too little forethought. I've seen better, and worse, in my day."

"Well *today* is my day."

"This PI really might be useful?"

"I'm sure of it. I met her yesterday. If she'd told me I lost my virginity on my sixteenth birthday with the camp director's daughter, I wouldn't have blinked."

"Maybe you're a little star-struck?"

"I'm no rookie, Brad. It wasn't just what she did. It was how damn fast, how accurate and sure. Never seen anything like it."

"Hmmm."

"And her ideas on the case—maybe they aren't all right, but so far she's one for one with the organ damage. We're crazy not to give her a look at the evidence. At least hear what she says."

Rosenberg shrugged. "You should never take the advice of an old man who lived in different times. So if I say work with this Gone woman, show her the bodies, let no one else know you're hallucinating."

Sacker squinted at the former detective. "Go behind Ladner's back? Risk my damn job?"

"Of course not! Like I said, *never* listen to an old man." Rosenberg patted him on the shoulder and stood, leaving Sacker to spin in his own thoughts.

Hill and Snyder inched closer.

"You think it's safe to approach now?" Sacker said.

God I'm tired of babysitting.

Hill smiled. "You didn't attack the old man. Figured you'd cooled down sufficiently."

"So, what did old Rosenberg say?" said Snyder.

"Nothing much. Just crazy old stories of what he did in his time."

"What did he do?"

Sacker grunted. "Nothing of use to us now. I've got a new assignment for the both of you. Go down to medical, convince Sutherland to run some tests on the mouth of the victims. pH test."

"pH test?" asked Hill.

"Yes. Tell him I'm wondering if the cause of death was carbon dioxide suffocation."

"What's that?"

"Nothing I'd run across before, but they use it to kill animals, small rodents and such after experiments. Enough of the gas in your blood and it knocks you out. Eventually kills you. Enzymes in the mouth can turn the gas into an acid. Lowers the pH."

Hill looked to Snyder and back to Sacker. "You get a Ph.D. in biochemistry over the weekend, sir?"

Sacker waved her off. "Just mention it to Sutherland. Remind him about the indentation around the mouth. Maybe left by an anesthesia mask. Maybe he'll be convinced enough to give it a try." Hill raised her brows. "Get! Time's in short supply, if you haven't noticed." The two rushed toward the examiner's office.

Ph.D. in biochemistry.

Sacker smiled. Did Gone have one? It didn't matter, she might as well. And computer skills. And light speed deduction from a photographic memory.

Fuck Ladner.

Rosenberg was right, about what he had to do and how stupid it was to do it. But this case would define his career, define an entire generation at NYPD and the 12th precinct. They would *not* be the group that failed to catch this killer. And Grace Gone was his ace in the hole.

Ace buried very, very deeply in the hole.

He didn't know how he was going to pull it off, but he was going to put her on the case. Unofficially, clandestinely, as a consultant, and hopefully no one the wiser. If they were discovered, he hoped their progress would earn him a keep-your-badge pass from the boss.

He dialed a number on his cell.

"Ms. Gone? This is Tyrell Sacker. We need to meet."

26

DROPOFF

A black van inched into a dim alley running between buildings of New York University. Several hours before dawn, the general glow of the city oozed across blocks and reflected off low-lying cloud cover, painting the concrete canyon with enough illumination to make out its decaying and aged state. A sign over the rusted doorway of one building noted "NYU Center for Reproductive Medicine."

The van stopped beside a collection of large trash bins. Above them a security camera dangled, its wiring rotted away and disconnected. The driver exited wearing black clothing, a mask concealing facial features, and proceeded around the vehicle. Opening the back, the dark figure removed a large and laden body bag, hoisting it on a solid shoulder, and shut the doors to the van with a free hand.

At the pocked and stained walls of the building, an old door was askew. A warp in the frame prevented the spring latch from engaging. The shadow approached the back entrance, pulled on the handle to swing the door out, and ducked inside with the body.

Four floors later, a stairway door creaked open, a concealed phantom glancing around the hallways before proceeding. The intruder panted, drained from hoisting the body bag four flights. But the hallways were dark and empty, all the laboratories closed for the night, and no scientists served as witnesses.

The broad shape dropped the bag to the floor beside a keycard reader, the object rattling the wall of glass separating the hallway from the laboratory space. Inside the lab, the lights were off, but computer monitors, centrifuges, and other scientific equipment painted the space with an eerie, bejeweled glow. A brass plate hung on the locked door near the body: *Linda Richards, M.D., Ph.D.*

The body bag hummed as the killer yanked the zipper from top to bottom. A rustling of fabrics, plastic and cloth, preceded the removal of a mummified form in white. Gloved hands peeled away the covering layers while propping the corpse in place, then stuffed the shroud into the black bag. The supporting arm jerked backward and flesh slapped the doorway and floor.

Stooping, the killer hung a plastic slider bag around the neck of the naked form, white pages visible through the translucent material. The shadow picked up the bag in one arm, removed a small can from a coat pocket with the other, and sprayed a mist over multiple surfaces—the body, plastic container, door, wall, and floor around the corpse. Retracing earlier steps to the stairwell, the retreating shape sprayed the handles and rails, coating everything touched.

Returning to the bottom floor, the grim figure exited the building, moved to the front of the van, and entered. The vehicle coughed, and without engaging the lights, the driver eased out of the alley and into the streets. Within seconds, the van rounded a corner, vanishing into the mist like a wraith.

27

PRISONERS

A soldier jerked off the hood, and Lopez squinted in the bright light. He breathed in small gasps. He hadn't resisted, but they had taken batons and gun butts to his ribs, anyway. He didn't think any were broken, but it hurt like hell. *Always gotta foul the big guy, huh fellas?*

They hadn't been taken far, some side room in the underground lair beneath the Iranian monument. He suppressed a smile imagining their engineers rigging something to get them up the elevator shaft. The secret to success and failure: always logistics.

Their captors dissected the structure of the strike team, separating the Special Forces troops from the members of INTEL 1. Iranian soldiers lashed them to chairs and hooded them, leaving the group in silence. Lopez heard the footsteps of guards patrolling outside, but could only make out staccato Farsi whispers in the hallway.

As his eyes adjusted to the light, he saw that the Iranian secret police had arrived. SAVAK or NOPO, what they called themselves mattered little. They were the elite governmental force, the black ops that took care of problems others couldn't. Beside the NOPO uniforms, a thin, suited man with a goatee glared down at them with a broad smile. Lopez recognized the face from briefings. *Mahmoud Karami*. The Butcher of Khorramshahr. Head of the NOPO and its most clandestine and extreme forces. Lopez assumed the enhanced interrogation would begin shortly.

"You Americans will never learn," Karami began, laughing with a rasp in his throat. "Failure, embarrassment. Every time your supposedly *special forces* operate in my country, we teach you your place."

Lopez didn't respond, nor did any of the group. He tugged at the ropes binding him. They did not give. *Professional.* He was not going to break them. His mind flashed back several years, when he and Houston struggled, tied to chairs in a similar fashion with little hope. Only the chair he sat on today was not rotten. He would make no dramatic escape. He did not try. His struggle became resisting the pull to look for Houston. He sensed her beside him, smelled her. But he dared not betray their bond and give these bastards any more leverage than they had.

"The circumstances of this raid puzzle even our organization." Karami gazed upward. "What is this place? Beneath our great tower? Not American. But then why are you here? Who tipped us off at the highest levels? Perhaps you three will be able to enlighten me."

He's good.

An experienced interrogator. His threats were palpable. He emitted a pungent will to violence. Basic survival instincts responded to it.

And you can suck air, amigo.

"No? I didn't figure this would be easy. We will likely need to go down some most unpleasant routes." Lopez tried not to tense as the man fixed his gaze toward the shape of Houston beside him. "And we have a *woman*. How easy they will break when we have our way with them." That grin again.

Houston moaned. "Please, no...."

Lopez stilled his muscles. *Sara, careful.* She was always playing the gender card with brutes like this.

Karami's eyes widened. "Indeed. And aren't you the athletic one." He bent down and stroked her cheek. She recoiled. "There is plenty of time to become much better acquainted." He straightened up. "But not now. My superiors need information. And your cooperation. And they need it now."

He whistled sharply. Footsteps sounded outside the door and two men dragged in Zaringhalam. His eyes went wide with terror.

"We know there are more in Tehran. We cannot afford to be blindsided. You will tell me the nature of this operation, the location and numbers of your other agents before we leave this room."

"Or what?" squeaked Houston.

The Iranian nodded. One of the soldiers removed his sidearm and fired. Zaringhalam screamed, the fabric in his pants ripped, the beige darkening as blood flowed into the fabric and began to run down his leg.

"Or we keep firing, removing limb by limb, until he is dead."

"Oh God..." whispered Houston.

"Time is of the essence," said Karami, focusing on Houston. "You'll tell me now or he dies." The soldier raised his weapon again.

"Wait!" cried Houston. "Whatever you want! Just don't kill him!"

Lopez played along, forcing a gasp. "Shut your mouth woman, or—"

The blow whipped his head backward. He tasted blood, felt it flow over his chin. He stared down the barrel of a gun.

"Shoot him if he speaks again," said Karami. "Speak, woman!"

Houston spoke in a high pitch, her voice trembling.

"There's a second team. Led by another of our intelligence group."

"How many?" he shouted.

Houston stiffened, her acting so raw Lopez felt a sting of anger.

"I don't know! Not larger than ours."

"Where!" A nod from the interrogator led to a baton across Zaringhalam's back. He crumbled to the ground, moaning.

"They don't tell us!" she stammered. Lopez heard tears in her voice. "The cells are kept in the dark. Only coded communications."

She's so good.

Even now, after so many missions, she could impress him.

Enough truth for them to swallow it, but enough omitted to protect the mission.

And she's dragging this out. Stalling. Move your ass, Angel!

"Then you can reach them. Provide the key codes. Arrange a meeting."

Her body slumped. "Yes. But only above. Everything's shielded here."

Karami smiled and jerked his head to the door. The men dragged the unconscious form of Zaringhalam out the door.

"What will you do—"

Karami struck Houston with the back of his hand.

Hail Mary, full of grace, the Lord is with thee. Don't look concerned. *Blessed art thou amongst women, and blessed is the fruit of thy womb, Jesus.* Look angry at her. *Holy Mary, Mother of God, pray for us sinners, now and at the hour of death.* She is nothing to you. Just another operative. *Amen.*

"You were not spoken to. You will learn proper respect, woman. I can assure you, you will learn it before you leave." His twisted face relaxed. "So will you all. You will all confess your crimes before the world. Once we have the others in hand, your re-education will begin."

He shouted in Farsi and guards swarmed into the room.

"Now, we will go outside." He looked at Houston. "You will make a call. And we will all take a ride to your new home in Iran."

28

DIVINE INTERVENTION

S unlight blasted inside as the doors opened to Monument Park. They'd cordoned off the area, the usual press of tourists nowhere to be seen. Secret police left positions near the hidden entrance and grouped with those escorting the captives.

The NOPO resorted to roped pallets to solve the exploded-elevator problem. Lopez didn't envy the men who'd hauled them up. He envied less the American special forces team, grimacing to see signs of violence on them. *Of torture.* But even such horror had to be pushed aside. There wasn't much time left.

The walkway broadened as they progressed. It ran a thousand feet from the base of Azadi Tower to the tree-lined edge of the park. At the end of it, the path opened to become a wide square.

Perfect for landing a helicopter.

The NOPO rushed. They moved their prisoners with an enthusiastic abandon. A great prize was to be delivered to dungeons elsewhere in Tehran, as fast as possible. The helicopter it was going to be.

"Call!" snapped the head of the Iranian secret police. Karami grabbed Houston by the back of the neck and jammed a mobile phone in her hand.

"This won't have proper encryption. Our devices are chipped, it's—"

"*In extremis*. You have codes for it. I know you do. *Use them*." He squeezed her neck. Houston cried out.

"Yes! *Okay!*" She dialed.

The conspicuous group marched forward. Regular Iranian police set blockades and redirected traffic away from the park, confusion on their faces. Trees lined sides of the walkway. A tunnel of colored foliage danced in the breeze.

They neared the square at the end of the path. Houston's voice rose in pitch.

"They're not responding!"

"You will keep trying. If you fail, you will be very sorry."

Houston grimaced, dialing again. As she looked forward, her pace slowed and she gasped.

"Oh, my God, *she's* here."

Lopez gazed forward. *God be praised.*

A wiry woman in desert fatigues approached from the center of the square. Bare, tattooed limbs swung from her sides, a scandal of skin for the Imams. The morning sun glinted off mirrored aviator glasses, the light competing with the shine from her shaved head. She carried no weapons.

Angel defenseless? Be afraid, Karami.

The soldiers rushed forward, leveling weapons at her and moving to intercept.

Karami removed his sunglasses. "Who is that?"

Lopez chanted, heedless of their captors.

"An angel of peace, a faithful guide, a guardian of our souls and bodies. We ask of the Lord."

The NOPO ignored him, focused on the figure sauntering toward them.

"Our lead agent," whispered Houston. "I don't understand. She shouldn't be here!"

The men approached the singular figure, a cautious shuffling replaced with increasing struts. Their weapons trained on her, the woman slowed to a stop, making no other moves. They padded her down. Satisfied, the NOPO chief confronted her.

"Who are you?" he shouted, his upper lip covered in sweat. "Why are you here? Where are the rest?"

The woman smiled and removed her mirrored shades. Her eyebrows glowed orange, the irises below a taunting, emerald green.

"One answer to all your questions." The man's brows furrowed. "Contingency."

Sharp spits sliced through the wind, bullets flying from the trees. Heads popped, blood bursting from the skulls of Iranian police as waves of sniper fire leveled the NOPO troops.

Never knew what hit them. With his bound hands, Lopez made the sign of the cross.

Karami spun in shock, jolted by the violence, gaping at the fallen men. He reached for his firearm, his motions robotic. The bald woman grasped his wrist from behind, wrenching it. He screamed, shoved sideways and disarmed, staring down the barrel of his own gun.

American commandos appeared from scattered positions in the trees and sprinted toward the group. They freed the captives, several maintaining an armed watch on their surroundings. The bald woman replaced the shades with her left hand as she aimed with her right.

"Hi, Sara." Her mirrored eyes sighted down the barrel.

"Angel Lightfoote," said Houston. "About damn time." Houston reached into her interrogator's suit and removed his phone. "The police?"

"Handful on the perimeter," said a soldier next to Lightfoote. "Neutralized."

"This is a NOPO dark op," Lopez said, rotating his freed wrists. "Law enforcement's clueless. We just killed a bunch of traffic cops."

"That won't last long," said Houston. She spoke to the soldier. "Tell your team to stash the bodies in the trees. Put on their uniforms. Nothing fancy. We just have to get the pilot to land."

"Pilot?" asked Lightfoote. "Ah."

Houston shoved the phone at Karami. "Your turn, asshole. Call in

the damn helicopter or she splits your fucking head open." Karami
gaped. Houston turned to the soldiers. "Farsi, anyone?" One called
back and she waved him over. "See he does it right."

Sweat poured down the spymaster's face as he took the phone.
His hands trembled. He dialed.

Lightfoote kept the weapon centered on the man's face. "You're
lucky they rushed this. No re-enforcements, or we'd be screwed."

Karami spit words into the phone, eyes darting to the soldier
watching him. The American gave a thumbs-up.

"How long?" she asked.

Karami's voice scratched like sandpaper. "Thirty seconds. A
minute at most. He was instructed to remain close."

Lopez gathered Lightfoote's men around the former captives,
their NOPO uniforms misfitting and blood-stained. On request, one
handed him a large knife. The deep beat of blades thumped in
his ears.

"Tag-team, Angel." He approached their prisoner, flashed a sharp
edge, and prodded him in the back. "Walk real slow. This thing
cuts deep."

Lightfoote lowered her weapon and turned to the square. The
helicopter approached and kicked grit in their faces.

"Knives are always scarier," he said. He prodded Karami again.
"Wave normally."

Karami waved to the aircraft.

29

BIRTH CONTROL

C amera flashes popped like fireworks around him, and Sacker downed two more ibuprofen with his cold coffee. The laboratory lighting summoned a tension headache all by itself. Row after row of ceiling-mounted, 1960s-era fluorescents forced him into a perpetual squint.

Then there's the dead body.

The corpse luxuriated in a decidedly uncomfortable manner against the entrance of Dr. Linda Richards' lab. The medical photographers buzzed, but Sacker didn't need to see photos or the body beyond a moment's glance. He knew the details.

Horrific bruising. Mutilation. Death.

The only variable was the new note from the killer. He scanned the empty lab. At least there wasn't going to be another PR disaster with photos and videos streaming around the net.

His cell buzzed. Again. He ignored it. Gone could wait. She'd understand why he stood her up this morning. He'd dangle the prospect of seeing this new body before her. He assumed that would dispel any ill will.

"Hey, Sacker, sir," came the voice of Snyder. "Dr. Richards is ready to talk to us now."

He rose from the body and stepped to a door on the other side of the short hallway. Inside a small office stood three scientists—Richards and two other members of her laboratory. Sacker introduced himself.

Richards followed suit. "I'm Linda Richards, and this is Thomas Dyer," she said, indicating a tall, Germanic looking male. "Thomas is my most senior postdoctoral scientist. He runs the lab when I'm traveling, which is often these days. His ideas and work are the cornerstone for much of our progress these last few years." She motioned to a short Indian woman who contrasted the blond Dyer. "This is Shilpa Reddy, my laboratory manager. Shilpa is the boots-on-the-ground, day-to-day manager of the lab, keeping things running, people in line, and stocks reordered. She has magic hands at the bench." She moved to the chair behind her desk.

"How many total in your group?" he asked.

She sat. "Sixteen."

"Where are the rest?"

Richards waved a hand toward the corpse at the end of the hallway. "They left this morning, soon as they saw *that*. Some never showed. Warned in advance, I guess. I can't blame them. A disaster for the lab."

"Yes, unpleasant for many." He glanced at the body.

"I don't do guilt, detective. Spare your energy. And it's not hard to guess the killer, now is it? Which means dead Joe Dickless is likely some serial rapist or child molester. Not much sympathy for him here."

"Duly noted. Explain to us then what the note was about. We couldn't make heads or tails of the technobabble."

She sighed. "It was a threat. The killer threatened me, my whole group, anyone working with me including collaborators at other institutions. He demanded we stop all work on our male contraception research. Demanded I *publicly* disavow continuing work, destroy all research samples. The letter said I have one week to comply or people in my group would start dying."

"Our killer is obsessed. What is this research?"

Richards exhaled, the muscles on her face loosening. Sacker thought she gained a hundred years in an instant.

"My life's work. My dream to find a biomedical solution to birth control, one targeting men. One to take some of the pressure off women who subject their bodies to hormonal bombardment over decades. To find a cheap and effective treatment not interfering with the precious male needs in sex," she said. "It's a long-term goal of the pharmaceutical industry and we are close. We *were* close. Now, it's all shot to hell."

"Why?" asked Hill. "Are you going to do what he asks?

"What choice do I have? Look at the pile of bodies flooding the city. This killer is serious. A complete psychopath. There's no way I'm going to subject my people to that sort of danger. My work is in the literature. Let someone else, somewhere else, pick it up."

"And steal your deserved glory."

Richards smirked. "As a woman in a man's world, dear, you'd better get used to it. I've got other options to pursue."

Sacker redirected. "Could it be a competitor? Someone who wants to take over the field?"

"Like this? I can't imagine even my most unpleasant colleagues undertaking this slaughter for a leg up. Besides, there's too much symbolism in the killings, don't you think? There's more to it than simple industrial sabotage."

"It would make a good cover."

"No way," she said, passing her hand over her forehead. "Don't waste your time on that idea. Anyway, so you can see why we're a ghost town in here now. It's either threat of death or the destruction of all their research. I suspect they're plotting their transfers at this very moment."

"Those two stayed." He indicated Dyer and Reddy.

"Like I said, they are the heart and soul of my group. They are the ones working until ten at night every day of the week, putting off social lives, families, retirement savings in this pitifully remunerated business. They needed big results. Their careers are as invested in this as mine, more so. I'm tenured. Now, where are they going to go?"

"We're collecting security footage from the building," said Sacker. "We're going to need statements from all your lab members, custodial staff servicing your floor, anyone who had access to the building last night."

"Are you suggesting it was someone *here* who is the killer?"

"We are suggesting and assuming nothing, but also leaving nothing unexamined."

This killing had narrowed the time of a crime—the body drop-off —more than for any of the other victims. He didn't want to admit how desperate they were, that they had zero leads, that this was the most promising thing they had come across.

She saw right through it.

"God, you've got nothing, do you?" She shook her head. "Sure. I'll get you names, contacts. You're wasting your time, but it's your investigation." She walked to the doorway and stared down the hall at the body and reams of police tape.

"Meanwhile, how long until NYPD gets this mess out of my hallway?"

30

GONE ALL IN

Sacker drove through Queens, cell phone in hand, on the way to see Grace Gone. He swerved to miss a delivery bike cutting from the left lane, missing the back tire by inches. *I need hands free.* He put the phone down and set it to speaker.

"Kathy, once again please. Nearly wrecking the wreck, here."

Hill's voice crackled through the phone. "It's bad news on the security footage. Nothing at all. We've got all the staff—scientists, maintenance, custodial, administrative—going in and out. Working with their HR, we've accounted for all of them. According to the footage, no one who went into the building on Monday stayed in it that night. Everyone was out by 11 pm."

"No footage of anyone else entering later?"

"No, but there's a hole in the system."

"Damn."

"Yeah. Back staircase and alleyway door for the trash. The camera's shot to hell and hasn't been maintained for some time. Nothing covers that stairwell."

"So our killer came in through the back."

"Only possibility. We've examined everything, but you can imagine, it's a mess of workers' prints and lots of garbage."

"Ode to Joy. How's the latest eunuch?"

"Sutherland has nothing new to add. Same old, same old. Oh, and he didn't do the pH test. Just ignored me like I never asked."

"We might need to take things into our own hands."

"What was that, sir?"

"Nothing. Anything else from the crime scene?"

"No. Back to square one."

Sacker sighed. "Yeah, where square one is serial killings and threats."

"We've started interviewing the staff. Whoever left the body, presumably the killer, also had a working knowledge of where to break in. Logical it could be a staff member."

"Concur. Although with this killer, anything goes. Maybe he just does his research."

"Or hers."

"Right." He was approaching Gone's block.

"Anyway, most have alibis, and those who don't are these Aspergers types living alone. They scream 'serial killer' so loudly it's too obvious." That brought a laugh. "In the backgrounds, no priors, no serious mental illnesses, nothing suspicious. It will take weeks to talk to them all."

"Okay," he said, pulling to a stop in front of Gone Investigating. "My guess is you'll strike out, but be thorough. Also, keep the list and data. Things might be opaque now but could gel with more information. Anything on the cathedral security footage?"

"The red tape on this is awe-inspiring. I'm hoping by the end of the week we'll get all the clearances."

"Whatever you do, don't talk to the Feds. This is too big now. They'll swoop down on us any minute and we'll be making them coffee for the next six months."

"Yes, sir."

"Keep pressing, Kathy. I'll talk to you later."

He stopped the car and closed his phone. *Even my damn eyes hurt.* He was beginning to run on five hours sleep a night, and it was adding up. Everyone was feeling it.

This is going to be one hell of a winter.

"THIS VISIT IS UNOFFICIAL, unlogged, and will be unacknowledged," Sacker began. He leaned forward in the chair toward her desk to emphasize his seriousness. Gone stared at him intently, her brandy eyes glinting. "You will be working strictly with me, reporting only to me, or it's over. Do you understand?"

"You're taking a huge risk on this, detective Sacker."

He leaned back in the chair and grunted. "Damn right I am."

"I appreciate the vote of confidence. But we need to get a few things straight. I will respect your rules only so much as they do not interfere with mine."

"*Your* rules?" *The nerve of this woman!* "Now *you're* making demands?"

"Given what I've read online today, I would characterize my negotiating position as strong."

It's out already? There were too many at NYPD taking green from the press corps.

She continued. "I'm not going to waste my time or yours without getting access to what I need to work effectively. And I will not do this as a freebie. I recognize this 'off-the-books' approach we're forced to adopt precludes financial compensation. I will require something a little different."

Oh boy. "Yes?"

"My rules are simple. First, you will grant me unfettered, uninterrupted, and complete access to crime scenes and evidence. This includes bodies, forensic reports and samples. *Anything* related to the case, including, but not limited to, databases, victim and suspect information, computer accounts, and interviews."

"There is no way I can—"

"This is *non-negotiable*, detective. This requires clandestine efforts on your part, meaning my access can't be in the light of day, so to speak. But I demand access nonetheless. You would want the same. If I am going to investigate, I must see all the data."

Sacker stared into the diminutive woman's smoldering eyes. She wasn't going to back down. *And, dammit! She's right.* He'd have insisted on the same. Any detective worthy of the name would.

"All right. I don't know exactly how we're going to pull it off, but you got it."

"Good," she said. "Second, if I solve this case, find the murderer, lead the police to the killer, then you and the NYPD will publicly acknowledge my role. You will name me as a consultant on the case and present my contributions fairly."

"Would be easier to raid precinct funds and pay you with stolen pensions."

"I'm serious, detective."

Sacker laughed. "So am I, Ms. Gone. You've got no idea how much hot water I'll be in for bringing you on board. It's against the demands of my superior. I could lose my badge. Even if you drag in the killer cuffed with a leash around his neck. Keeping my job is pretty high on my priority list. Strong-arming a bunch of angry dudes at NYPD to wax eloquently about Gone Investigating isn't."

"Whether or not NYPD officially says anything, then, I want your word that *you* will. That you will put my name and my contributions in your official report. Fired or not, you'll be required to submit one."

"Ah, I see. And then one way or another, the information will find its way out to the press." He smiled. "Might be the end of me, but you would earn yourself some choice advertising."

"I don't run a nonprofit," Gone said, smiling. "At least, that isn't the intention, whatever the current figures."

Damn. He couldn't blame her, but *damn!* This wasn't just doubling down, this was all in.

"Done."

Gone stared at him for a split second and blinked. Sacker suppressed a smile. She hadn't anticipated his quick capitulation. *Didn't figure everything, huh, little genius?* But, like everything with Gone, her recovery was fast.

"That's good to hear! And since we'll be working together, can we drop the formalities and go with Grace and Tyrell?"

"Done, Grace," said Sacker, the corners of his mouth twitching upward.

"So, Tyrell, when do we start?"

31

FLYING LOW

Dalir Afshar set the helicopter down in an outermost section at Azadi Square. The landing space was more than adequate, the weather conditions optimal with blue skies and a mild wind. Only the circumstances spiked his adrenaline as he caught the monument arcing skyward in his peripheral vision.

The NOPO? He'd worked some sensitive missions, but nothing like this. Nothing with those shadows and killers. He didn't even want to see what he would be transporting in this military sized aircraft.

But that he couldn't help. The two soldiers opened the back hatch and lowered the ramp. Figures beneath the monument captured his attention. Weapons out, NOPO in their dark uniforms raced toward him. They herded a group of bound captives. Sending a chill through him, the bearded form of Commander Karami accompanied the prisoners.

God protect us.

Who are these prisoners? Why are they in Azadi Square?

Why is the NOPO here?

He tried to focus on the flying machine, its rhythms, its needs, its complicated and emotionless mechanisms. This calmed him. He'd only be flying. It didn't matter what he carried. It'd be over soon and he would return home to his wife and children. Forget this day.

Then the screams began.

~

"CONTROL THE PILOT!" cried Houston. "Secure this bird! We've got minutes."

Lightfoote darted past to the co-pilot's seat and aimed a gun at the frozen form of Afshar. "Calm down. Don't try anything. How's your English?"

The pilot is key.

They either forced his cooperation or they died. Houston focused on him as Lopez tossed the second Iranian commando from the helicopter. Behind her the American soldiers lined the transport. A medic tended a pale Zaringhalam, blood everywhere.

"My English?" came Afshar's strained words. "Three years. I have watching the televisions."

"Passable," said Lightfoote, studying the pilot's eyes. "Might piss himself, though."

Houston sat beside an unconscious Karami, his arms tied behind him. He bled from the back of his head. She shouted over the noise of the aircraft to Afshar.

"Time is short. You know who this is." Afshar swallowed. "He lives only if you do exactly as we say. *You* live only if you do what we say. We've got nothing to lose. We're desperate."

He shook his head up and down, displacing his headset.

Lightfoote's eyes flashed to Houston. "Watch him."

As Afshar stared in shock, Lightfoote reached forward and smashed the control panel with the butt of her gun. She ripped back the front facade to expose the instrumentation.

"Wait, no, you cannot—"

Sparks flew as she yanked a series of wires from the circuitry. The HUD before him popped and blackened. They tasted acrid smoke.

"What—"

"I fried the GPS and other triangulation systems."

"No navigate!"

"No one can track us! You don't need GPS. Fly the old fashioned way."

"You are crazy!"

Time to raise the threat level.

Houston turned to Lopez. "Gabriel, cut off Karami's small finger." Afshar's eyes grew wide. "Work your way up to the larger ones if needed."

Lopez removed a large knife.

Afshar screamed. "No! *Yes!* I fly! *I fly!* Where?"

She gazed out the window. "North. Due north, keep low, and don't respond to any hailing." He gaped. *"Fly!"*

The helicopter lurched upward, the passengers jolted, equipment crashing in the back of the craft.

"And there she blows," called Lightfoote.

The base of Azadi Tower exploded. The grand monument plunged, its majestic curves dissolving like sand into a growing eruption of dust from the ground. Afshar screamed again as thunder rolled over them, straining to steer the craft. They climbed skyward.

"Shame," muttered Lopez. "Beautiful monument."

"Damn," said Houston. "Supposed to take out the underground structure. Leave nothing for Mirnateghi or the NOPO." She sighed. "But you know me and explosives."

One side of his mouth twitched. "Yeah, you really need to go back to school for that or something."

The Seal captain stared at her. "When did you—"

"When you were searching for an escape route underground."

"Next time consult a specialist. *Jesus!*"

"Next time, maybe. But I'm kind of in a vindictive mood, today."

Houston felt a deep tug in her stomach and scanned the skies around them.

"We bought some time," said Lightfoote, leaning back in the chair. "Thank God for NOPO secrecy."

"Time?" asked the soldier.

"Our only hope." Houston shook her head. "The government didn't know. Mirnateghi went straight to Karami. And right now it's 9/11 down there and we're just some bird in the sky. Might slip through the smoke."

Lopez looked at the sprawled body of Karami. "We just kidnapped the Iranian head of intelligence, blew up one of their most prized monuments, and pissed off Nemesis. Again. She knows her information's compromised. We've got a head start, but the manhunt is going to be something fierce."

"I know," she said. "Not likely going to be a next time, but I'm still taking notes."

"You think we can make it?" His gaze bored into her.

She turned forward. "I don't know." She prayed the blur ahead was the blue of the Caspian Sea. "To the sea, maybe. Port of Nowshahr is seventy miles as the helicopter flies. We're not carrying any heavy equipment. I'm guessing this bird's got two hundred miles in her at least before we drop out of the sky." She smiled. "Sure, we'll make it. Piece of cake."

"And when we get there?" he asked. "It's landlocked by hostile countries."

Lightfoote interrupted from the front. "Don't you read the mission preps? CIA contacts have a ship. Last line evac."

Lopez laughed. "That's why you're here, Angel. Last line for everything, it seems." Lopez nodded at the back of the pilot's head. "Can't have that get out, though. Looks like we have one more passenger."

Lightfoote sighed. "Inevitable. He's seen too much. We dump him to the locals once we're clear."

Static popped on the radio and voices in Farsi called out. Lightfoote glared at the pilot, who kept his gaze locked forward.

"If we can make that ship," she continued, "they smuggle us through Georgia or Azerbaijan. It's going to be a bit *on the fly* from here. At least out there we've got a chance to get lost."

In silence, they left Tehran behind them. The urban landscape shifted to the rough and jutting foothills of the Alborz mountains, a wall of rock looming. No pursuit followed.

Houston checked the restraints on their captive and leaned back in the seat.

They flew toward the mountains.

32

GONE MENTAL

Sacker backed away from the bristling scientist. Dr. Richards had just about had it with Grace Gone.

"Look, gumshoe," she began, a vape-pen dancing in a fog of some cinnamon flavoring turning Sacker's stomach. "I don't care if the NYPD brought you in. I don't care about his recommendations. You don't know shit about my crew, understand? There is no way in hell any of them had anything to do with this."

Gone stared unblinkingly at the raving woman, her face an emotionless contrast to the beet-red researcher towering over her.

She's vulnerable.

He grimaced. *Don't get personal.* Cardinal rule in police work. Never, ever works out well. He'd seen the truth of it and he was no rookie. So, what the hell?

It's that damn foot.

He'd noticed it the first time they met. The limb, the way she dragged it around. Some accident? But no cast, no brace. *Congenital defect? Wasn't she a dancer?* Few answers, and it didn't seem to matter then.

But damned if it hadn't started to matter. She'd struggled to move through the alleyway, the leg like some loadstone. By the time she'd insisted in walking up the stairway, her breath rattled.

She didn't care. The little tyrant ordered and questioned and sampled every aspect of the crime scene. The area around the busted doorway, the fried security camera, the railings and steps, the location around the body. She spared nothing. Gone toted her own evidence case, complete with sample vials, blue nitrile gloves, knock-off smart-glasses shooting the scene.

But she *was* human. In Dr. Richard's office, he could see a trickle of sweat run down her cheek. With raging Richards screaming over her diminutive form, he winced. The real question was why the hell he gave a damn.

"Why entertain such a simplistic hypothesis?" Richards fumed. The derision crackled like a force field. "It's right out of a TV show. Based on what?"

Gone dropped one of her logic cluster bombs.

"The facts present this as the most probable scenario. First, the killer, a strong man who is also well acquainted—"

"Strong *man*?" scoffed Richards. "Jesus."

"The elevator cameras show nothing. The front entrance the same. The only other way up is through the back door. It happens to be broken and with an inoperable security camera. Not only does this indicate the killer is familiar with this building, but it means he carried the corpse up a stairwell. Four flights. Few men could do it and leave no sign. Many fewer women. Probabilistically, a very strong man."

"Why not a team? Why one?"

"A ritualistic serial killer. Methodical with a giant ego, staging and taunting the police. Surgical mutilation and effective destruction of evidence. You're dealing with an intelligent psychopath. Statistically, such killers work alone."

Sacker couldn't help himself. "And how to recruit for this job? Craigslist?"

Richard's mouth tightened. "Gangs? The mob?"

"Hire some mobsters to drop a corpse in a federally funded

research lab?"

Gone continued. "Statistically, such killers are predominantly men. Combine these facts and the conclusion is inescapable. A single, very strong male was responsible."

Richards frowned. Sacker smiled. "I'm convinced," he said.

"In summary, the killer is a very strong man who knows this building well. As noted, he's an expert in concealing any information about himself or his methods from forensic investigation. He's therefore knowledgeable of forensic science. I sampled the route he moved the body." She gestured to the grid of vials in her evidence box. "There's nothing evidentiary. No prints. No DNA. No proteins." She indicated a magenta liquid. "This vial shows significant quantities of chlorine. The killer bleached everything. You can't smell it here. All the research chemicals overpower it. But some simple assays show it's coating the body, the door handles, the railing. Anything the killer could have touched is bleached. Evidence erased."

Sacker jumped. "What?" *How did we miss this?*

"Therefore, we have a highly educated killer, fluent in forensic science. He's intimately acquainted with the research building and the lab and knew he could erase his presence chemically. That no one would realize. I'd say the chances of him working here are high."

Richards paled. "Maybe. But not one of my people. I know them. Certainly none of them are ritualistic serial killers. Why destroy my scientific career and theirs?"

"Maybe someone in another lab," said Sacker. "Another floor? A frustrated Ph.D. dropout janitor? Good Will Hunting meets Hannibal Lector?"

She leaned back and closed her eyes.

The woman is near the breaking point.

"Maybe it's ideological. Political."

Gone's eyes narrowed. "How so?"

"God, I'm not a psychologist." Richards passed a hand over her forehead. "But think about it. This...*man* clearly has it out for rapists. *That's* obvious."

"Granted," said Sacker.

"It happens some labeled my work a rape drug. A tool for degrading women by removing consequences of sex from men."

He shrugged. "A male contraceptive?"

"Yes. Pop a pill, enjoy all the unprotected sex you want. Never fear some slut is going to come after your bank account with a kid in tow."

"I see. So, some got upset?"

"Oh, sure. We got letters. Screeds online. A few threats of violence. Threats of *rape*. How's that for irony? These idiots can't see anything. Unwanted children are the single biggest drag on a woman's life. Placing the burden of preventing children on women is unfair. So is the health cost they pay for many of the hormonal treatments. Maybe this killer's hung up on it."

"How does your male contraceptive work?" asked Gone.

Richards laughed, but her eyes were dead. "A lot's kept under wraps because of my company. But this psycho's setting fire to it all. I guess secrets don't matter. It's a viral treatment. An infection with a benign virus targeted to the testes. Testes-specific promotors in our recombinant virus turn on a set of proteins. Screws up sperm production. Side effects are minimal. A small percentage get cold symptoms. Seminal fluid is unaffected. Arousal, performance, the same. Just no functional little genetic missiles swimming to target. Immunity's a problem. Threatened to make it useless. But we're working around that."

Sacker straightened in his chair. "You mean you're working on an infectious birth control for men?"

"Bothers you, detective? A harmless virus scare you more than hormone treatments for women and the cancer risks?"

"Well, ah, I didn't mean it—"

She cut him off with an imperious wave of her vaping device. She glanced at Gone, one eyebrow arching.

"What about you, little Sherlock. You figured it all out now?"

Gone snapped shut her evidence box.

"Thank you for your time, Dr. Richards. This visit's been very interesting." She turned, and offered her arm to Sacker. "Detective, would you be so kind?" She inhaled, glancing from her foot to his face. "Leg's on its last legs."

Her brown eyes caught his. The emotion flowed again. He coughed and nodded.

"Thank you," she said, smiling for the first time that day. "The only thing more interesting than this visit would be to have a go at the corpses now."

He helped her out of the office toward the elevators, leaving Richards in a stunned silence.

33

NARAKA

Partho Ghosh beseeched the goddess in delirium.

But sacrilege drowned him. His heartfelt prayers reeked. There shouldn't be blood and vomit on her statue. He shouldn't stink so, fouled from endless rounds of diarrhea burning through him like poison. The comely breasts of Parvati should not sway! She shouldn't blur from the sweat stinging his eyes like some river of fire.

My eyes!

The fever beat in his head, a lunatic's gong pulsing. And he saw them. Demons curdled from the stained carpets, their black forms dripping blood and tar dragged from Naraka. They whispered his name. They hummed like some demented choir, unholy vibrations shaking his soul. Red eyes burned through him.

His vision tricked! It mocked. It closed in on him. The bloodshot eyes in the mirror no longer saw themselves. Only the ever-widening blur. He stumbled through the rooms of his New York apartment by fragmented memory.

Yet his *other* eyes, his *ajna*, the sixth chakra opened wide. It discerned the demons. It perceived the deeper planes, even as his body crashed into walls and furniture. Blind.

But not blind! No! I see you, monsters! Now I truly see you for the first time!

"Didn't I call Deepa?"

Deepa had left in a storm last month.

Or was it last year?

Deepa. She cradled him sick with flu. Deepa of the sing-song fairy voice. Deepa of the large heart. Amla tea, spiced with cinnamon and sweetened with honey.

Where is Deepa?

Part of his damaged mind tried to speak. It clawed past the degenerating neurons, the dissolving blood vessels of his brain. It screamed a last warning: *Partho, this is not the flu.*

Yes. The voice was right. This was serious. Something terrible. He needed to call the hospital. *I'm a nurse!* Certainly he must know this! What was he thinking? Silly.

Move, Partho, move!

Ghosh crawled. He crawled across the fetid carpet soiled in his own excretions. His filthy robe caught on the statue, yanking him to the side. He flailed like some netted fish and overturned it. His scattershot mind ignored the crash.

Phone. Where is phone?

Kitchen! Yes. Fool. Fire. Friends laughing at the clinic. Friends joking. Policemen. Men with holes. Men with holes in their crotch. Was it funny? He knew it was supposed to be funny. His friends laughed and laughed around him. Especially when he'd cut himself with the scalpel.

"Jim. Sally?"

They didn't answer. They just stared at him and laughed. Their heads moved apart from their bodies. *Laughing.*

"What's so funny?" Silence. "Tell me!" he screamed, his face collapsing to the tile floor.

Darkness. He opened his eyes.

Where am I?

The white squares stretched, an endless field toward infinity. They chilled his bones. Indifferent. Miles away. Ten thousand centuries away blurbed the refrigerator. Its form spanned parsecs and dwarfed the nebulae. Its low churning hum rose from the black bowels of the cosmos. Blurbing. Searching like the claws of the demons...

Phone.

Of course. Yes. I'm sorry Amma, yes. I'll find the phone. It's here, Amma. You're right. I'll be better. I promise. Can I have pinni, now, Amma? Amma, please? Pinni?

Phone.

The room retreated from infinity. Regained its dimensions. The kitchen stopped the mad charade of being a tiled universe and behaved itself.

Like I will.

Amma would forgive him for breaking the diya. He would have pinni.

I'm on the floor.

Dear God, something was wrong with him. He shook his head. Sweat slung against the cabinet doors, a languid molasses creeping to the ground.

The counter with the phone!

He needed help. The voice inside screamed. Time was short. His thoughts cleared. For a last moment, he found himself again in the midst of a decaying mind. He placed his hands on the cold tiles.

Act now.

Focusing, pressing with all his remaining strength, he lifted his body. His arms shook like some frightened bird's wings, but he brought himself to a crouch against the counter. He gasped for breath, the effort Herculean. His entire body shivering.

What happened to my arms?

Trembling, he held out his hands. The robe fell back to his elbows, revealing a blue and red patchwork of bruised skin. Some thug had beaten him. Over and over and over. What else could explain it?

Did I fall so much?

He couldn't remember. He couldn't remember the important

plan. The plan he must follow *now*, before it was *too late*. Too late. *For what? For...*

The phone. He could see it now. Right above the stool beside him. "No...."

It towered. Loomed. *Impossible!* A skyscraper above him. Mocking. Gloating with the hideous chants of demons.

Ghosh wept and gasped from the pain. *Too high!* Too far. How could anyone be expected to climb so high? For what? What could be worth such effort?

Life.

Yes? Life. Had it come to that? Yes. Despite the shadows encroaching, he knew it had. His body was broken, the window of time closing.

I'm dying. Dear, Amma. Beloved Deepa. I'm dying. Maybe I will see you? Are you both waiting?

He had to focus. He knew he had to scale that mountain, climb the towering stool, hold upright, find the phone and dial the numbers. He could not slip. He could not fall. There would be no second chance.

And he could not wait. Death slunk beside him, exhaling a rotten cloud down his neck.

He knew what he had to do.

And he knew that he couldn't do it.

34

HALF-A-DOZEN!

"I'm Frank Borden with Canid News, live in New York City next to Suite Tower."

The reporter shivered in his parka, a scarf pulled below his mouth. Clouds of vapor rose from his lips. His voice fought over the angry chanting of a wall of protestors behind him. Signs and fists rose in the air, directed toward a forty-seven story building. Its glass reflected spotlights, the darkening evening lit by one word in enormous, golden lettering: "SUITE."

"Thousands are gathered, clogging city traffic and hurting local businesses. Some threatening violence against the man who would dare challenge the imperial presidency of Elaine York. Mostly young, unemployed or college students, these liberals believe in their cause, and are shouting it to the penthouse."

"No Suite! No KKK! No fascist USA!"

The voices cried in unison, slogans and caricatures of the businessman-candidate swirling around the block. Across the street the Secret Service patrolled. Officers of the NYPD lined the avenues and sidewalks, sandbagged trucks shielding the block.

"And we'll send it back to you at Half-a-Dozen!"

The screen cut to a television studio. Five suited men and a black

woman were seated around a half-moon table. A blond man in the
middle spoke toward the camera.

"Changing of the guard? Will the Left stop at nothing to thwart
the will of the people? I'm your host, Brock Allen. With me to discuss
the continuing protests against the candidacy of Daniel Suite are
Howard Roitman, John Mason, and Phillip Logan. Filling in for
Alfred Cleave, our new voice from the Left is Lewa Ajayi, bestselling
author and activist. Nice dreads there, Lewa."

The black woman smiled, shaking the cascading strands of hair
around her face. "Always gracious, Brock. Good to be here."

Allen turned to a heavyset man in a blinding red blazer. "Let's
start with you, John. Are we looking at another Occupy movement?"

Mason's baritone boomed over the room. "It's worse. Candidate
Suite dared challenge the liberal stranglehold on America. He's
promised to take the fight to those eroding America's place in the
world. He's stood up to thugs erasing our culture and heritage with
politically correct foreign religions and customs. Sharia Law. Homo-
sexual agendas. You bet the socialists and feminists aren't going to
take this lying down. This is war."

"Phil, your take?" Allen flashed polished teeth.

Thin, in his thirties with a receding hairline, Logan placed an
elbow on the table and leaned in. "York represents the ruling elite.
What happened during this so-called *coup*? Let's be honest, with the
White House cover-up, we're never going to know. But we must ask,
what are they hiding? This president rules like a tyrant. Suspending
normal Congressional actions. Declaring martial law. It's classic
Leftist autocracy. Lenin and Stalin in the USA."

Ajayi cut in. "The national infrastructure had collapsed! A coup
ensued. It was the biggest crisis since the Civil War. You might cut her
a little slack for saving the country."

The old man among them, Roitman, adjusted his glasses, a
strong Brooklyn accent clashing with Ajayi's Nigerian cadence.
"Saving it for whom? Herself? Other Washington elites? Our military
fought her! Instead of demonizing them, maybe we should consider
why they did? Now most are dead. And dead men tell no tales.

Maybe York presented a danger they had to stop to save the republic!"

Logan hopped in his seat. "Exactly! Exactly! The witnesses are conveniently dead."

"Conveniently?" Ajayi blinked. "Half a million died just in the Kansas City area. Nukes your *noble generals* launched to kill York!"

"That's never been proven!" shouted Logan.

"You visited Kansas, recently, Phil?"

Roitman sighed. "Stop playing games, Lewa. Nukes were launched. People died. It was horrible. But who really gave the orders?"

Logan pointed a hooked finger toward Ajayi. "Alex Jones believes it was York herself! A false flag!"

"Jones? That nutcase? Next you'll tell me we didn't land on the moon."

"Mocking us won't win you any arguments," said Roitman.

Allen chuckled and tossed several yellow locks from his forehead. "I can see that we're going to have a live one tonight! Let's turn then to the question of—"

"Hold on just a minute, Brock," said Ajayi, leaning forward in her chair. Her index finger pointed across the panel. "You asked a question. You wanted to know if the protests are a new movement. I can answer that for you."

"I'm sure you can," mumbled Roitman.

Ajayi's bright teeth shone in a snarl against her dark skin. "These protestors march for a simple reason. Daniel Suite is *not* an ordinary political candidate. He represents the worst of America."

"There she goes—" began Logan.

"His rap sheet is a mile long," she continued. "He's a serial liar and fraud. He's slandered entire ethnic groups and religions, threatened their First Amendment rights, threatened to shut down mosques and deport millions."

"Enforcing standing immigration laws!" said Roitman.

"Ethnically cleansing America!" Ajayi shot back. She pounced on the moment of shock. "And that's what it is. The whitewashing of

America. The *bleaching* of it by a man who has surrounded himself with known bigots and white supremacists."

Allen's smile was gone. He waved his arm toward Ajayi.

"We're here for a reasoned debate, not to insult presidential candidates."

"That's all the Left *has*," scoffed Logan. "That's all they do. Deny freedom of speech. Cleave at least had respect."

"Cleave? Your token liberal who plays nice because you pad his bank account? That's not me, friend. There's no reasoning with white supremacy. No civilized debate about ethnic and religious cleansing. Just look at you. Another white male panel of judges. You don't understand this movement because you can't see through your privilege and abuse of it."

Allen spoke in a monotone. "I'm going to cut your mic."

"Cut it then, Brock. Silence *my* speech. But if you want to know what this movement is, I'm telling you: A fight for decency, against racism, misogyny, and fascism. A fight against corporate greed and plutocracy. Suite is no man of the people. He's a child of a billionaire, born with a silver spoon in his mouth. He's off-shored jobs, made his products abroad, shafted workers, and hasn't paid a dime in taxes for decades! He's everything Occupy was against. And far, far worse. If he's elected on a platform of hate, then I promise you—"

Her voice became a whisper in the background. The camera focused on Allen's teeth-grinding smile.

"Apologies to our loyal viewers. At Canid News we try to be balanced and present a fair look at all sides. But it's always hard to entertain the extreme voices of the Left. Half-a-Dozen will return after a commercial break. With a new panel. This is Brock Allen."

35

CONNECTIONS

"Rebecca?"

Savas stared at his wife. She was draped like a thick coat over the office chair, brown hair a caramel river flowing over the seat-back. Her eyes were shut, her breathing slow and deep.

Enough with all this. Let her be.

In the middle of this crisis, for one long moment, he stopped caring about the rest of world. He stopped caring about his team and their enemies. He'd tuned out the voice of the US President on the speaker phone of his office.

"John!" cried York.

Cohen snapped upward at the president's shout, her eyes wide and confused. Bloodshot. She waved at Savas to ignore her and eased herself up.

"Where are they *now?*" repeated the President.

Savas rubbed his temples. "CIA safe-house outside Ankara. The Agency intel was right. They came in from the Caspian. The report is fragmented. Communications were minimized as they went into hiding. Smuggler's ships. God knows what happened. Once in Turkey, it looks like it went relatively smoothly."

"Looks can be deceiving," scoffed York. "Erdoğan's been a total prick. He nearly held it all up, was going to deny clearance and hold them. I had to give in to his blackmail, promise we wouldn't back the UN resolution on the Kurds."

"I'm sorry, Elaine," said Cohen. She lowered her head.

Savas felt the weight of her guilt drag on him as well. The collateral damage of their royal mission screwup was growing by the hour.

"UN resolutions are like politicians' promises. Worthless. But with Iran announcing the big reveal and blaming us for the destruction of Azadi Tower—we had to clean up this mess fast."

"What about Iran?" asked Savas.

"This won't be forgotten. Not for a long time. There is enough circumstantial evidence to convict us in the courts of international opinion. But they're quieter than I expected."

"Nemesis," said Cohen, emptying the contents of a thermos into a mug. She buried her face in the steam. "Almost certainly. She'd love to hurt us more, but too much investigation might shine light in places she doesn't want. She must have pressured the government. Shut things down. But it was damn close."

Savas ground his teeth. "Ugly and a mess. And I take full—"

"No time for that," York cut in. "The double agent?"

"Zaringhalam? He's alive. Agency assets pulled off some miracle field triage. He's hospitalized in Germany. Going to lose the leg."

"Damn."

"Could have been worse."

Cohen spoke. "We nearly lost them all."

Static popped on the speaker. York's voice was distorted. "Yes, but worth the risk. INTEL 1 pulls off another stunner from the jaws of defeat. The data Lightfoote sent. You've verified it?"

Savas glanced at Cohen.

"Yes," she said. "It took some analysis to figure it out in the first place. Bringing the confidence up, that was harder. False companies, shell games and money laundering. A trail of shadows."

"But there is no doubt."

"There's always doubt," Savas answered. "But we're pretty sure.

Money funneled to SuperPACs, individual think tanks. Even some core advisors of the Suite campaign are paid lobbyists. Several internet-based news organizations, too. They popped up over the last two years, doubling their numbers over the election cycle. They're basically running on this money. All their news is highly critical of your presidency. Some of it is just wild conspiracy theory material. But it's everywhere. It's damaging."

"Foreign powers have tried different things to manipulate US elections before," said York. "But this is unprecedented. I'm biased, no doubt. But I also try to believe in the meaning of our system of government. And it's under threat."

"I can't disagree with you." He sat down, the fatigue overtaking him. "Then there's the local connection."

"You still don't know who that's going to?"

"No. It's not any known organization. No business. Might be an individual account. We're looking into it. But the money's from her organization. Her tentacles reaching out over the seas, through the wires, tended by some hands in New York."

He exhaled and set his jaw.

"Nemesis is here."

36

GONE ON

Two in the morning and the 12th Precinct was as quiet as the morgue they were headed to. Sacker escorted Gone through the loading dock. An old friend in security looked the other way, only the precinct cameras recording. An investigation would reveal everything, of course. He knew if it ever got to that, his career was over.

What you can't change, you don't think about.

First he brought her to his desk. The footage from the security cameras around Saint Patrick's had come in. He played it for her, the choppy still images enough to make out the approach of a hooded man. *A very large hooded man.* The tall shadow carried a body toward the cathedral, concealing himself in tree-lined walkways. He returned slowly, struggling with the concrete doughnut. Few pedestrians roamed at that hour, and the killer took care. Delaying, hiding, and springing into motion when the opportunity presented itself.

"He took a terrible risk," said Gone.

"It happens sooner or later, especially with the more clever ones. They've got to go and make a damn show, rub our faces in it. Prove they're more clever than the rest of us. That's how we usually catch them. They push the envelope too far."

"His build matches my assessment. But we can't see anything in detail from this footage. We'll get nothing more here."

Sacker yawned. "Okay, Grace. Then I think that means the bodies."

Gone smiled. "I thought you'd never ask."

They took the stairs. Fewer cameras. Maybe it didn't matter. They'd been recorded several times already. But the less stress he felt under Big Brother's eye, the better.

One way or another, maybe this case means early retirement.

He was burning through his favors fast with Gone. As he'd arranged, one of Sutherland's techs had left an examination room open. In his hand was a strip of paper with the current code for the cadaver room and cooler box. He would get the body, roll it to the open room, and, God help him, let this nobody PI have a go at the corpse.

Yeah, my career is probably over.

He decided he might as well unplug the smoke detector and light one up while he was at it.

"Wait," said Gone as he keyed in the code, yanking open the door to the morgue. "Take me to the examination room first."

"Let's just get the body. Door's open and I'm nervous enough."

"No," said Gone, with a firmness that gave him pause. "I want us in biohazard gear."

Sacker's eyebrows danced. "Biohazard?" *What is this woman on?*

"A hunch, Tyrell. I want to be careful. Just humor me."

"Sutherland didn't wear anything. He's fine. His techs are fine."

"The bodies are cold, nearly frozen. Maybe they got lucky. If we're careful there should be little risk of contact. But I want to be cautious."

"Contact with what?"

"Not sure yet."

I should just have gotten the patch. Mainline the goddam nicotine.

"Alright, Sherlock. Let's go."

It took ten minutes to find the boxes. By the end of it, he was covered in sweat. What were the odds that someone wouldn't come down and discover them? Would his contact above phone, warn them in time? As they hunted through lockers, closets, and storage boxes, a sickening claustrophobia took hold of him.

Gone found the gear in a hallway closet. Ebola or no Ebola outbreak a few years ago, the NYPD wasn't too concerned about meeting biosafety specs. Dusty, unopened boxes were shoved into the rear of the room, covered with random paraphernalia of medical forensics. A small miracle they found the suits.

Or maybe because this crazy genius is with me.

She bobbed around, a foot shorter than him, her form in the biohazard gown and mask like some post-apocalyptic sprite on a mission. He rolled the body into the examination room as she hopped behind him, bulging bag in hand.

Unaccustomed to moving bodies, he managed to get the corpse of Jack Reaper on the table without embarrassing himself. He turned around, beads of perspiration dripping into his eyes. Gone brushed past him. She unzipped the bag, removed a host of instruments, tools, vials, slides, and items he didn't recognize. He'd gotten a taste of her mad scientist vibe at the NYU lab, but this stepped it up to some new level of crazy.

Grace, you're either fucking Asian Holmes or a total nut job.

The thought chilled him. High-functioning crazies preyed on the desperate. With just enough plausibility, and tons of con, they lured those who needed what they sold.

And I need a breakthrough in this case. Please, Grace, be the real thing.

She went to work.

37

GONE DARK

The following symptoms characterize a multisystem cascade, including prostration, nausea, vomiting, abdominal pain, diarrhea, chest discomfort, labored breathing, coughing, nasal discharge, conjunctivitis, postural hypotension, edema, with headache, confusion, even coma.

The lab results danced in her mind along with the entries in the medical diagnostic manuals. Words and phrases, microscope slides and biological assay readings. A terrible sense of danger and madness lurked behind every drop she pipetted and every instrument reading. Every movement she made vibrated with tension. She'd never felt so disturbed in the quiet order of her lab work.

And when upset, Grace Gone made tea.

Others took walks. The movement and scenery change, the repetitive biomechanics, the solitude created mental spaces to process the difficult. Some knitted, or fixed cars, or played a musical instrument.

Making tea was not so different. Any kind of tea would do. Black, green, even these faddish fruit teas. It was as much in the making as drinking.

It is more in the making than in the drinking.

And when very upset, she made tea with *effort, gongfu cha.* Today was a day for serious tea. Her hands shook from the anxiety burning through her.

Hemorrhagic manifestations occur as the illness matures, with petechiae, ecchymoses, discharge from venipuncture sites, mucosal hemorrhages, and post-mortem evidence of visceral hemorrhagic effusions.

She broke out the small Yixing teapots, thermometer, and her favorite caramel-smoke Oolong blend imported from a small shop in the Wuyi Mountains. *Black dragon tea.* Her mother insisted she determine the temperature by bubble monitoring, but she was too much the modern scientist. A disturbing day in her private lab haunted her. Precision and care meant everything when examining a murder victim's tissues. For *gongfu cha*, she would match those efforts. The thermometer it would be.

She laid the pot and cups on the table, warming and sterilizing them with hot water, the excess discarded. She examined the tea, inhaling its powerful and musky fragrance, gazing on its dark hues and texture. All her senses strained to appreciate its complex nature.

"The black dragon now enters the palace."

Her voice hummed, full of memory. *Childhood. Before the chaos. Before the men with guns.* She saw her mother's beautiful and sorrowful face.

She filled the pot with the dried tea. The small vessel received a weighed eight grams of leaves, promising a rich and potent brew. Gone liked her tea strong. Underneath the pot, she placed a catching bowl, raised hot water a hand height above it, and poured the steaming liquid over the leaves to rinse them. Raising the pot, she decanted the water inside.

"Xuan hu gao chong."

Glancing to her left, she noted the thermometer in the large bowl read 96.7 degrees Fahrenheit. Grasping the bowl, she poured the hot water until the pot overflowed. With a jade spoon she scooped away the top layer of bubbles and debris.

"The spring breeze brushes the surface."

Several days into the disease progression, erythema and desquamate with maculopapular rash can be observed. Terminal stages include shock, convulsions, acute metabolic dysfunction, and disseminated intravascular coagulation.

She decanted the first brew into the cups, liquid never to be drunk.

"Drifting clouds and flowing water."

She filled the pot again with the remainder of the hot water. The sound of her mother's voice filled the air around her.

"Zai zhu qing quan."

She removed the bubbles at the top and closed the pot with the lid. A minute later she poured the tea into a set of clean cups, repeating the process for the second and third cups. After that, it was drinking water.

Laboratory diagnostics include early leukopenia, lymphopenia and neutrophilia, thrombocytopenia, spikes in serum aminotransferase concentrations, hyperproteinemia, and proteinuria. Diffuse intravascular coagulopathy will manifest in detectable proteolyzed fibrin with extended prothrombin and thromboplastin time courses. Secondary bacterial infections can cause elevated white cell counts in advanced stages.

She stared at the row of cups, steam rising from the tan brew within. Hints of caramel and peat danced in the air.

Success.

A near-perfect brew. A taste of divinity.

Then why am I so sad?

Why had the joy risen away from her like the fragrant steam?

She knew the answer but wished it were different. She would enjoy the tea. But it was an echo. A fogged memory of the joy of the making.

It is more in the making than in the drinking.

But now she was calmer. She drank the tea and returned to the laboratory. She would call Sacker.

GONE REMOVED the blue gloves and dropped them into an orange biohazard bag picked up on eBay. She'd raided the odd sales from shuttered biotech and university labs. But those were hard to find, and too often the school or governmental red tape made them impractical. But online markets amazed. Centrifuges, PCR machines, the odd HPLC and mass spectrometer. Most were either vintage or unsupported by the manufacturers. Fixer-uppers requiring epic quests for spare parts.

Necessity, motherhood, and invention.

Whatever the challenge, investigating with the power of modern science was priceless. For the Eunuch Maker case, she'd performed a long list of tests on the surreptitious NYPD samples. Some of the more in-depth genetic analyses still ran, but the pathological tissue microscopy shook her.

I was right. God help us, I was right.

She fitted the Bluetooth headset over one ear and tapped the smartphone surface on the table beside her. With her other hand she dimmed the bright lights in the cellar lab.

"Uh, yeah. Hello?" The voice on the other end sounded hoarse.

"Tyrell?"

There was a short pause. "Gracie? Well, how the hell you doin' girl? Just thinkin' of you. Yeah. You on my mind, honey. And damn! Here you are callin'."

Is he drunk? They didn't have time for this!

"Tyrell, we need to talk."

"Mm-hmm. I've been thinkin' that. I didn't want to be the one to say it, you know."

"Tyrell, stop. Sober the hell up. We need to talk about the case."

"The case? Yeah, that case. *Fuck* the case."

Jesus! "Tyrell, I'm serious. We—"

"Fuck the case and fuck the Eunuch Maker and fuck the Mayor and fuck the goddamned FBI!"

"FBI? Look, Tyrell, this isn't a good time. I see that. Sober up. I'll call tomorrow. But we have to talk! I've had a look at the samples. It's my worst fear."

"A look at the samples." His voice slurred. "You QuestLabs now, too?"

"Tyrell, this is possibly a medical emergency! People's lives are at stake!"

"That's what happens when you got a serial killer castratin' bros left and right. Dumping them all over the motherfuckin' city."

This is impossible!

Gone pressed her fingers to her temples. How was she going to get through? Collaboration with an alcoholic brought risk, but she'd assessed him as more stable!

Unless something has happened...

"Look, Tyrell, I think we need to redouble our efforts. You need to convince NYPD. I need to brief you—"

"Might not be any point now."

She strained to decipher his words.

"Not a point? Why?"

There was a deep sigh and a belch.

"Fucking Feds called. We're outta time."

GONE TO SEED

F*uck the Feds.*
He'd hated to rabbit, but he couldn't take any more of her positive, *can-do!* spirit. The flood of confusing technobabble. Her holier-than-thou critical tones.

Yeah, babe, I've been drinking.

He'd told her the FBI called. Didn't she get it? G-boys didn't make social calls. One thing and then another and soon they'd be damn interns. But she wouldn't shut the hell up. She wouldn't see the truth of it. She just went on and on with medical terms and bleeding and infections and God his head hurt!

Doesn't she know what drunk means?

She was young and hungry and talented and wanted to make a difference. She hadn't had the world laugh and kick her in the teeth. Rip every ideal to shreds before her eyes year after year.

Maybe she's seen more than you think.

That voice inside. Arguing, pointing out missed facts, weak assumptions. Like Gone, too often right.

Fuck that voice.

The room wobbled. He braced on the armrests of the chair. His stomach lurched. He swallowed more whiskey.

Fuck the bottle.

Sacker stared at the medicine cabinet in the bathroom down the narrow hallway. He'd left the light on. The blue glow from the LCD screen on the wall mingled with it somewhere in the middle of the dark tunnel between them. He knew what was behind the mirror.

Fuck the meds.

He fought down a spasm from his throat. Stomach acids burned. His thoughts blurred. They bounced around like some kid's mad superball.

Murder, television, police, Gone, autopsy, hormones, smokes, FBI.

It was bound to happen. He'd known that. The case was too high-profile. The NYPD getting nowhere. Somewhere, someone demanded something be done. Some agent saw a chance to make his bones. They start with the phone call. The collaboration. They send field agents. Share data. Move in on crime scenes and evidence.

Steal the damn case out from under us.

The room spun again. He fought to hold focus on the medicine cabinet.

Why tonight, Tyrell? Because you're fucking drunk? Because the case of your lifetime just got swiped? Because you can't face that damn mirror anymore?

What price for the alchemy behind that mirror? What did normal people see when they looked in a mirror?

Normal people.

He laughed. *Embrace the metamorphosis!* So what if he had played mad scientist with his body and brain? Who the hell hadn't?

Pills and potions. Hair dye. Hair growth. Skin whiteners in Asia and tanning booths in America. Makeup and hairstyles. Clothes for the job, for the crew, for the country club. Glasses to look smarter or contacts to look dumber. Valley accent or faux-British, lose the street slang. Up your damn vocabulary. Facelift, boob job, penile-pec implants. Steroids. Piercings. Tattoos and nail color. Swing those hips, walk like a man, firm grip, teasing fingers, shoulders back, legs open. One thousand different masks.

All acts.

All for each and every person to fit into some preconceived and bullshit icon of self or society. From the moment the cord was cut they dressed, instructed, and adapted us to some internal gyroscope, instilled a desperation to fit in with others and with ourselves.

Fuck all of them.

Another smirk as his stomach dared him to laugh. Images of mutilated bodies blended with visions of the crimes those bodies once perpetrated. Multiplied by the teaming mass of humanity committing crimes high and low, consistently and constantly, all congealing to an obscene satanic idol.

Fuck the medicine cabinet.

To hell with all the pharma, impossible demands of mind and flesh and confusions and *why is my bottle empty? What the ever-loving hell!*

Sacker fell out of his chair. He groaned on the ground a long moment, dizzy and sick. The bottle spun on the wood floor inches from his face. Unbroken. Mocking. Absurd.

He crawled. Across the small carpet in the living room, down the wood floor of the hallway, sweat building on his brow. He crawled to the light of the bathroom.

Steadying himself on the door frame, he rose, swaying, planting one foot in front of the other. He lurched inside and confronted the mirror of the cabinet.

"You look like shit, brother."

A slurred voice he didn't recognize. Eyes glared, fissured with red, his skin an oily and sweaty mess. His mouth hung open like some idiot's.

He dropped toward the toilet, the vomit roiling through him like an angry express train. A jet of orange and pink splattered the porcelain sides and splashed into the water. He heaved again, gripping the sides of the bowl, soiling his hands and shirt. The stink sickened him more, bringing a third wave.

He fell against the wall panting.

Just let me die.

He closed his eyes to stop the spinning. In the darkness, the words of the Chinese detective flitted in his mind. What was it she said?

High-functioning alcoholic.

Grace. Her name was Grace. Gracie. Gracie Gone. Small. Sharp like a tack. Vulnerable. She'd called him. What had she said? *Hemorrhagic* something or the other. God, his head was pounding!

High-functioning alcoholic.

His eyes fluttered to a view of the ceiling. Another wave of nausea built. Maybe she wasn't so bright. Maybe just being kind. But reality had him by the gut, tonight. Whatever all the others in this teeming and mad world were, he knew what he was.

Alcoholic.

39

PAPER TRAIL

F *ollow the money.*
Savas shook his head, weary eyes gazing through the tinted glass of the rushing black SUV. Manhattan flowed. Yellow and green cabs darted. Pedestrians, accordion buses, and the concrete canyons churned into a confused mess in his mind. His life blurred along with it.

Here he was, having stepped from the NYPD to the FBI to this covert and probably illegal reincarnation of INTEL 1. Here they all were, a quirky and damaged group of talent, having gone through a modern civil war, unearthing and somehow defeating a global conspiracy. Now they operated from underneath the city like Batman's deputies to root out what remained of that organization. Insane resources waited at his fingertips. A frightening lack of oversight primed him to resign at the first sign of abuse of power. Here John Savas sat, rolling over the streets of Manhattan in a black SUV with dark windows like some sinister head of an underground police force.

And despite this formidable arsenal of intelligence and investigative weaponry, back to Gumshoe 101.

Follow the money.

And *boy*, where the money had led.

"Don't focus on the politics," said Cohen, her hand brushing his. Her deep intuition of his moods still shocked him despite their many years together.

And many trips to hell and back.

He leaned his head back against the seat rest. "It's hard not to, Rebecca. Angel's sure opened up Pandora's box with those files from Tehran."

"The box has been open a long time. This is just the latest incarnation."

"Sure. Some nasty bugs, with nasty stingers. But millions, *millions* of dollars pouring into this election, into Suite's campaign. Can we say *Manchurian Candidate?*"

Cohen sighed. "This isn't new. Foreign powers are always meddling. We just got a look under the rock this time. And we're hardly *unbiased*. York gave new life to INTEL 1. Without her, we're done."

"To hell with bias. Maybe York's right. Maybe INTEL 1 *should* get shut down. But after what happened in Kansas, I'll never doubt her again. And this *isn't* complicated. A level of foreign meddling that's unprecedented. It's unbelievable. And we *know* who's behind it. That alone makes Suite's candidacy corrupted."

"He might not be aware of the history of the cash. Politicians don't *want* to know. Don't look."

"Does Suite seem like the kind of man who doesn't know where his money's coming from? He's a tycoon with a reputation of balance sheet malfeasance and fraud!"

Cohen's brown eyes darted away.

I'm ranting. He tried to calm himself.

Cohen opened her tablet and flipped through case files. "For *all* these reasons," she said, "I'm glad the political investigation is in other hands. Neither one of us wants to start investigating York's political enemies. Even if it's clear crimes are being committed. It's a hot mess. Not our problem."

"Too close to Nixon's playbook. Honest work could blow up in a scandal." He turned his body toward her in the seat. "And what if we end up in the same place today? More political money."

"Maybe, but this account's an outlier. Nemesis was up to something very different here. No big organization. No famous agitator or politician. An unknown, single account. Chump change compared to the other money transfers."

"All the more intriguing for it."

She glanced at him, her eyes smiling. "Now that's the old NYPD detective I like to see. Yes. Something very different is going on with this guy."

"Assassin? Spy? We've struck out on every possible correlative search on the account name, bank, location, you name it. *Nothing.*"

"It could be any of those things. The name's an alias. For sure. It might not even be a *man*."

The SUV pulled to a stop in front of the large Citibank building. The driver awaited their instructions. Savas reached into his briefcase and removed a false Secret Service ID.

"So, let's review. We're part of their Financial Crimes division looking into major fraud. York guarantees all background checks will clear us with the bank. NSA code in the bank computers will scramble any video footage during our visit, so we're free to play."

Cohen removed her ID and closed her purse. "Right. Hopefully no robbery during the next hour. There'll be no record, no evidence of two shadow agents." She sighed. "They'll want to freeze the money. You know that."

"We can't let that happen. He'll learn his source is compromised. Whatever he's up to, he's our best link to Nemesis, wherever she is now. We can't lose that."

"Losing her in Tehran was a disaster," said Cohen.

"The entire mission was a disaster." Savas slid toward the door and gripped the handle. "Whatever they say, the account stays open."

Cohen nodded. "We push them to disable online access. Force him to show in the flesh. He'll *come* for the money."

Savas opened the door, the cold air hitting his face and bringing his senses to full alert. "And we'll be waiting."

40

SCHRODINGER'S IMMIGRANT

"*Hail, holy Queen, mother of mercy, our life, our sweetness and our hope. To thee do we cry, poor banished children of Eve.*"

Lopez left his seat in the military transport plane again, continuing to mumble the litany under his breath. He'd lost count of how many times he'd paced the length of the aircraft. The movement and prayers brought no peace.

"*To thee do we send up our sighs, mourning and weeping in this valley of tears. Turn then, most gracious advocate, thine eyes of mercy toward us, and after this our exile, show unto us the blessed fruit of thy womb, Jesus.*"

This time he was determined to walk off whatever was plaguing his mind. He passed the sprawled form of Lightfoote, dangling over two seats, her eyes hidden behind mirrored glasses. He passed Houston, who watched him with growing unease.

She's going to ask me soon. I'm not ready to talk.

He steadied himself on two nearby seats as the plane shook through a bout of turbulence. *Holding on in turbulence.* It was symbolic. A summary of his life in the years since his brother's murder and its CIA coverup. Since he became a fugitive from the US government. From the time he worked, ironically, within this very government to protect the nation.

"O clement, O loving, O sweet Virgin Mary! Pray for us, O holy Mother of God, that we may be made worthy of the promises of Christ. Amen."

His head swam. They'd departed Ramstein Air Base in southwestern Germany several hours ago. It was a surreal and staccato change of environments. The deserts and mountains of Iran, violence and escape. The cramped hold of a smuggler's ship. A wild ride into Turkey. All the while trying to keep a wounded Zaringhalam alive while they maintained their cover. Finally, to the US global center of drone operations, the historically central and strategic Ramstein.

After landing in Germany, they'd handed off the wounded man to a medical crew, eaten, and followed marines on a plane bound for the United States.

Dizzying.

"Okay, *Paco*," said Houston as he sat. "What gives?"

"Only my brother called me that. Let's keep it that way."

"Archangel Miguel looks over you. He's worried. And you are in one hell of a mood. Paco."

He frowned at her.

"More like St. Bloody Francis of Assisi," said Lightfoote from behind. "How's a girl gonna get some shuteye with monk-man haunting the aisles?"

Houston ignored her. "Tehran rattle you?"

"Sure," he said. "As much as any of the lunatic things we've done the last few years."

She leaned against his arm, staring forward, her brown hair disheveled from the chaotic trip. "It was a close one. You always said we'd die on one of these missions. I thought that might be it."

"The Lord heard our prayer." He paused, but couldn't contain it anymore. "But I wonder if it was a sign."

"Oh, Lordy," came Lightfoote from behind. There was an impact on the backrest as she sat up. Her head poked through the space between the seats..

"Okay, how many times do we have to almost die together?" she said.

He grunted. "It's not about dying. Or about risk. It's about making a difference. *How* we live."

Houston looked up at him. "Francisco, we *have* made a difference. A *huge* difference."

"Maybe."

"Maybe?" Houston sat upright in her chair. "We stopped the conspiracy of all conspiracies! Saved the country. We freed humanity!"

Strawberry scented gum smacked as Lightfoote chewed.

His voice deepened. "Did we? Or do the rich still rob the poor? Do the powerful still abuse the weak?"

Lightfoote blew a large bubble. It popped between them. "So what *is* this about, Hercules?"

Lopez looked out the window. "Those I left behind in Alabama. The Latino mothers and children and workers who are paid nothing for the labor of five men. Those across America who are being scapegoated, demonized by some rich kid's stab at playing TV Hitler."

"Daniel Suite?" asked Lightfoote, pulling gum out of the piercings in her lips. "Nasty piece of work. He's going to win. You heard it here, first. Going to be bad."

"It's nothing we haven't heard for decades. We began as second class citizens. And the illegals—God help them with the hate I'm hearing. It's insane. First they're lazy immigrants freeloading off the government. In the next breath they're stealing American jobs!"

"Schrodinger's immigrant," laughed Lightfoote, her hands on their shoulders.

Houston squinted. "What?"

"Schrodinger's cat?" Lightfoote tipped her glasses down, her green eyes sparkling. She smacked the gum. "Quantum mechanics? Uncertainty principle?" Houston blinked. "Never mind."

Lopez continued. "How quickly people forget. Mexicans fed the damn country in the Second World War. Bracero Program. Ever hear of that?"

Houston shook her head. "What was it?"

"US government plan. Brought truckloads of Mexicans in to grow the food. Millions over two decades. Marriage of convenience between the US and Mexico. White Americans hated the visuals of it. Hated the poor migrants—those invited by their own government—hated those breaking their backs, feeding the nation." He scowled. "Spic, rapist, job-stealer, gang-banger. I watched families in my parish work themselves to death while America scorned them. Now, this candidate, this *monster* is legitimizing the hate, wants to ethnically cleanse the whole country."

"Never going to happen," said Houston. "That's not America."

"Sara, being white is blinding. You don't know a lot of America."

She pouted. "Maybe I don't."

"You *can't*. You can't know the ugly underbelly. But I've seen it. Felt it personally. It *can* happen. It might. Don't underestimate the death-throes of a racist and privileged population."

Lightfoote stopped chewing. "I see. You need to help."

Lopez stared forward. "I told Sara when we signed on to this York resurrected INTEL 1 that I didn't like it. Big, secretive government programs that kill people rub me the wrong way. And after Bilderberg, *Suite?* Black ops that bring down one tyranny for the next leave a bad taste in my mouth. Mexicans, all Latinos are under threat. Hell, anyone with brown skin. God forbid you wear a turban or hijab. Hate crimes are spiking with Suite encouraging violence and discrimination. I need to be on the ground with the endangered Muslim and Latino communities."

"He's always got a vague escape clause," said Houston, her voice low.

"Of course he does. And vague is good for him. It's exactly what he wants. It puts the choice of how monstrous to be in the hands of others. He's got his 21st century Jews, his boogiemen for a tyrannical state."

"And women," said Lightfoote. "He despises us."

"I'm ready to fight all of it." He turned to Lightfoote. "What about you?"

A large bubble expanded from her mouth, blotting out her face.

She pinched it from her teeth and held it over her head, staring up at the pink sphere.

"We're going to fight. Dark times coming. But only once this serial killer thing is stopped."

Houston turned toward her. "The Eunuch Maker? What's that got to do with anything?"

"We'll see," she said, her eyes distant. "But we won't talk about him."

"Why not? You brought it up."

Lightfoote sprung backward and thudded against her seat, kicking both of theirs.

"Because I say we don't!"

Lopez frowned. He'd never heard her voice so shrill. Lightfoote popped another bubble and sucked the deflated strands into her mouth.

"Okay, Angel," he said. "But you said we'd fight. Why?"

"Because Suite's going to win, like I told you." She smacked the gum. "And then INTEL 1 won't be working for York. It'll be working for *him*."

41

TORCHBEARER

The reek of whiskey pummeled Carl Miller, but the young aid smiled. He smiled through the spittle that rained on him as the large man bellowed, his tongue locked in place.

Miller melted in his suit. He obeyed the strict codes of the Suite campaign, even as the tycoon's campaign manager flouted them. Stan Brennem lounged in oversized pants, fly unzipped, shirt untucked and food-stained, his face a grizzled lawn of unshaved stubble.

Miller sat unmoving, upright, holding the laptop forward for Brennem to see the numbers. He would await the imperious commands, withstand the shouting and insults. He would continue to remain indispensable to his boss, because one truth he knew: this coalescing power was going to make history. And Miller was sure as hell going to be part of it.

"God damn!" shouted Brennem, staring at the monitor. "Holy God damn!" Miller flinched at the burst of pickled vapor. "The Russians are running with this. They've got some line into her people's files. My God! Look at the reports from the hack! We can grab some of the more extreme statements out of context and make York look like Hitler himself! Gentlemen, this could be it! This might be the kill shot!"

Miller smiled back at the maniacal grin in front of him. He spoke. "And the bank transfers—"

"Yeah, I see them, Miller. I can read, goddammit." Brennem took another swig of the brown liquid from his glass. The smile returned. "But they *are* spectacular. With all this money pouring in, we won't have to do much fundraising. We'll explain it all away. Dan's a billionaire. We'll deep-six all the records. Hide any financial information of his. No one will know where it came from."

A man in the back spoke. "What about the Iranian money?"

Brennem held a half smirk on his face as he spoke. "Well, we don't actually have a clear source on that."

Miller blanched. "You don't know where it's coming from?"

"No," said Brennem. There was some murmuring. He raised his voice. "But that doesn't *concern* me."

"But sir," said Miller, unable to catch himself. "It's *Iran*. Russia is one thing, I know, but Iran is *Muslim*."

Brennem laughed. "And so I'm even happier to take money out of the pockets of those towelheads." The large man leaned forward and stared into Miller's eyes. "You think the money's tainted? You think money gives a shit about whose hand it's in?"

"Well, no, sir, I—"

"Maybe you think we'll be *compromised*? That those towelheads will have something on us? We'll owe them or they'll blackmail us?" Silence. "Well, let's get one thing clear. *We don't owe shit to anyone.*" His voice was a snake's hiss. "They're going to owe *us*. Every last one of them from the dickless pants-pissers in Congress who wouldn't back us to the donors and voters who think we work for them."

"The voters, sir?"

Brennem chuckled. "God you're a fucking idiot." He threw back his head and downed the rest of the whiskey. "We've got a vision for this country," he said, wobbling as he stood. "We're gonna reclaim what's ours, what they've taken. The right people are gonna set our course in history." His arms whirled. "We're going to use *every* tool to win. Russian mob money, hacking, secret Iranian donors, disinformation, voter fraud, you name it. If you think they're gonna give you your country back without a fight, you're *sadly* mistaken. We're a nation with a culture and a reason for being. And I'm on a mission to save it."

He slammed the glass on the table. Miller jumped, amazed it didn't shatter.

"Nobody's going to stop us."

42

CONSPIRACY THEORIES

S hutters chirped like angry birds in the NYU press room. Dr. Linda Richards stalked into the cramped space in a frumpled pantsuit, her long, graying hair in disarray. She dropped into a chair behind a table covered with microphones from major news outlets. The mayor, chiefs of the NYPD, the president of NYU, and several unidentified men and women in suits were arrayed behind the table.

Richards surveyed the crowded mass of reporters. The room stank of wet clothes, steam still rising from those who had dashed through the rain. She put on reading glasses and exhaled. The clicks intensified as she unfolded a piece of paper and read.

"Good morning. My name is Dr. Linda Richards. I'm Head of the Department of Reproductive Biology at the NYU Center for Women's Health. I'm here to make an announcement related to the spate of killings in the city over the last few weeks."

The cameras hummed now, video streaming into the datasphere, reporters in rapt attention. Ratings were being made.

"I've been contacted by the so-called *Eunuch Maker*, the serial killer mutilating male victims by complete removal of their reproductive anatomy. The killer left the body of a convicted rapist in the hallway of my laboratory several days ago along with a typed list of demands."

She sighed and adjusted her glasses.

"The killer has demanded that I end all work on male contraception, the cornerstone of my research career. In addition, I'm to destroy all samples related to this research. If I do not comply, the killer has threatened to murder me and the people in my group." She paused. "However, because of Federal Law, I cannot destroy the research produced with taxpayer funds. I can't personally challenge the government on this, and I hope that the killer understands. But I've removed all such material from my group and put it in the hands of the authorities, who themselves can negotiate with the killer. Therefore, from this day forward, I've shut down my research program into male contraception as demanded." She removed her glasses, her eyes wet, and her voice hoarse. "I'll take questions."

"Dr. Richards, Dr. Richards!" The swarm of voices hit her like artillery blasts.

"Yes, yes," she said, indicating a lanky man from CNN in a sweater-vest.

"Did you speak with the Eunuch Maker? What else did he say?"

She shook her head. "It was only the written note. It's been turned over to the NYPD, part of their investigation. I've said what I can, what I've been cleared to say to protect the investigation." More shouts from all directions. "Yes?"

A man in a suit and tie waved his hand. "Dom McCanell from the Daily News. The new victim—was the body also mutilated?"

"Yes," said Richards. "So it appeared. But I did not inspect the body. Examination was by the NYPD. But it was like the other cases. Naked corpse. Removal of genitalia obvious. I assume the other elements like the prostate and such."

A woman in a striking red dress stood. "Laura Conley from Canid News. Who was the victim?"

Richards turned to chief Ladner from NYPD who bent down toward the microphone. "We'll reveal that in short order."

The woman in red persisted. "Then tell us: why you, Dr. Richards? Why your work?"

"I don't know for sure, but—"

"Because of your male sterilization pill?" Silence dropped. "Are you one *eunuch maker* too many for him?"

Richards smirked. "The conspiracy theories never die, I see. Especially at Canid. For those with some journalistic standards, my work is focused on a male *contraceptive*. Like the pill, but different. It doesn't sterilize men. It doesn't impair their sex life or their ability to father children once the treatment wears off."

"Then why has the killer tried to stop you?" asked Conley, her tone triumphant.

"Serial killing castrators aren't my specialty, Ms. Conley," said Richards, drawing several nervous laughs. "But some here might remember that my work's been controversial. The Left called it a rape drug. The Right, chemical castration. It's neither chemical nor castration, and it's a *contraceptive*, not some date rape drug. The Eunuch Maker has a thing about men who abuse women. Fits in well with the Leftist conspiracy theories. Maybe he thought it was all some evil plot to enslave women." She shook her head. "I hope NYPD finds him and we find out."

"Dr. Richards, what will you do now?" A young woman from NYU press.

"To be honest," said Richards, "I don't know. I start over. Pick some other projects unrelated to my main work. Try to build them up to something worthwhile. Or head in a new direction. I'll have to figure that out."

She smiled and pushed her chair backward. "For now, I'm going home. Put on some jazz and open a bottle of wine. I'm going to say goodbye to this insanity. Leave the Eunuch Maker to the authorities and the Information-Entertainment Complex."

She rose and bowed toward the officials, turning back to the reporters.

"Fuck this shit."

Dr. Linda Richards exited, stage left.

43

BLUE-EYED ANGEL MAN

hy? Why didn't I follow protocol?

José Perez sat on the cracked tiles of his Bronx apartment bathroom. Another round of bloody vomiting. Another beating at the hands of this illness. Whatever ibuprofen he kept down failed to lower his temperature. In a matter of hours, perhaps minutes, he'd be delirious, unable to help himself as he sickened.

Berating yourself is pointless.

Why hadn't he followed protocol? Such a simple answer.

I needed that job.

Dr. Sutherland was a jerk. A racist one, if mild. A problem, but one like many he'd learned to manage. The medical examiner had ridden him on everything he did, only hiring him because of the technician shortage. He made every hour on the job a minor hell.

But it paid.

Because with the Eunuch Maker case, they needed more hands to free the doctor from the mundane forensics. Because of the killer, staffing needs rose. But if he'd taken off work to heal, the coroner would have replaced him.

One clumsy moment. It's not fair.

He'd slipped on the ice outside his housing project. *They never salt our neighborhoods.* The city didn't care, not enough about the dingier boroughs. Not until they'd seen to the others, polished the broad avenues gilded with gold and towering glass.

And I fell.

His hip gleamed blue, bruised. But his hands opened the gateway. He'd tried to catch himself, peeled skin back like a knife to an apple. The razored ice breached the most protective layer available. No way he should have been in a forensics lab. Broken skin, *patches* of broken skin, collected microbes like a vortex. And clean cadavers were scarce.

I should've called in sick. Taken medical leave.

Such luxury. Medical leave belonged to another class. Doctors, medical students. The right kinds of nurses. Not those from the Bronx. Not those with families to support. Not those named *Perez.*

He stared at his hands. The bruising spread, extending up his arm. *Growing.* It made no sense. The fall couldn't be the cause. Something much worse burned inside him.

Poison?

Had one of the bodies been poisoned, the toxin slipping past his best efforts to remain sterile? Had those patches of raw epidermis brought in something dangerous?

He knew the answer was yes. Whatever invaded his tissues, death approached. A forensic scientist, he recognized the signs of a serious immune reaction. Time slipped through his bruised fingers.

Perez moaned, pushing himself up. His body shivered from the climbing fever. The room spun, his vision beginning to blur and casting a fog over everything. He pulled the door open and stepped out of the bathroom, leaving a bloody handprint on the knob.

A loud thumping startled him.

The door? Who could it be this late?

The paramedics! Of course. Yes, he'd called them. An hour ago, perhaps.

Dear God, I'm losing it.

He'd called and told them he had acute poisoning. Given his

address. Left the phone dangling as he had lurched to the bathroom to vomit again.

He tried to speak, but the raw swelling shut his throat. His voice clawed out a whisper no one could hear.

I've got to get closer.

He staggered toward the door.

"Hello?" came a male's voice. "Mr. Perez, are you in?"

The pounding stopped. A woman's voice.

"Sr. Pérez ¿Hay alguien en casa?"

"¡Sí!" His yell was a breath of forced air.

"Sr. Pérez!"

He reached the door gasping and dropped to his knees. The room spun like a child's ride at Coney Island. Somehow, his hand found the doorknob. Somehow, he held himself upright, fought the spinning gravity pulling downward. Somehow, he turned the knob.

The ceiling is so filthy. Must get ladder. Do something. Shameful. What would Mama think?

"Mr. Perez! Can you hear me?"

Who is this handsome gringo? Mama will be angry. No boys after hours. No gringos! It was a shame. A family shame. *Boys!* How would he give Mama a grandchild? *That's* why he had to leave. It was better in America.

"No lo conozco, Mama," he gasped.

"My God, look at his arms." The woman's voice again. *Not Mama.*

The man spoke. "Subcutaneous hemorrhaging, but I've never seen anything like this." Flashing lights. Strong blue irises floating above. But so blurry. "God, his eyes! They're *bleeding!*"

"What was the poison?" asked the woman. *Still not Mama.*

The man pulled something along his arm. "I don't know. There's nothing in the call log. Nothing I've ever come across, that's for sure. Not even in school. Let's get him on the gurney!"

They're counting! Like English school. "One, two, three!" He flew! Up! And down. Moving, racing down a tunnel, the voices dancing overhead, out of sight, little ghostly voices bobbing and weaving. Lightbulbs and wood and heads poking out of doorways.

Darkness. Then flashing lights. Red and blue and a wall of white and he flew into the mouth of the creature. A stab in his arm. Something hung over his head. Doors slamming.

"Secure! Let's go! His heartrate's erratic!"

A deep tug inside as they flew again.

Mama, the angels came! The blue-eyed angel man lifted me into the air and so many lights and colors and the wind! So much wind. Mama, Mama, I'm flying. I'm scared. Something's wrong.

"Be calm, my child," came his mother's voice. *"I am sorry. Sorry for so much."*

"No, Mama. No lo lamentes."

"He's trying to speak," said the woman. "I can't make it out."

"Sorry for my hard heart. So much you have carried. Soon, it is over. Soon, you will have peace, my sweet boy."

His mother's voice soothed the fire inside. The trembling in his limbs slowed. Ceased. All fear flowed out of his body. He closed his eyes a final time.

The ambulance strobed the dark evening as it sped down the highway.

44

DRUG LORDS DON'T SEQUENCE DNA

A black car pulled out from the main traffic approaching the Holland Tunnel. Uniformed officers diverted it through a line of construction zone pylons and under a net of opaque scaffolding that never left the rocky face on the New Jersey side. The officers glanced at the readout on a wrist device, ignoring what was behind the tinted windows of the car.

Inside the vehicle Savas fidgeted. His suit chafed his neck. He was developing a rash across his chest. His eyes refused to focus anymore. Several years of constant existential threats were tearing him down.

We can't let Nemesis escape now.

His driver electronically passed the required codes to the hidden security forces. A doorway concealed from outside eyes opened like some secret passage from a fantasy novel. The vehicle accelerated toward the artificially lit tunnel behind it.

What is she plotting?

The last leader of the powerful Bilderberg group was on the run. The most fanatical of the shadowed puppet-masters remained free. Increasingly cornered, she was more dangerous than ever.

We'll root her out just like the others.

Savas didn't fool himself that INTEL 1 owned the credit. Bilderberg's demise began with Fawkes. The genius hacker threw down the facade, revealed the hidden forces pulling the strings across the world. INTEL 1 simply completed the kill.

Except for Nemesis.

Steady light replaced strobing ceiling fluorescents. The clandestine second tunnel under the Hudson vanished. He entered a large underground cavern, vehicles carpeting a space before a set of doorways in the granite underneath Manhattan.

He hopped from the car the moment the driver stopped. Security confirmed his credentials, fingerprints, retinal scan, and DNA analysis. All pro forma. They knew him well, chief Morlock of President York's literal underground agency. He passed the ID checks and was ushered through the blast-proof doorways.

"Captain Overlord returns!" rang a woman's voice to welcome him.

Three figures approached him as he entered the heart of the INTEL 1 operation. Computer screens, windowed offices, corridors and high ceilings surrounded them. A buzzing background of agents, computers, and air compressors assaulted his senses. The female voice spiked as a strong signal in the background noise.

"The country burned down yet?" asked Lightfoote.

Savas stopped in front of her. Her green eyes burned as always, her tattooed and buff body bulging through tight fatigues. The light danced from several places off her shaved head.

"Not yet, but God knows we're trying."

He turned to Lopez's broad form. "Gabriel." He pivoted to the left of Lightfoote toward Houston. "Mary." Code names for fugitives on the Most Wanted list who could never admit their true identities. Personally selected by the President to work in a secret, underground force hidden from all other branches of government.

Lunacy.

"Glad to see all of you alive," he said.

Lopez clapped a powerful hand on Savas's shoulder.

"Glad to have survived!" he boomed. "But we have to be smarter.

Nemesis is playing for keeps. We wanted the mission in Tehran too much."

"We've just arrived, too," said Houston. "They told us you were coming in. Heard Rebecca has some leads."

"Bank records," said Savas. "She called me in, so it must be important."

"In from where?" asked Lightfoote. "You moonlighting?"

He smiled. "The city's totally worked up about this serial killer."

"The Eunuch Maker," said Lopez.

Lightfoote straightened, her entire body tense.

"Yes," said Savas. "The FBI's been called in, which should be good enough. But our contacts are spooked. I was asked to consult, whether INTEL 1 might get involved."

"Bad idea," snapped Lightfoote, her tone drawing glances from the others. "We need to focus on Nemesis."

Her eyes were wide and Savas tried not to stare. *Is she frightened of the Eunuch Maker?* He'd known Angel Lightfoote to express a broad spectrum of emotions. Laughter. Tears. Anger. *Fear?* When the closeness of imminent death made such fear rational, yes. At the mere mention of the disturbing or dangerous? Never.

"York knows about this?" asked Houston, cocking her head to one side.

"No, and if you morons behave, it will stay that way."

"She's got a lot on her plate right now," said Lopez.

"I told them the truth," Savas added. "This is not national security and we have a wildfire we're putting out. I told them to handle it."

"The less we waste time on that case the better," said Lightfoote, her voice strained.

"Right." Savas squinted at her. "The election's turned into a storm. Politics is like nothing anyone has seen, gone full tribal, out of control. Oddsmakers at a loss. Pundits look like idiots." He shook his head. "Once we removed the steadying hand of Bilderberg, all hell's broken loose."

Lopez laughed, a twinkle in his eye. "Sounds like you miss them already."

Savas glowered. "Like hell I do. *Live free or die.* I hope it's not coming to dying, but freedom's sure gotten crazy."

"Let's see what Rebecca's found," said Lightfoote, turning toward the broad hallway behind her. "If she yanked you back like this, must be juicy, and we're wasting time."

She is *afraid.*

He didn't have time to analyze it. Lightfoote was right—they had to move. He also needed to see Cohen. *Privately.* He needed her help and they'd keep that from the others. Someone had called in a favor at NYPD, one he couldn't refuse.

"Juicy?" said Cohen, glancing up from her desk, her glasses on the bridge of her nose. "It's something."

They sat around a desk in Cohen's office, a room she'd designed near the data centers of INTEL 1. All intelligence streamed by her, agents and analysts only steps away in adjoining spaces.

This is my domain.

Despite everything the group had been through, despite her real heroics, some ending at the barrel of her gun, she belonged here. Comfortable as an analyst, orchestrating the hunt for criminals.

Give me data and time. Let Angel and Sara blow things up.

"They just handed over private banking records?" asked Lopez, an eyebrow raised.

"It wasn't easy." Her eyes darted to Savas. "John and I had to lean on the bank. But they knew something was up. The transaction history of the account didn't fit any AI models. It couldn't belong to any sort of normal person with a job, debts, rich or poor. It was an anomaly. Along with the hints of nefarious associations and our fake clearances with the Secret Service, they caved quickly."

"And so?" sighed Savas, rubbing his eyes.

He's so damn tired. This is killing him. Cohen felt a rush of sympathy.

"So, the transactions are indeed bizarre. No wonder the pattern recognition algorithms were at zero confidence levels." She tapped a smart screen on the wall behind her chair. A spreadsheet appeared, columns of data filled with numbers. "Discrete, massive cash influxes at irregular intervals. All of them untraceable, buried in nested phony shell companies and other accounts."

"Nemesis," said Savas.

"Undoubtedly."

"And the cash out?"

"Not the politically motivated expenditures from her other activity. Here it's really odd."

Lightfoote squinted at the screen. "Medical supplies?"

"Lot of them," continued Cohen. "Hospital items, monitors, isolation chambers, pharmaceuticals, research equipment and reagents."

"Unsettling," said Lopez.

Cohen nodded. "We're still trying to find out what some of the companies sell, get records from them tied to this account. If we can get the shipping information, we'll have a real lead to the contacts, to whoever is working this."

"Sounds like a drug operation," said Houston.

Lightfoote frowned. "No. That's not right. Sure, some of that stuff. But hospital equipment? Basic biotech research? What the hell? Drug lords don't sequence DNA."

"They didn't used to," said Savas.

Cohen shrugged. "We don't know what we're looking at. But it's Nemesis, so it must be disruptive. As we've learned the hard way, she plays a very long game."

Lightfoote leaned back in her chair and put a combat boot up on the desk.

"I've got a very bad feeling about this."

45

STAKEOUT

"So this is staking out," grumbled Lopez, drumming his fingers on the dash. "Can you verb that?"

Savas suppressed a sigh. Four hours outside the main branch. *To be honest, I'm not cut out for this anymore, either.*

They'd arranged things with the bank. Online access to the account was disabled. The mysterious account holder, the man in the pocket of one of the planet's most dangerous individuals, had no other means to access that precious money. He had to show.

"So, given all the presidential resources we've got at our fingertips, why are *we* here?"

"You know why, *Gabriel*. Whoever is working for Nemesis is likely a professional killer. An assassin. Someone we can't trust to just anyone. I'm not sure *I* should be here, but you're our secret weapon. You're the damn wrath of God."

"Lord grant mercy."

"And patience is a *virtue*. A little longer."

"Much longer and we're going to need a solution to *solution*," said Lopez. "What do you guys use? Gatorade bottles? I didn't touch coffee. Some sips of water, but biology is biology."

"He'll show," said Savas. "Online withdrawals had a pattern, Angel found it. He's overdue. We've forced his hand."

And on cue his cell vibrated.

"Savas!" he answered. "Perfect. We'll move in. Tell them not to—"

The door of the bank burst open, sunlight flashing across them as the glass reflected the bright sun. A man in a fog coat and pulled down baseball cap raced out of the bank, sending pedestrians flying. He darted toward a nearby alleyway.

"Damn!"

They denied him the money, didn't they? He turned the ignition. *Idiots!*

"On foot!" yelled Lopez, the ex-priest's door opening. "Subway line two blocks down!"

He's right.

The car would just slow them down. He leapt out and slammed the door, turning to follow Lopez across the street. The blaring horn of a cab stopped him short, a yellow blur inches from his sidearm. Savas inhaled, scanned the street, and raced across.

The chase was brief. Lopez stormed ahead, his broad back twisting like a pass-rusher pursuing a quarterback. The prey bobbed even farther in front, the man's head higher than Lopez even at a distance.

That is one tall man.

People screamed as they rushed past, cell phones whipping out. He approached the next street and glimpsed the green sphere of the metro ahead. The baseball hat disappeared down a stairway next to it.

"Don't let him board!"

Lopez didn't respond, disappearing himself down the subway entrance.

Savas gulped air, his mouth a parched desert. He reached the stairway, grasping a lamppost for support, catching his breath. A crowd pulled back from the entrance, their eyes wide.

"FBI," he gasped, giving them a practiced stare of reassurance.

A gunshot shattered the calm. He drew his firearm and

descended the stairs, his fatigue wrecking his balance. Sweat clouded his vision as he stepped into the underground station.

I'm getting too old for this.

NYPD officers entered from the opposite side. Their eyes locked with his, his gun raised toward the ceiling, his face dripping. They drew on him. He held up his false FBI identification, hoping that this afternoon wasn't going to end with friendly fire.

"FBI! Special Agent in Charge Thanasis Papavasiliou!" he shouted, praying he'd got the ID right in this madness.

The officers approached with their guns trained on him.

"Put the firearm on the ground! Now!"

He put it down, going to his knees and holding up the ID. One of the officers grabbed it.

"What the hell is this?" the policeman asked. "Saw two men run down toward the N train. Shots fired."

"Fugitive with terrorist connections. The tall one. FBI agent in pursuit. The short one."

"Jesus!" whispered the officer.

A warm blast of air hit them, pushing up from the lower level.

The train!

"Let me through!" cried Savas.

The man nodded to his partner, who handed Savas his firearm. He took it and stumbled over the turnstile, dashing down the stairs underneath a sign labeled "NQR."

Too late.

Halfway down the deep roar of acceleration began, the repetitive clacking of the wheels over the tracks speeding up. He landed on the platform, his legs buckling, his gun arm shaky.

The tube was empty. The receding glow of a subway car disappeared into the blackness of the tunnel.

"He got on," came a gasp from his right, around the stairway column.

Savas turned to find Lopez against the wall, doubled over and holding his stomach. His weapon was on the ground several feet from him.

"Francisco! Are you okay?"

"*Gabriel*," he wheezed. "Not okay. Not quite. Was waiting for me. I came down the stairs. Too fast," he panted. "Should've been smarter. I got a shot off. His fist was faster." Blood trickled along Lopez's ear.

"Your head?"

"Lifted me off the ground with that hit. Slammed into the wall."

Jesus. Lopez was a heavy man. Muscular, broad. A short tank. For a man to have thrown him into a wall with a single blow?

"Sorry," said Lopez, rising and placing a hand on Savas. His voice grew in strength. "Knocked the wind out of me. I couldn't breathe. He got on board." He grimaced. "We lost him."

Savas put his shoulder under Lopez's arm, helping the man walk. The NYPD officers arrived with backup.

There's going to be a lot of explaining to do.

Savas sighed. "I hope the ladies are having a better day."

46

HOLY ZOMBIE APOCALYPSE, BATMAN

H ouston pulled the black car to a stop beside a block-spanning series of brick buildings in the Bronx. She pushed the dark sunglasses to her head, tufts of brown hair sprouting around the lenses. Piercing blues gazed out in their place, through the window.

What a shit-hole.

Riding shotgun, Lightfoote glanced between a smartphone and the building, popped a giant bubble, and sucked the gum in. The piercings running up her face and ears glinted in the afternoon sunlight.

"You sure this is it?" Houston asked.

"This is the address the shippers had." She laughed. "Merchants seemed *way* too happy to tell us everything once we flashed ID and mentioned *terrorism*. It's like a magic word. Opens a lot of doors. And addresses."

"And jail cells."

Lightfoote smirked. "I guess you'd know. That's my point. Fear-factor has the whole system screwed." Her gaze darted through the window. "But, yeah. This is a dump. Why ship products from reputable medical distribution centers at biotech prices to what looks like a gunrunners' warehouse?" She popped the door open and spit her gum to the curb. "I'm *very* interested to see what's going on."

Houston exited the vehicle, scanning the deserted streets. Wind-blown refuse and dilapidated cars populated the block. Houston wasn't taking any chances, either with local criminals or with some unexpected killers working with Nemesis. Her Browning 1911 bulged on her left side, her boots stiff from sheathed knives. She'd seen Lightfoote holster a Glock.

The girl kills just as well with her hands and feet. Or her brain.

"Loading dock's open for business," said Lightfoote. A black leather coat and cargo pants lent her the appearance of a worker on a cigarette break.

Houston motioned toward the middle of the block. A large metal door opened in a four-story brick monolith.

"No one outside. No signs. No logos. They don't advertise much."

Lightfoote cast her a sharp stare, and the pair strode toward the ramp and opened entrance. They crossed the street and jogged up a set of stairs, entering the building without seeing a soul.

Inside was a different story. Workers darted back and forth, carting boxes and crates through two broad passageways. Down the halls, Houston saw steel cages with multiple levels, each holding rows on rows of boxes.

"Hey!" cried a heavyset man with a clipboard, ambling over from a forklift. "Who the hell are you? This is private property!"

Houston flashed a fake FBI ID - *how sweet that felt* - and decided to cast the spell, looking to the nametag on his shirt.

"Terrorists, Mr. Kogan."

Lightfoote choked back a laugh.

"Terrorists?" came the hoarse reply.

"Special Agent Mary Borden with my assistant, Jane McKeegan. FBI."

The half-shaven foreman stared at Lightfoote. "She's a girl?"

Lightfoote winked at him.

"We're pursuing a lead. Highly suspicious packages were deliv-ered to *this* address, Mr. Kogan."

His eyes widened. "Bombs?"

"These terrorists are capable of anything, sir," said Lightfoote, who pressed herself against the foreman. She placed a hand on his shoulder. "Anything."

Kogan pulled back, his eyes darting between Lightfoote and Houston.

"Look, we're just a storage facility. We get packages. We store them. We don't ask questions."

"The law requires you ask certain questions, Mr. Kogan," said Houston. He licked his lips. She shoved a piece of paper with a number on it in his face. "I need to see this location."

He took the paper, sweat beading on his upper lip. "Yeah, sure. No problem. No problem. This here's one of the sheds in the back."

"Sheds?"

"Yeah. Some clients store a lot, or want more privacy." He forced a smile.

"We'd like immediate access to that shed by authority of Section 802 of the USA PATRIOT Act, domestic terrorism. Will you allow us access?"

Foreman Kogan retrieved a small electronic device and ushered them through the cavernous central storage facility. They continued out a back doorway to the interior of the block. There, surrounded by monotonous red brick on all sides, a grid of metal sheds rusted. Most were subdivided into separate, private storage rooms. He led them to one of the few standing apart with a single lift and slide door. The number 441 glinted above it.

"Here it is," he said, aiming the controller at the unit and keying in a code. The door rattled and slid upward, tucking itself into the ceiling of the trailer-sized shed. "I don't need to see what's inside," he said, walking to the side. "Don't want to see."

The interior was dark. Houston felt for a switch on the side wall and pressed a button. Fluorescent lighting bathed the crowded space.

"It's a damn hospital junkyard," said Lightfoote.

Houston gazed over the equipment, most of it covered in plastic or still boxed in wooden crates. She recognized some items. Vital sign monitors, gurneys, IV stands. Others she didn't, but they radiated a clinical function.

But shapes pulled her eyes elsewhere.

"Holy Zombie Apocalypse, Batman." Lightfoote whistled.

Biohazard suits dangled from racks like radioactive fashion statements. Houston shivered. The plastic face guards, goggles, gloves, and boots possessed a nightmarish gravitational pull on the psyche. Lightfoote moved toward them.

"Careful!" hissed Houston.

"Doubt there's Ebola in here, *Agent McKeegan*." She touched the suits, twisting them back and forth. "No. Not in *here*, anyway. But who's playing outbreak?"

Houston swallowed. "We need to call this in." She reached for her phone.

"Ten-four." Lightfoote read from the boxes. "Air filters. Double-door autoclave. Ultraviolet light passbox. Disinfectant dunk tank." She gripped a thick curtain of plastic. "Lot of this all folded up. For *containment,* I'd bet."

The chill inside Houston reached the freezing point.

"Containment? For *what?*"

Lightfoote turned, her green eyes flashing like a cat's.

"Something pretty damn bad."

47

R NAUGHT

A tone rang on the coffee machine, and a broad hand grasped the handle of the pot and lifted it toward a dark mug. Steam rose as the black liquid flowed, a chemical molecule drawn on the side of the mug changing from white to black and disappearing as the cup filled.

A tall form turned to the window and drank, staring outside into the cold morning fog and downing half the hot fluid uninterrupted. An ironed white coat stretched across his broad shoulders. It matched a set of similar coats hanging from a bar along the wall. He placed the mug down, opened a new box of surgical masks, and headed toward a thick metal doorway embedded in the kitchen wall. He tapped a keypad, a metallic click sounded, and he yanked on the handle. The door shut behind him as he descended a flight of stairs.

The cellar was dim compared to the windowed kitchen, long fluorescent bulbs on the ceiling failing to reproduce the full spectrum of sunlight. A mask obscured the man's face, tufts of blond hair protruding from a cap worn on his head. At the bottom of the stairs, he passed a large waste container on the left filled with purple gloves. On the right was a table with a box of fresh gloves and a plastic face shield. He grabbed two gloves from the box, stuck his hands inside them, and lifted the face guard, fitting it over his head. The bright lights above reflected off the plastic, further concealing his face.

In front gleamed a wall of plastic, the entrance a zippered gash down the middle. He grabbed the pull-tab, yanked the teeth apart from top to bottom, passed underneath, and zipped it shut. Inside the plastic, he pressed a button connected to a maze of tubes and dials out of some steampunk novel. A loud hiss of air rushed through the inner chamber along with a gas fog. After several seconds he unzipped the next chamber, entering and sealing that as well.

Two layers inside, he approached a floor-bolted hospital gurney in the middle of an open partition. Plastic surrounded him. A dying creature twitched on the gurney, a naked man of indeterminate age, the final stages of a horrific metamorphosis rendering him alien and monstrous.

His skin oozed, a mottled impact zone, bruising and burst vessels a macabre series of continuous tattoos covering him from head to foot. Blood pooled in many locations, the vasculature failing in some spectacular fashion, the tissues unable to hold themselves together. Crimson gel leaked from several orifices, the mouth, nose, eyes, and penis. The man's lips drew back over bleeding gums and loose teeth.

The form convulsed at the sound of the large form entering the space. A distorted whisper escaped him.

"Kill me."

The figure covered in the biohazard gear stared at the battered body. Instruments around the form beeped in alarm. The killer straightened, his voice muffled.

"I am sorry for your suffering," the large man began, stepping around the figure and removing equipment and tools. "Your disease progression was unusually rapid. I didn't think you would reach this level of morbidity until tomorrow. The hemorrhaging is particularly pronounced." He sighed. "There is such patient to patient variability. It complicates my studies."

The near-corpse moaned as the man fitted a mask connected to a thick tube over his face. But he offered no resistance.

"I do try to be as humane as possible, even if you do not deserve it." He snapped the fittings of the mask in place, creating a tight seal. The dying man squirmed, generating little movement.

"Don't panic. It's carbon dioxide. You'll fall asleep and it will all end."

He reached with his gloved hand and opened a valve. A compressor churned with a soft hiss.

"I haven't thought of a way to present you to the world. My theatrics are draining time from research." He clicked his tongue on the roof of his mouth. "In some ways, I shouldn't bother. The new world that is coming will set its own priorities. Make its own histories. Determine your value and mine. But it's hard not to preach. I've taken history into my own hands."

The form on the gurney relaxed. The muscles stopped twitching. One arm fell to the side and hung motionless.

"But I simply can't get the statistics required! I can't know the real value of *r naught*. It underlies everything." The lights and sounds on the monitors climbed to a panicked state. "Simulations tell me I'm in the right order of magnitude with some confidence. But if I'm wrong, too low, if I don't seed enough patient zeros, there won't be full penetration through the population. There will be a recovery. The revolution will never occur."

The monitors flatlined. There was a warning tone. He reached over and silenced it.

"Not that it will matter to you." He stared downward. "How many women did you abuse? How many have we all? How many centuries of horror and hell on earth for half the human population?" His gloved hand slapped the wet shoulder of his victim. "That's what matters."

The man rose and opened a tool box. Scalpels, forceps, and specimen pans lined the interior. He moved the cart toward the pelvis of his victim and placed the tools in a tight line.

"And yet you may be near useless, if your disease progression is an indication." He shook his head. "An outlier. A data point to skew the norm and discard. And so I lose precious time."

He raised an electric scalpel and positioned it over the man's crotch. A tingle of voltage buzzed in the air.

"But let's see what the tissues say."

He began to cut.

PART III

GONE VIRAL

"Among insect diseases, the androcidal disease of fruit flies are of special interest. The SR-spirochetes exerted a lethal effect on XY but not on XX individuals, regardless of whether they were phenotypically males, inter-sexes, or females."

—Harris and Maramorosch
(*Pathogens, Vectors, and Plant Diseases*)
and Miyamoto and Oishi,
(*Genetics*. 1975 Jan;79(1):55-61.)

48

OLD FRIENDS

S acker watched the brunette lecture the 12th precinct with a detached amusement. It wasn't the air of a graduate school seminar she projected, square glasses and long hair working overtime to cast a West Coast protest girl vibe over the formal FBI pantsuit she sported. It wasn't the expressions of his fellow NYPD officers, mostly male, dancing between professional respect and unprofessional leering. *All these years and training, and they still can't hide it.* No, it was because he knew Rebecca Cohen as only a trial by fire could accomplish.

"So, let me be clear before I wrap this up," she said, removing her glasses. Her brown eyes scanned the crowd before her. Sacker noticed how bloodshot they looked. "We're not here to take over or scoop you on the Eunuch Maker. We're here to collaborate with the NYPD to lend our expertise and resources to help you make the collar. We're here on invitation, not invasion. I hope in this spirit you can work with liaisons from the FBI and other agencies to catch this killer."

Less than two years ago, when all hell broke loose, when Anonymous began blowing things up and gunning down Wall Street CEOs, he'd been onsite at the Citigroup building. Bodies strewn around the square, police tape like some spider's web, crowds and cameras massing around the crime scene. *Insanity.* A black town car pulled up and announced the arrival of the Feds. In the midst of the chaos, a stunning brunette stepped out of the car, cell phone stuck to her face, bag in hand. *Built like a damn brick house.* He understood the glances the men around him gave her. He'd done the same that day even as death encircled them.

Nothing like a real professional to get one's head out of one's rear. She'd taken control of the scene, asked the right questions, and sized him up as someone the FBI could trust. So had begun an inter-agency collaboration that landed him before a military tribunal during Civil War 2.0. That madness ended with nukes dropped in Kansas and the nation snatched from the cliff's edge. *By Cohen's group at FBI* from what he could determine in the aftermath.

The stress of those days returned in waves of panic. He remem-bered hanging on a thin thread, his freedom uncertain. One wrong answer could have led to—*who knows what?* A time of rashness and the pinnacle of his performance in law enforcement.

The past and present superimposed over her form. Before him, in the now removed from that chaos, Cohen dismissed the men in blue. She fielded a few final questions from detectives and the brass, stretching with exhaustion as the last left her. But that other time hung like a swirling halo around her, pregnant with an unnerving truth: Rebecca Cohen had nearly gotten him executed.

He smiled and shook his head, rising from a chair on the side of the room. He approached as she stuffed papers into a bag.

"Agent Cohen. It's been a while."

She paused, manila folders in hand, her face turned away. Cohen placed the papers down and turned, a broad smile on her face.

"Detective Sacker. I *wondered* if you'd be here."

She damn well knew I'd be here.

"Thought I'd keep a low profile. Didn't want to tip off anyone to our sordid relationship."

Her eyebrows danced. "Indeed. A crazy time of rules bent and broken. Oaths voided. People killed. I understood your silence after it all ended."

Did she miss me?

"Well, we have a serial killer castrating victims on the cover of the Post and Daily News. Things are getting back to normal." He saw corners of her mouth twitch. "So, did you mean all that up there? You gonna let us work this with you?"

Cohen sighed, her fatigue returning like a tsunami. "Absolutely. And I *did* know you were coming. I prepped. You're leading things now. Wise move by your chief." Her smile flickered.

"He might be reconsidering. Gotta crack this soon. Jack-booted thugs like you showing up would've ruined my year, normally. So, I *am* glad *you're* here."

"You helped INTEL 1 out a good bit back in the day." She met his eyes. "I know this investigation's in good hands. If you ever need backup, on the street or in the halls here, we'll make the calls."

"Folks from INTEL 1?" he said, trying to keep his tone flat.

"Um-hmm." Her sharp eyes held his.

"Papers said INTEL I was closed down after the madness."

"Yes. They did say that."

Nice poker face.

"But you're still with FBI, it seems. You didn't say which division."

Cohen dropped the last folders into her bag and zipped it, hoisting the satchel over her shoulder. She brushed past him, moving toward the door.

"No, I didn't."

49

GONE MOGGY

G race Gone startled out of deep concentration. The blows were heavy, a sense of irritation in the sound of fist to wood.

Tyrell.

Only he'd feel familiar enough to knock so rudely.

Either that or a collection agency.

She stumbled from the chair in her office and limped to the entrance of her rented space.

"You need to get that damned ringer fixed," he grumbled, slipping in through the open door. She closed it and turned the bolt locks.

"Sure, Tyrell. You want to spring for my rent this month? Or last month's while you're at it? DNA analysis isn't cheap. None of this is. I'm broke, in debt, and tired. I don't need the attitude."

He straightened. "Gracie." She grimaced at the new nickname he'd become enamored with. "Now that's what I'm talking about! Mike Hammer stuff there."

They stared at each other a moment, eyes locked. He smiled from one side of his mouth. She half-expected him to wink.

What is it about him? I need to figure that out soon.

"Worst deduction I ever made was teaming up with you," she said, turning away from the door. A wry grin crept over her face.

Then she fell.

One moment she buzzed in the presence of Sacker, the next she was sprawled on a rack of out-of-date magazines. *Hail irony*. The collection was intended for the clients who had yet to materialize outside her office.

Strong arms grasped her waist and side, turned her over—floor, wall, ceiling.

Tyrell.

He was staring down at her with wide eyes.

"Gracie! Are you hurt? What happened?"

She tried to slow her breathing.

Damn.

It was getting worse. More and more of these. Soon, she wouldn't be able to hide it any longer.

I need to figure out that soon, too.

"I'm okay. I'm okay." She made a heroic effort to sit up, appear normal and unscathed. "Always was clumsy! Tripped on that ragged carpet edge." She pointed downward.

"Uh-huh." His brows knitted over his eyes. "My spy file said you were a dancer."

"Bad intel." She pushed herself up.

Turn the leg away, Grace.

She did. Sacker noticed.

"Look, maybe we ought to have that looked at—"

"Tell me about the FBI." She sat on one of the lounge chairs.

He took her hands in his. "Gracie, I'm serious, let's—"

"So am *I*."

He let go.

Too harsh. Damn. "I'm okay. We need to talk. I need you to under-stand some things. But first, do we still have a case?"

Sacker sat across from her and exhaled. His gaze didn't waver.

"Miraculously, yes," he said. "Long story. Long bloody story, but during the crisis a few years ago, I worked with a special branch of the FBI. Called themselves *INTEL 1*. I haven't talked much about them to anyone, but those guys about saved the country. Several died in the process."

"Savas's group?"

His eyebrows rose. "Yeah, that's them."

"It's not all they're known for."

"Well, guess who shows up today to take over our investigation? Lovely lady from INTEL 1, Rebecca Cohen. Except she's not with INTEL 1 anymore and I can't figure out who the hell's she's working for. But she's there posing as FBI. Tells us they will help. Tells us it's still our case."

Gone's eyes glowed. "God, good to hear. Because things are very serious, Tyrell. You need to understand."

Sacker frowned. "Yeah, about the other night—"

"No time."

He grimaced.

"Look Tyrell, you've got a problem. And yes, it concerns me. But later. Not now. Things are serious."

He set his shoulders back. "Okay. I'm all ears. And more brain this time."

Gone gestured to the stairway descending to her laboratory.

"Maybe better if I show you."

SACKER SQUINTED into the eyepieces of the stereo microscope. He tried adjusting the focus with the knobs on the side. He tried twisting the eyepieces. He tried moving his head back and forth. He gave up.

"So, I'm supposed to see *what* here, exactly?"

"You can't see the tissue damage? Even some necrosis? Signs of massive trauma, hemorrhaging, immune infiltration."

Sacker stood and shook his head. He put his hands on her shoulders. "Just tell me what it means."

She blushed and closed her eyes to keep balance. "These men are *not* victims of a beating, Tyrell." Her lids flicked open. "Sutherland's *wrong.* I've done the tissue pathology, some initial panel screening for viral genomes—"

He cocked his head. "Wait, viral what?"

"The conclusion is inescapable. These men died of an acute infection with a hemorrhagic virus."

"A hemorrhagic virus." His mouth hung open. "You mean like, what? *Ebola?*"

"Marburg family of viruses, actually, at least as far as my genetic markers tell. But, yes."

"Genetic markers for Ebola? Why the hell do you have that lying around?" He blinked. "Hell, I don't even understand how there's a working medical examiner's office in your damn basement!"

"These weren't just lying around. I *ordered* them specifically because of my suspicions in this case. From all the other evidence. I was hoping to God that I was wrong."

"Grace," he began, holding the words back, hesitating. "Are you sure about this? What in the world are you talking about?"

Well, there goes 'Gracie.'

"I'm one hundred percent sure! I can't nail the virus down without access to more sophisticated DNA sequencing. And a hell of a lot more money. But the tissue pathology, the viral markers, everything —these men died from viral damage to their bodies."

Sacker exhaled. "This doesn't make sense. What's the killer's play here? How could he get his hands on it? It's crazy!" He straightened, his glare focused at a distance. "We need to get the CDC or somebody on this."

Her stomach dropped. "What can *they* do?"

"What can they *do?* I don't know, quarantine or something? These things are contagious, right? We can't let something like this spread!"

"Quarantine what? We don't know where it's coming from. The bodies are on ice in the morgue. The CDC can't do anything."

"Whoa, hold on girl. This all sounds nuts, but if there's any chance you're right, we've got to bring in the big guns. Verify, at least. You could be wrong. And God! I hope you're wrong. But this is beyond you or me or NYPD. And we've got to tell Sutherland about the bodies. Someone could infect themselves!"

She sighed. "True. But they'll shut us down! The guys with the space suits will come in. They won't be friendly like the FBI woman you have a crush on."

He pulled back. "Wait, what? Have a crush—"

"They'll take over completely. Kick us the hell out. We'll lose it."

Gone bit her lower lip. *I'm being a monster now. And I can't help it!*

Sacker reached over and put his hand on her shoulder again. She wanted to cry.

"Gracie, then we lose it."

"But I'm making progress!"

His hand wouldn't move. *Damn him!*

"Come on, girl. Ambition's good, but you can't go down that road."

Her mind raced. "This sexy FBI woman. Do you trust her?"

Sacker gaped. "Sexy? Gracie, what—"

"Do you *trust* her?"

"Yes. I told you. I've got history with INTEL 1."

"Or whatever it is now." Her eyes darted like lasers. "Set up a meeting with her. We tell them everything. We let this mysterious *new* INTEL 1 decide. They'll control the evidence. The bodies can be quarantined. They can lock it up, get CDC to work on the samples. Do the science. Or nuke the site from orbit. But your girlfriend will let us stay involved!"

"But—"

"Someone is behind this. Someone dropping men dead from a hemorrhagic virus in New York City. An investigation the CDC isn't up to." She smiled, tapping her finger on the nape of her neck. "But a shadowy intelligence organization might be exactly what we need."

"Gracie..."

She reared up on her toes and grabbed his collar. "Do you trust *me,* Tyrell?"

"Trust you? I—"

"Don't overthink it. This is a fulcrum moment. Yes or no. Do you trust me?"

His eyes widened. "Um, yes. Strangely enough. I do. But—"

"Then give me a chance! Someone's infecting sex offenders with a hemorrhagic virus, making modern art of them. Whatever sick game is playing out, this is *dangerous*. More than ever, we've got to crack this case. We must find the killer. We may not have much time."

"Time until *what?*"

Gone could feel the chill in his voice.

"I don't know, and that's what scares me. Something's going on, a lot bigger than some serial killer with gender issues."

Sacker didn't take his eyes off her, his body unmoving.

"Alright, Gracie," he said. "I'll talk to her. Jesus! We'd better not be responsible for the next damn plague."

"Thank you, Tyrell!"

He passed a hand over his face. "Maybe I *should* lose my job. Better yet, go to prison. *Damn!*"

Gone limped over to a workbench and removed several items, walking them back toward the detective.

"I need to ask a favor."

She placed a needle, several sample vials, and a rubber tube on the bench beside him.

"What favor?"

She began rolling up his sleeve.

"Blood. I need some samples."

"From me? Why?" His eyes widened as she tied a rubber hose around his bicep.

"Experimental controls." She thumped the skin below the muscle. "I can't keep using me."

She looked into his eyes.

"Make a fist?"

GONE ROGUE

B lindfolded, dumped in the backseat of ciphered black town cars, whisked through Manhattan with deceptive and dizzying driving, INTEL 1 wasn't taking any chances.

The speed of their response shocked Sacker. A call to the number Cohen left him, a message recorded, a return call in minutes, and *in the same call* an arrangement to rendezvous. On their terms. Blindfolded.

The immediacy of the meeting pumped adrenaline through him. He'd imagined several possible responses, laughter the first and most likely. Maybe, just maybe they might consider that a deadly virus was turning a killer's victims into pulverized pink goo. *Maybe* they'd say they'd look into it, Cohen indulging him for old time's sake. Helping her save the nation might buy some tolerance to madness.

And what's sane about Gracie's idea?

But, no. They told him to hold, turned tense, and pushed for a meeting. *Immediately.* And so his protective scaffolding around that black pit of doom collapsed. INTEL 1 took the hypothesis so seriously there was only one possibility: they had *already* considered it. He coughed a laugh in the car. *Ridiculous.* Terrifying. The black pit loomed in front of him as the car sped.

Toward something underground.

The cacophony of New York traffic yielded to the rush and reverb of a tunnel.

But which?

Several were within striking distance. But all had tolls and the associated sounds. Sacker heard none of it. Might as well be a private gate with Lex Luthor himself directing them into the bowels of the earth.

Wherever they were and however they got there, the journey ended. The vehicle jerked to a stop and the doors opened. Hands helped them out, ushering them forward. There was a short pause in front of what felt like a wall, followed by the unmistakable sounds of massive doorways opening. They moved forward again.

The doors closed behind them, fingers danced behind his head and the blindfold came off.

He blinked in the light.

"Well, I'll be damned."

——

ONCE THE SHOCK WORE OFF, federal agents led them through this Manhattan NORAD to a spacious office belonging to his old friend, Rebecca Cohen. She and two others he'd never met sat around a broad table.

Cohen chaired the meeting at the front of the desk. Two intense faces glared at him on either side of her. *The man named Gabriel is Latino.* Probably Mexican from his Aztec features. Built like an express train, he emitted a strange aura combining a reflective and deadly silence. Across from him a woman slouched back in her chair, short brown hair and blue eyes with a gaze reminding him of a bored cat. *Mary.*

He and Gone sat at the other end of the table. The polished wood grain reflected surreal, wall-sized flat-screen monitors spinning images and data out like some scene from a Matt Damon film. He returned his attention to the conversation. All eyes centered on Gone.

Gracie doing her thing.

"Numerous clues, data along the journey, Agent Cohen," she said, her voice weary. The long walks through this underground labyrinth had drained her. "It's not rocket science. You're a covert operation funded and run by the Executive Branch, staffed with former members of the FBI division once called INTEL 1. This was run by John Savas of *Mjolnir* fame. He likely still runs things, even though he's not here today. I'm sure you realize, all this is in violation of numerous laws and precedents. I assume it happened during the constitutional crisis, Civil War 2.0. Your operation's sequestered somewhere under the Hudson or below Manhattan—the trip out to New Jersey used to disorient us, or maybe because access is limited to one direction. Finally, whatever else you're doing, you've stumbled on data linking the Eunuch Maker to biological hazards. Which means my own research is correct."

Cohen's eyes darted between him and Gone. She said nothing.

I hate long awkward silences. Especially in secret underground lairs. Time to break the ice.

"Pick up your jaws and move on, people. That's Gracie for you. Don't think too hard about it or you'll just get a headache." He rubbed his jaw. "Got any whiskey?"

Houston's glare flicked to Lopez. "Man after my own stomach."

A striking woman entered the room. Bald, muscular, tattooed and pierced from head to foot, she sported some odd combination of military garb and what could only be described as post-apocalyptic chic.

Holy Mad Max, Batman!

She strode up to Gone and stopped cold by her chair, staring. The silence stretched. Gone swallowed, gazing up at the green, unblinking eyes.

"Yes?" Her voice was a whisper.

Lightfoote held her hand out palm first as Gone tried to stand.

"No, don't get up. I know it's getting harder."

Gone furrowed her brows. "Harder? What do you mean?" Sacker saw fear in her eyes.

Cohen stood, interrupting the moment.

"Ms. Gone, let me introduce Agent Lightfoote. She's been...indisposed for most of the day, but she's deeply involved in everything relevant to our meeting."

"Angel," said the wild-eyed bald woman.

"I'm sorry?" asked Gone. It was the first time Sacker had seen the PI so flummoxed.

"Call me Angel." She kneeled beside Gone. "It's going to be hard. Dangerous and painful. But you're right. The killer," her voice caught. "It's all related. To what we're doing. To something terrible. There isn't much time. You have to move quickly."

"We're going to, Angel," said Cohen. "That's why she's here. We've all got to put as much together on this as we can." She glanced at Sacker. "Team up."

Lightfoote rose and shook her head. "Not this time, Rebecca. No Angel on this one. Angel must go. Angel cannot fight the Eunuch Maker." She bent down and kissed Gone on the forehead, the PI too stunned to move. "He'll be alright. Check the samples. Don't worry."

Lightfoote turned and walked out of the room. Sacker saw tears in her eyes.

Houston snickered. "Well, that's Angel for you. Don't think about her too hard, either. But I second the need for whiskey."

Cohen refocused the conversation.

"There's an important international case we're investigating. I can't tell you much about it. One thread leads back here to New York, to bank accounts and medical suppliers. It leads to biohazard suits and virus containment. The source of that money is one of the most dangerous people in the world. This source would do almost anything to gain power." She stared at Gone. "We'll help you. We need to trust each other. We need to see your data. We need access to all the samples. We will use our cover with the FBI to obtain everything from NYPD."

"You'll let us continue to investigate?"

Houston and Lopez leaned forward. Cohen nodded.

"If that is what you want to do, yes."

Lopez rumbled. "After what we just saw, we'd be crazy to cut her out." He gazed out the door. "Especially with Angel flying off. Not to offend INTEL 1, but we need the brains."

"We'll help you with whatever line of research you want, within reason," Cohen added. "But we've got to involve the CDC, other US and international agencies. I hope you understand. The stakes just went from a few vics to the population of NYC. Or worse."

Sacker exhaled.

Thank God Almighty.

Gracie had done it. She'd talked her way into the super black-ops club. INTEL 1 would bring in the medical experts. Win-win.

"As long as we don't lose access to the case," said Gone.

The corner of Cohen's mouth twitched upward. Sacker looked away.

Yeah, Agent Cohen, she's got big damn ovaries.

"As a measure of good faith," said Cohen, "let me give you some intel. Two men involved in the Eunuch Maker case fell ill with symptoms matching your diagnosis. One was a nurse who handled one of the first bodies. The other was an assistant medical examiner working with none other than Dr. Sutherland of the 12th Precinct."

Sacker bolted upright. "Seriously? Who?"

Cohen walked back to her desk and lifted a piece of paper, fitting glasses over her eyes. "One José Perez. Did you know him?"

"No. Must have been one of the new hires. Sutherland brought in a bunch when the bodies started piling up. *Jesus!* We've got to get those bodies out of the morgue and in some locked down lab!"

"We're on that as of your phone call. We've got a lot of influence. Men in space suits are descending on the 12th as we speak."

He stared at Gone. She smiled.

Nice play, Gracie.

Gone unlocked her tablet, pointed at a set of DNA sequence alignments she'd brought in.

"And I need *your* resources, Agent Cohen. I need access to top-flight academic and governmental virology labs. We need to find out what the hell we're dealing with here. We have the samples. The right labs have the means. We need to sequence the virus and find out exactly what it is." She met the gaze of the members of INTEL 1. "One of the most dangerous people in the world, you said. So, this is *beyond* the Eunuch Maker. Something much bigger. Much worse."

Cohen removed her glasses. "Yes, Ms. Gone. Much worse."

"Then we don't have a second to lose."

51

FALLEN ANGEL

T he hum of machinery grew. Cohen entered the office and let her eyes adjust. Only the numerous monitors tiled around the desks and walls cast any illumination.

Lightfoote's sickly blue.

Behind her, Houston burst in, not adjusting to anything.

"Angel, what the fuck?"

The ex-CIA agent made a motion forward, but Cohen put her arm up.

Wait, Sara. We're defusing a bomb.

Lightfoote packed. Computers, paraphernalia, and odd items of clothing flew into satchels. She didn't look up.

"Bugging out, girls."

Houston crossed her arms over her chest. "Like hell you are. Not like this. We went to hell and back and you never once *blinked*. What in God's name has you so spooked?"

Metal growled as Lightfoote zipped a bag shut, tossing a firearm on top of a bulging canvas. She spoke from a crouch, toward the wall.

"You remember that night in Princeton? After your man gave last rites to those thugs? After we burned that damned museum to the ground?"

Houston eyed her at an angle. "Sure. Well, *no,* actually. I got hammered."

"You sure did." With a laugh, Lightfoote stood. "You passed out in Francisco's arms. But before that, we had a talk."

Houston stiffened. "About monsters."

"About monsters." Lightfoote gripped her firearm and stared down the barrel. "About my dad. About seeing him die. I told you then it was complicated."

Cohen squinted. *What the hell is going on?*

She didn't dare interfere. The pair had been through an ordeal. She knew that. They *all* had when things went to hell after Anonymous. Pursuit. Murder. *War.* She didn't doubt deep bonds had formed between them, but Lightfoote's pain went deeper. Happened earlier. And not even Houston seemed to know the full story.

Does anyone?

Houston's voice dropped. "I remember. Confession time."

"In front of *the priest*," smiled Lightfoote. It faded. "Only I didn't. Confess, I mean. I stopped there."

She walked up to Houston, the gun still in her hand, her face inches away. Cohen felt light-headed. The tension sucked the air out of the room.

"Fawkes found out." A quick smirk from the side of her mouth suppressed a rising pitch. "They tried to erase it all, bringing me to INTEL 1 all those years ago. But that fucker dug it out and put it together. In the middle of that shitstorm, he tried to bleed my brain out. Summon the monsters again."

"Angel, what—"

"Shhhhh." Her finger pressed Houston's mouth. Tears filled her eyes. Then she kissed her. Her mouth explored, famished and desperate. Their bodies met and pushed, curves zippering with the scrape of fabric. Houston closed her eyes and moaned.

Blanked and dazed, Cohen simply gaped.

"Don't tell Francisco," Lightfoote gasped, pulling away. Both swallowed air. "He'll go all guy on you."

She spun and grabbed the bags, slinging two over her shoulders, the weight creasing her exposed skin. She swung toward Cohen.

"Tell John, I'm sorry." Tears rolled down her cheeks. She touched Cohen's face. "And I'm sorry for what's coming."

"Angel," said Cohen, her pulse racing, "what's coming? The Eunuch Maker?"

"Not only. But he's just a tool. He's insane. But still, I can't face it. I can't face another monster with cages, dissections, you and those you love. No. I just can't. Even if the analogy's wrong, the motives are different, the time new." She gawked at the ceiling. "It's just my mind. It's a kernel panic."

Cohen's eyes widened. "I don't understand!"

"The PI's the real deal. She's got his number. But Nemesis is plotting. So many threads. The election—darkness is coming." She shook her head. "You and John will be so brave. Angel should be with you. You'll be so alone. But Angel can't stay. Angel's broken."

She pushed past their stunned forms to the doorway and stopped, exhaling. Her head pivoted, mirrored sunglasses over her eyes reflecting the silver in her face.

"Fallen Angels are cast down for a reason."

She turned away and marched down the hallway.

52

VOLUNTEERS

The killer in the biohazard suit removed a mask over the blood-soaked body. The monitors beeped and flat-lined. His victim died, released from an excruciating journey. Now the precision work.

His mind struggled to focus. His thoughts couldn't pull away from the sound of feet slapping pavement. The moment of terror at the bank, when he realized he'd been discovered. The clinging stink of sweat-soaked clothes he'd fought to later remove. A day ending with his assets frozen and the noose tightening around him.

So close. Everything nearly lost.

The killer eased around the fleshly horror in the center of the plastic room. The suit chafed. It restricted motion. It stunk of some vile DuPont synthetic material. And it mixed with other nauseating smells. The air filter in the Biosafety Level 4 positive pressure suit let in the stink of the dying body and corpse. Small molecules, processed by his olfactory system. Much, much smaller than a virus, thereby passing through the filters. Rationally, he understood this, deduced there was little danger. But tell that to a primitive brain reflex honed by millions of years of evolution. Rationalize away the automatic release of stress hormones and the elevated heart rate. Mixed with the suit reek, it was all he could do to keep from vomiting.

But such concerns had little impact on his will. He was so near to reaching his goal. The viral titers increased with each new round of infection and protocol alteration. Before the final release, he would do all he could to maximize the impact.

And no one was going to stop him.

Damn the police, or whoever had chased him down. Damn the amazon women and their queen, who had all too happily funded his scheme. They'd been the first to track him down, zero in on the birth control research, lure him, ask questions and pull out the answers. Secretive and deeply resourced, unknown motivations driving them, they played him expertly. He knew that. Sex, physical threats of killers, and money—he'd revealed all. And they'd gone all in with him. If he triumphed, it would be their world.

If the damn virus chimera would do more than kill and truly go airborne!

I must focus.

Time contracted. Someone pursued him, tried to corner him. Would have killed him. But he would do *everything* within his power to succeed.

And change the world.

The medical instruments waited, and he prepped the body. He shaved the groin hair and sterilized the pelvis. A broad laser scalpel hummed to life. He opened deep incisions. Without the pressure from the heart, the blood mimicked crimson honey dripping over the plastic to the floor.

The entire process felt too routine. Complacency must be fought. He entertained no delusions about his final fate, but he must remain healthy so close to his goal. He monitored the readings of the suit, kept the cutting edge aligned, activated only when positioned. He would remove this sample without incident.

The fat challenged him the most. This child abuser was significantly overweight. He struggled through the adipose tissue, the stink of fried steak sickening in the air. He swallowed a retching reflex and cut around the prostate and seminal vesicles. After so many brought to justice, he was a practiced professional removing the male reproductive anatomy—a fisherman filleting a catch. Out popped the tissues and he dropped them in a pan, the flaccid penis hanging half over the metal edge. He pushed it back inside with his index finger.

Shuffling to the work bench, he opened the top of a large Waring blender, dropping the organs into the glass chamber. He dumped the contents of a fifty-milliliter plastic tube in after, enzymes and chemicals to help liquefy the tissues. He capped the blender and pressed a button. The industrial machine screamed as it turned a rapist's prized parts into a flesh smoothie in minutes.

The killer decanted the homogenized sex organs into plastic bottles, tightening the caps. He waddled in the bio-suit toward the blinking lights of a table-top centrifuge, placed the bottles in holders in the rotor, closed the lid, and set the spin for half an hour. He pressed START.

The motor hummed to life, the low sound climbing in pitch until it stabilized at its normal annoying whine. The man removed his gloves, sterilized his hands in the fluid of a tank, dried them under hot air, and then re-gloved.

He leaned against the table, his head back and eyes closed. Exhaustion labored to incapacitate him. *I can't screw this up now.* After this prep, he would store the samples and sleep. Sleep long and hard for the rest of the day, leave the lab, leave the men tied to stretchers for tomorrow. The poor bastards likely needed tending, some sort of half-hearted gesture toward humanity. But they were as good as dead, injected with the highest viral titers yet.

"Good news, gentleman. I think we've got the bugs worked out. With this next harvest and the new construct, we might just be ready. Of course, we'll need a final set of volunteers to verify before we seed the actual vectors."

Who am I talking to? They couldn't hear him in the other sections of his make-shift facility, behind the humming wall of refrigerators filled with samples. They couldn't hear him because their fevers made them delirious, because their bodies were dissolving, because they had no useful mental processes anymore.

Let them die. Let them suffer. It would be justice for their monstrous crimes. And he was too tired to give a damn.

The machine slowed. The pitch dropped. The lights on the control panel blinked. A moment of silence followed, the r.p.m.s at zero, and a pop as the lock on the lid disengaged.

He retrieved the samples. World changing plans brewed.

53

KILLER PROMISES

E unuch Maker Promises New Victim
        Sandra Ruf, New York Daily News

THE EUNUCH MAKER, *the now infamous serial killer leaving a trail of mutilated male bodies across New York City, has announced through anonymous means to several major news outlets that a new victim's body will be
left in a prominent public place today.*

*Mayor Logan has locked down major tourist attractions and land-
marks, stationing police and other emergency personnel at numerous locations. Federal, state, and local law enforcement were scouring museums,
subway stops, nightclubs, and monuments looking for the promised next
victim in this gruesome series of murders.*

*NYPD representatives would not disclose the method of communica-
tion, but were firm that they are taking the claims seriously.*

*"We have an unprecedented series of killings in the city," said 12th
Precinct Chief Michael Ladner. "We are working with federal and local
agencies to identify and bring this killer to justice. He is intelligent and obviously ruthless. Public exhibitions of the victims indicate a flair for the*

theatrical. We are convinced he means what he says and have mobilized a city-wide manhunt to find him and the body of the next victim."

Criticism of the police department's handling of the case has intensified. As little progress has materialized, the continuing trail of high-profile murder scenes has made a mockery of law enforcement efforts.

Divisions within the 12th Precinct recently came to light when junior detectives publicly questioned the performance and leadership of those handling the investigation.

"There are senior agents who shouldn't be involved, who are known substance abusers in and out of rehab," said a source from the 12th who requested to remain anonymous. "It's all politics and seniority. Meanwhile, there's a killer out there and we're dropping the ball."

THE LATEST CORPSE summoned the locust plague of press, police, and public to his grisly circus show. The ratings-starved media excelled at its job. Time to do his.

The blond man approached an alleyway on the NYU campus, his features concealed in an overlarge fog coat and wide brimmed hat. Staring at the university buildings, grinning beneath the brim, his fogged breath billowed skyward like some unclean brew.

So few guards.

His distraction thinned the NYPD presence at the Richards lab, set there on behalf of the NIH to guard the scientific products the Eunuch Maker demanded be destroyed. Officers milled about the main entrance, the fools not learning, still focused on the front door. A single, young man in blue shivered outside the back door in the alley. The police assumed the crime scene dead to him. They understood little from his last deposit at the labs.

Now theatre.

The killer took on a staggering gait, stumbling and catching himself on the brick walls of the old buildings. In his right hand he drank colored water from a whiskey bottle. The policeman sighed and approached the drunk's bent figure.

"Hey, buddy, see the yellow tape?" he asked, pointing behind him, his right hand on the butt of his firearm. "Crime scene. Off limits. Get plastered somewhere else, okay?"

The young officer was careful to keep his distance, an instinctual caution in the presence of so towering a man a force field pushing him backward.

But he's close enough.

Click. Two blurred lines shot out toward the policeman, striking his face and neck. He convulsed, dropping to the ground, a series of low grunts escaping his lips.

The massive figure swooped over him like some bird of prey, bringing the bottle down over the young man's head. It shattered and blood sprayed, the form on the ground twitching while sporting a vacant expression.

The killer removed the taser wires and stuffed the device inside his bulky coat. He jogged to the broken back door, still not repaired, yanked it open, and dashed up the stairs.

Breathless near the top floor, he approached the door and turned the knob, peering through a thin opening. He saw no one. Passing like some vampire in his overlarge garments, he ignored the crime scene and entered the laboratory. The security system beeped, a green light flashing as he swiped a card.

Inside, he rushed, one by one opening the bench gas valves across the lab, a putrid stink overpowering his nostrils. Returning to the door, he set a device on the ground, flicked a switch, and a digital timer glowed and began a countdown from eight minutes. He checked the fuse and flint, spun and dashed out of the room, down the stairs and into the alleyway.

The downed policeman hadn't moved. Still alive, the killer left him with a major concussion and taser burns. His radio crackled with calls from other officers. They wanted to know why he wasn't answering.

It didn't matter. The police guarding the lab would soon have something bigger to deal with than a downed officer. The killer sprinted down the alley, paying no heed to sights or sounds on his left or right. Eight minutes left little to chance, and he was going to make sure he cleared.

He turned the corner, reaching halfway up the block when the ground shook. He put his hands to his ears and covered his face in the coat. The blast wave knocked him to his knees. Windows shattered above him. Glass rained.

He opened his eyes to dust and stark shadows from a flickering orange light behind. People screamed. Car alarms blared in the cold air. He stood, picked up his pace, and rounded the next block, disappearing into the evening chaos.

54

THEIR FILL OF AMBROSIA

"Well, there's something we didn't think of."

Sacker stood with junior detectives Hill and Snyder gazing from the South Street Seaport into the East River. Lights from Manhattan behind them and Brooklyn across the water danced over the waves. Camera shutters stuttered and a helicopter hovered over the water. A murmuring crowd of onlookers pressed from behind, NYPD officers shoving them back.

Small police boats, red and blue lights strobing the river, escorted Lightship LV-87, a New York tourist attraction. Christened *The Ambrose*, its sides glowed a deep crimson, the white letters of its name bright in the port lights. But all eyes focused elsewhere, ignoring the helicopter, police boats, and the painted sides of the ship.

Lashed to the forward light tower, just below the beam shining from the lightship's lantern, hung the latest victim of the Eunuch Maker. The garish corpse gleamed in the spotlights and swayed. Sacker closed his eyes and imagined thousands of images circulating the web at the speed of hype. He tried to block out the photo captions and how the NYPD would fare in them. Despite the warnings, despite police preparation and manpower set across the city, the killer again made them look the fool.

Snyder gaped. "How'd he get it up there?"

Why should I answer you, you little bastard?

Sacker was wise to him now. The Daily News article made it obvious. The anonymous criticism of the 12th precinct. The flood of leaks soaking the press. Too many details. The smug little brat pocketed Benjamins while he undermined Sacker's standing before the public. *Bad enough.* It was harder knowing the personal nature of the attacks, the slander of his character, poisoning him with the NYPD.

A simple thank you for the mentoring would've done, asshole.

"He really knows how to jerk our chain," whispered Hill.

Sacker wanted to hug the lady. He'd taken two rookies under his wing and tried to mentor them in one of the most difficult cases of his lifetime. One betrayed him, using Sacker as a possible stepping stone in a case of myopic ambition. But Hill was a model trainee. Thoughtful, hard-working, and minus one stabbing instrument in his back.

And it will be the asshole who gets promoted.

Hill should've been a guy. Better odds.

He turned away from his young charges. Feet tromped behind him. The Feds poured out in force for this kill, sealing off the area. The team emerging from a black van with hazmat gear really got the crowd buzzing.

"What the hell?" said Snyder.

Hill looked between the federal spacemen and Sacker.

"Any idea what's going on, sir?"

He kept a poker face, lighting a cigarette. "Government works in mysterious ways. They'll let us know when they're good and ready." He blew the smoke toward Snyder. The kid coughed.

A new commotion drew his attention to the crowd behind. Onlookers congealed around a focal point, a raised arm waving, besieged by the NYPD and bystanders. A sheen of black hair surfaced from underneath the sea of bodies.

He winced. *Gracie, what the hell?*

He'd agreed to let her near the crime scene. He'd promised to give her access along with INTEL 1.

But later, girl.

"Detective Sacker! Tyrell!" she cried above the noise.

"Ah, hell."

Snyder and Hill stared his way. He had to do something.

Marching up through the blue wall, he reached Gone as men began to haul her away. A few quick words and he led the diminutive woman down to the seaside railing. His trainees approached with great interest.

"Ah, detectives Hill and Snyder, this is a former NYPD consultant, Grace Gone."

"Consultant?" asked Snyder. Hill blinked.

Gone flashed a smile their way. It dropped.

"No time, sorry." She turned her back to them and addressed Sacker. "This is all interesting, but we've been played."

"Played?" His stomach dropped. He pressed her elbow, trying to distance her from the other detectives. "Maybe we can talk a little later? As you see, I'm involved in—"

"All this!" She waved her hand at the approaching corpse above their heads. "The killer needed a diversion. He targeted the science."

Hill scribbled in a notebook as Snyder glanced between them. Sacker's head spun.

"Gracie, this is a hell of a *distraction*. What science?"

"Dr. Richards! Remember the Eunuch Maker's demands?"

"Sure. Stop working on the male pill."

"And *destroy* your science. He asked her to destroy her work."

"Right. But she didn't. Federal property. It's all under lock and..." His face fell.

"Exactly. Explosion on the NYU campus. The lab's gone."

He bent down and stared into her eyes. "Wait a minute! How the hell do you know this? I haven't heard a thing!"

His cell buzzed. *I can't believe this.*

"Ladner, right? Your boss?"

"You're infuriating."

"While we're huddled around kill number five, he's erasing the evidence."

"The science? How's *that* evidence?"

Gone limped, tugging him to the side and whispering in his ear.

"It's all too coincidental, don't you think? Hemorrhagic virus in the victims, killer demands a cessation of work and destruction of samples of a *viral* approach to male contraception."

The detectives strained to hear. Sacker wanted to scream.

Gone continued. "No, it's *not* a coincidence. There's a link. I need to review Richards' work, find out what kind of viruses they used." Her voiced dropped again. "See if there is any link to the Marburg family."

"She said it was harmless," said Sacker. "I'm thinking, no?"

"Yes. You're right. It can't be that trivial, of course. But something less obvious, but a real link. Why else would he demand all her work be destroyed?"

"Because of the rape-drug theory?"

"He just blew up the place, Tyrell. It's got to be much more than that."

"Well, what, then?"

Gone shook her head. "I don't know. But the key to this entire case is in the Richards lab."

55

GONE MENTAL

G one adjusted the volume of her headset. "Agent Savas, can you move your mic? I'm getting a lot of noise from the fabric of your shirt. Clip it on your tie or something."

Thunder rolled and scraped over fabric. Then voices.

"Much better, thanks."

Adrenaline coursed through her. *The difference a month made.* In September, she drowned in desperation, nearing the end of her rope. Broke, without a client, and for the first time questioning her life's choices.

"You'll never make it on your own, Qiānjīn. You can't leave home."

Her father's confident words echoed in her mind. She fought the old response, tried to deflect the bubbling anger. *Qiānjīn.* Always with him it returned to money. But she'd shown him. Shown them all with one wild night in Mexico City and out of the cartel's *protection.* The only downside—she never saw his face when he learned the news. Learned just how wrong he was.

INTEL I sequestered her in a small office at the 12th precinct. A radio transmitter linked her to the interrogation in the adjacent room. Savas and Sacker questioned Dr. Richards. Cohen worked elsewhere, following up on the biological analyses of the virus Gone requested.

They actually did what I asked.

The adrenaline spiked again, the percolating data and what it might reveal raising goosebumps. Maybe she couldn't sit in the interrogation room with them, but *she was there*. Live. With the FBI—INTEL 1 in reality—on her side. She was privy to law enforcement efforts to stop one of the most notorious serial killers in a century. Grace Gone was central in a chain of investigation closing in on that monster.

Sacker's voice crackled through her headset.

"But we're having trouble understanding the main event, Dr. Richards. Why would this killer risk so much, perhaps even his own life, to blow up a building? Why would he target your work?"

The frustration and fatigue in his voice pained her. She wanted to raid his apartment, throw out every last bottle of whiskey and ship him to rehab. She couldn't for a number of reasons, the most important that Sacker had the right to wreck his own life. But he was killing himself. Watching it, living the truth, hurt.

Richards sounded even more frazzled than Sacker. Her voice rose in pitch. "We've gone over and over and over this same damn question for an hour! If you don't like my ideas, then let me go! I've told you, I'm not a psychologist. The maniac threatened to kill *my own people* if we didn't destroy the research. *You* and these Feds posted *guards* around the damn place because of the threats. And he still managed to get past all of you and erase my life's work!"

Metal rang in Gone's ears. *Is she pounding the desk?*

"He's fucking insane! Okay?"

Savas spoke, his voice steady.

"And the work he demanded you destroy—"

"That is now *destroyed!*" snapped Richards.

His voice didn't waver. "My understanding is that this was based on using a virus to infect men and render them infertile?"

Richards sighed, her voice an octave lower and hoarse.

"Temporarily, yes. A harmless virus, limited in replicative ability. It spread to reproductive cells specific to the testes. There it shut down the production of sperm. *Voila!* The perfect condom. The male pill in a shot. Early testing in humans showed that it was male specific. Women were not infected efficiently, and men had very few side effects besides low sperm count. Honestly, adenovirus is much nastier."

"Adenovirus?"

"Common cold. Still had to work out dealing with immunity, but there was progress."

"But the killer obviously had major issues with the treatment?"

"*Obviously.* I feel like I've gone over this one hundred times." There was a long pause. "Some celebrated our work—yay gender equality! Women don't have to bear the brunt of contraception! But others had a darker view. With men freed of the fear of fatherhood, sexual assault would increase."

"Rapists don't care about babies," scoffed Chief Ladner. His voice boomed through, popping and distorted, for the first time in the interrogation.

Richards scoffed back. "The overwhelming majority of rapes are committed by people *known* to the victim. It's not some slobbering election-prop thug. It's the clean-cut boy next door who thinks he owns women's bodies. Friends, lovers, relatives. Smirk away, but those are the stats. That's what people call rape culture. Some fear it will get worse if there's one less risk."

We're getting sidetracked.

Gone's alarm bells clamored, her intuition churning through the facts, catching a scent it couldn't quite identify.

"We're missing something here. It's right in front of us. Ask about the prison experiments."

No one interrupted as Richards continued a long sociological discussion in the background.

Did they hear me?

She pressed. "Remember? They began limited testing in humans. Prison records. We have them. Something went wrong with one of them."

"That's all very interesting," said Sacker. "Can we return for a moment to the studies at the women's prison?"

Finally!

"Bedford Hills Correctional Facility for Women," said Savas, his voice neutral. "That's the place?"

"All ethical protocols were followed," said Richards. "By the book. We needed blood samples to test early versions of the virus. We needed blood from men and women. Prisons were available in both cases. Whatever your personal code, it was legal."

"One of your subjects died at Bedford Hills," said Sacker.

"It wasn't related to anything we were doing. We just took blood samples. From what I understand it was a suicide. He jumped from a window and fell to his death."

"He?" Papers rustled. "I thought this was a women's prison?"

"Sorry, yes, *'she.'* The inmate was born male but identified as female, having undergone hormonal and physical alterations for many years. She happened to be arrested as a woman. I'm getting a little old for all this gender bending and tend to focus on the biological sex."

Gone caught her breath. "Wait a second!" Her mind raced. "We've got to get to the prison. We've got to—"

Her cell vibrated. A text message from Rebecca Cohen.

"Virus sequencing completed."

56

GONE HAYWIRE

W *hen it rains, it pours.*

Gone unplugged the headset from the transmitter, pressed her smartphone screen to call Cohen, and flipped open her computer. She plugged the headset into her phone, dropping the volume on the unit as the ring tones exploded in her ears. Her fingers typed the password for her computer and she opened DNA sequence files.

"Ms. Gone," came Cohen's voice. "That was fast."

"Call me Grace, please. I'll call you Rebecca."

"Okay with me. Aren't you participating in an interrogation with John?"

"Was. Remotely. I don't exist at NYPD, remember? They were wrapping up, but dropped something big at the end."

"What?" asked Cohen.

"Later. I need the data. Now."

Cohen laughed. "You're intense. I'm sorry, but I don't have the data. I got a call from the labs at CDC and Columbia. They've been coordinating and verifying each other's work. But you need to reach out to them. INTEL 1 isn't a bioinformatics center. Well, maybe if we still had Angel. Unfortunately, she's—"

"Okay, how do I reach the labs?" Her head pounded.

"I sent you an email. All the information's there."

Gone opened an email app and scrolled through messages. Cohen continued.

"But I did get a summary if you're interested."

"Yes?" Cohen's email flashed in a window.

"Your work's confirmed. Viral DNA's definitely there. So, hat-tip to the Queensboro PI who just broke the infection-crime story of the century."

"Thanks. Anything else?"

"This Marburg virus you mentioned—there are sequences like you found, but the story is bigger. The virus isn't Marburg, in case you wondered. Not a virus they've ever identified."

"Didn't think so." Gone squinted at her screen. "Too many phenotypic differences. Several Marburg markers not there. But, *wait*—your email. Am I reading this right? There's *human* DNA in the viral genome?"

"Yes," said Cohen. "They called it a chimera or something. That's what had both research groups very concerned. They're convinced we're looking at a synthetic virus. Not a natural one."

My God.

Gone sat back in the chair, staring forward. Her thoughts split into a thousand branches of a logic tree, each predicated on answers to chains of questions. So much connected, impossible to move through, until enough nodes were satisfied. Then an avalanche. A thousand puzzle pieces tumbled into place before her eyes.

"Rebecca, this is bad. I need those sequences."

"The scientists had a moment, too. Could it be a bioweapon?"

Gone typed into her web browser. A map of Westchester county in New York State appeared. The browser window zoomed in on a patch of land east of the Saw Mill Parkway.

"We have to get to that prison."

"Prison? Wait, you mean Richards experiments?"

"Yes!" A compound grew in the middle of a forested sea, the red pin on the map screen labeled *Bedford Hills Correctional Facility*.

"What's the connection?"

"Think! Male victims butchered with some sort of serial-killer level misandry. A link to a lab doing male contraception. A *viral* contraception specific to *male* physiology, presumably specific to the male genotype. Throw in a *synthetic* Ebola-Marburg-who-knows-what mash-up." Silence on the phone. "The prison study included obtaining blood samples from women. One commits suicide and surprise! She's genetically male."

More silence.

There isn't time to walk her through it!

She had to talk to Sacker. She had to get those sequences, analyze them herself. Prove or disprove this nightmare hypothesis.

Cohen spoke in monotone. "Are you saying the Eunuch Maker created this? Some designer virus, combination of a hemorrhagic virus and human DNA, only killing men?"

Gone squeezed her temples. "Yes, Rebecca. But what I'm saying is much worse."

"Worse?"

"Yes." She snapped the laptop shut and stuffed it into her bag, pulling the strap over her shoulder as she stood. He legs shook. "I think these victims are the test subjects for a much, much bigger plan. And what happened at Bedford Hills might be the key to the killer's identity."

"Bigger?" Cohen gasped. "Dear God."

Gone turned, moving toward the door. "Exactly. I'm going to talk to Tyrell. If you can get INTEL I to pull some strings, I think—"

Air rushed, light flashed with an impact, and she blinked at the fluorescent bulbs on the ceiling.

Not again.

Her head throbbed. Dizzy and nauseated, she caught a woman's voice calling her name from a great distance.

"Rebecca?"

She felt around for the headset. It was gone, the wire still in her hand and connected to her smartphone. The door to the room opened, the sharp edge brushing her hair.

"Gracie!"

Tyrell. Once again staring down at her with those wide eyes. She couldn't help but smile up at him.

"Hi, Tyrell. What're you doing here?"

Sacker looked at an older man in a suit beside him.

That's Savas. Her mind was clearing.

Sacker knelt beside her head.

"We hadn't heard anything from you for a while," he said. "I was worried."

His hand was on her shoulder. She touched it.

"Thought maybe you'd had enough of me," she said.

Savas spoke. "Should we move her?"

"No need," she half-whispered. "I can move myself."

Groaning, she sat up. Sacker braced her back with his other hand. She suppressed the urge to vomit. She tried to suppress the growing despair welling within her.

It's getting worse and worse. How much time's left?

"Time's short," she managed, catching her breath and preparing for the next hurdle: *standing.* "Time might be short for millions."

57

A GONER

The tree-lined Saw Mill Parkway in Upstate New York exploded in autumn colors, the reds and yellows interspersed with frequent green towers of pine. Sacker angled the police cruiser off the parkway and to Harris Road, the hour-long ride with Gone beside him painful. He'd learned his lesson. The same focus and stubbornness that made her such a relentless detective made interpersonal relations a minefield.

Don't bring up whatever the hell is going on with her leg.

And he wouldn't even think to ask about the odd twitch in her left arm.

Off the ramp, a few minutes passed until they ducked into a more forested stretch. After a curve the car emerged from the shade, the Bedford Hills Correctional Facility perched at the top of a hill.

In all its brick and barbed-wire glory.

It might be for the ladies, but the design still screamed *stay in or die*. Bedford Hills held some of the most notorious female killers in the country. *Women committing acts of violence!* Was their notoriety from the crime or from society's shock? Men owned the lion's share of the hitting, shooting, stabbing, and killing. *Boys will be boys.* When mothers ended lives instead of creating them, people just lost their shit.

Bedford Hills enjoyed a softer image on the inside. Papers loved to run stories on the mental health programs, addiction counseling, and child care available. *Look, a nursery!* People working overtime to turn murderesses into mothers again.

After security, they met Savas and Cohen outside the office of the prison superintendent. The agents of the mysterious INTEL 1 division had arrived separately.

Secretly departing from their hidden base in a cloaked jet, probably.

The entire arrangement made him uncomfortable. It was one thing working with a known division of the FBI, even during the chaos of the Anonymous Event and what followed. But who were these people now? Who was running this show?

Someone way, way up the chain of command.

INTEL 1 had extraordinary access at the wave of a magic wand. It spoke of immense power. And a dangerous lack of oversight.

"So, where are the other members of Team X?" he said, smiling at Cohen.

"Agent Lightfoote—*Angel*—is taking some personal time." A glance passed between her and Savas. "Gabriel and Mary—they work undercover for the most part."

"Undercover?" His smile broadened.

Savas scowled. "Yes. We'll leave it at that. Look—here comes our lunch date."

A broad woman in her fifties approached from the office suite. Bifocals dangled from her neck over a blue pantsuit. Her hair was short and mostly gray, her eyes sharp. She put out her hand to Savas.

"Agent Savas? Betsy Donovan. I'm sorry to have kept you waiting."

Savas took her hand. "Thank you for seeing us on such short notice."

The woman huffed. "Couldn't very well say no, could I? I don't remember the last time the *governor* called me out of the blue for a favor. You folks are some high rollers."

"This is FBI agent Cohen," he said, tilting his head. "From NYPD, Detective Tyrell Sacker."

"Oh, yes. I've seen *your* face on the news, detective. You look better than I thought you would." She stared at Gone and her smile dropped. "And who is this?"

Sacker spoke. "Grace Gone. Private consultant on the case."

"Hmmm." Donovan gave Gone a side eye. "Why don't we continue in my office?"

She ushered them into a cramped space filled with legal books, photos of grandchildren, and eccentric items from animal skulls to polished geodes. Donovan sat regally on one side of a desk piled with papers. The other four were sandwiched together across from her. Donovan got straight to business.

"So, the Richards volunteers. I guess I'm not surprised somebody would chase this down for completeness, what with that killer so focused on that poor woman's work." She placed her glasses on her nose, scanning papers in front of her in a bound notebook. "But I didn't expect Seal Team Six, or whoever they hell you are. And I'm not sure what you might be looking for. Anyway, all the records are yours. Should've been available publicly. You didn't have to bother yourselves to come all the way out for a visit."

Sacker stifled a frown. *I'm really beginning to dislike that grin of hers.*

He could feel Gone fidgeting next to him. She itched to ask questions, likely as irritated with this woman as him. But they had agreed —the INTEL 1 agents would run the show. They had the clout. And Gone especially would be quiet. Madame Superintendent did little to hide her suspicions.

Or am I being paranoid?

"We've seen the files," said Cohen. "We're interested in Dawn Lodmell."

"The suicide?" Her face fell. "We've worked hard to reduce the numbers of suicides. Lodmell was unfortunate."

Cohen continued. "She was part of Richards' experiment?"

"Yes, it's all in the files. Quite horrible. Somehow she escaped to the high tower, stood at the top of the damn thing and jumped."

Savas eyed her. "Reports mention serious internal bleeding, bruising."

"That's what happens when you hit the pavement swan diving. Helluva mess."

"I'm sure. No autopsy was performed?"

"No. No need. Cause of death was obvious." Her brows furrowed. "What's so special about this jumper?"

"Anyone here who saw the body before it was removed?"

Donovan leaned back in her chair and shook her head. "It was late at night, a few years ago. Guards rotated out, and the crew that cleaned it up was from out of town. We have a record somewhere on the company."

"It would be great if you could look that up," said Cohen.

"Oh, and Jenny. I completely forgot. Jenny Bargmann, one of our janitors. *The* janitor. Been here since forever. She found the body. Called it in. She's still here."

Sacker couldn't help himself and cut in.

"We would really appreciate the chance to speak with her. Is she here today?"

"In fact, she is."

THE REDHEAD SPORTED MORE gray than red, long, gnarled strands of hair flowing midway down her back. Fissures erupted in an earthquake zone across her face, blue eyes twinkling back from sunken sockets. Her hands had every bit the appearance of a woman who had scrubbed floors for most of her adult life. The damn witch's cackle was going to give Sacker nightmares.

"Heh!" barked Bargmann, her yellowed teeth jutting forward. "Ran out naked is what she did! Stark naked. I knew something was up so I tried to follow her, but then she started climbing. That was it for me."

"Did you see her body? Her skin?" asked Sacker.

Bargmann looked askance at Sacker. "Why you interested, colored boy?"

Wonderful.

"You know when Suite's president, he's gonna deport all you. Wetbacks, too. I sure as hell am votin' tomorrow."

Cohen swooped in.

"Ms. Bargmann, this is important. Did her skin have anything unusual about it?"

Still giving the evil eye to Sacker, she spoke through the side of her mouth.

"Well, it sure did. Poor girl was bruised all over, like someone had taken a sock full of rocks to her." She turned to face Cohen. "That's my guess. She'd crossed the wrong people. Been near killed in a beatin'. Lost her damn mind and ended it. Splat!"

Sacker bit his tongue. He felt nauseated, not sure if it was more from the open racism or callous disregard for Lodmell's death. Of course, his discomfort only encouraged her.

"But that weren't nothing compared to what I saw on the concrete. No, sir. Broken bones pokin' out, body all blowed up like a balloon, face opened up so as you could see everything inside. Everything one big bruise, purple, streaks of red and black. Ain't seen nothin' like it before."

"One big bruise," said Gone, speaking for the first time.

"Who's the chink?" said Bargmann.

Gone ignored her. "Signs of hemorrhagic fever consistent with what has been seen in the other victims." She glared at Sacker and the others. "We know what this is."

Donovan squinted at Gone. "Know what *what* is?"

Gone stared back at her. "Where was Lodmell buried? It wasn't in the files you sent."

"I don't know," stammered Donovan. "Once she died, it was out of our jurisdiction." She removed her glasses. "What's going on here?"

"There's likely public records, county records," said Sacker. He eyed Gone. "But, hold on. You're not thinking—"

"We need that body."

58

ANDROCIDE

" **G**od. What's going on?"

A voice over a speaker blared nearby. The bearded man cracked his eyes open, squinting at an overhead fluorescent lamp. His skin was bronzed, his lips chafed from exposure to the elements. He was naked. He turned his head. A small flatscreen on a table framed a man screaming at a lectern before thousands of people. A political rally. The man's voice hurt his head.

"Tomorrow we make history! Tomorrow we take back America from those who have stolen your country, your culture, your history. Tomorrow we make this country great again!"

Distorted applause over the speakers made him wince.

"Help. Where am I?"

He tried to raise himself, but restraints yanked him back to a plastic surface. He peered over his chest to his arms and legs. They were shackled. He arched his bare body and pulled at the restraints. His veins bulged, his face contorting. The gurney shook, but the locked wheels didn't move, the shackles held, and he collapsed gasping for air.

"Let me out!" His deep breaths choked him.

"Stop it. You can't get out."

A muffled voice emanated from a speaker lodged within the moving plastic bag of a biohazard suit. The cheers of the crowd and the voice of the politician nearly drowned it out.

"They took your jobs. They live off your hard-earned money. They drop babies here and bring a foreign culture. But their time is over! The corrupt and enabling Left is finished!"

The shape inside the suit positioned medical monitors behind the man and three others who lay unconscious on his right. To the left another wheezed, his body flushed with extensive bruising. The captive broke out into fits of coughing, the last spraying a mist of blood on the side of the yellow suit.

The suit-speaker cracked. "You're going to make me sedate you, too."

The bearded man gawked with wide eyes at the coughing creature.

"What the hell's wrong with him? Is it catching?"

"Indeed. It's very much catching. *How* much is actually the point of today's experiment." The killer switched on the monitors connected to the bodies in front of him.

"Experiment? Whoa, whoa, buddy. You told me two hundred and all I had to do was give blood!"

The suit paused and turned toward him.

"I lied."

The man screamed and again strained to free himself, falling in exhaustion. His deep gasps for air panted over the cries from the television.

"We'll return our nation to safety, peace, and prosperity. To law and order. We're in a time of great crisis for our nation. The attacks on America's police, terrorism in our cities, all are threats to our way of life. My political

opponents don't understand this threat. They're not fit to lead our country!"

"My head! Turn it off!"

"The others behaved similarly. It's unfortunate. Your breathing is suppressed under sedation. It will skew the test of infectivity."

The restrained man gasped. "Infective what?"

The killer attached leads from the monitors to the unconscious men, his motions slow and awkward in the suit, yet practiced and confident.

"There isn't much time left with the authorities zeroing in. This is the last data to see how airborne I've been able to make the virus."

"Virus? What virus!"

"The one that's killing this man, that I hope will kill the four of you very soon."

The man shouted, his voice pitching upward. "No, no, no! This isn't real. I can't be here. Not like this. You can't do this!"

"Ah, the anger of the powerful made powerless."

"Fuck you! I'm not powerful! I'm nobody! Let me go!"

"Two balls and a dick between your legs," scoffed the killer. "You're powerful. We're powerful. We've ruled our species for ten thousand years. We've enslaved half the population, forced them to prostitute for us, bear us children, clean our homes, cook our food. We've raped them, beaten them, burned them, and sold them. We're the first and truest slave owners."

The captive turned to the killer, his eyes bulging. "What the fuck are you talking about?"

"My fellow Americans, you've seen chaos and violence in our streets. Domestic disaster. International humiliations. But I bring a strong message: that time is coming to an end! On Inauguration Day, when Daniel Suite is sworn in, safety will be restored!"

"I'm talking about everything you consider normal. In this most *enlightened* of nations, this country of *rights,* half the population couldn't vote less than a hundred years ago. Think about it. Their spouses could legally *rape* them until fifty years ago. That's around the time we granted them the right to own property. *Radicals."* He laughed. "But let's not judge too harshly—we'd just stopped burning women alive at the stake! Such progress. We still make their lives such a hell they paint their faces and dance for us, fear us, *still* are beaten and raped and murdered by us."

"America will come first again! First with safety at home, neighborhoods, borders secured from terrorism. There WILL be law and order. And jobs. So many jobs. The best jobs. We'll rebuild America. You, the forgotten men and women of America, you who work and struggle without a voice—I AM YOUR VOICE."

The killer sighed and pushed a button on the flatscreen. It went dark, the plastic tent quieter. "This lying windbag and his Nazi minions—another ocean of mad men, of course. They can't even stomach the infinitesimal progress made. They will steer America deeper into the darkness. But not when I'm finished with them. And you're going to help me change things."

He connected the last leads. The graphics on the monitors beeped to life, cardiograms and other data blinking in the dim light, reflecting off the wall-to-ceiling plastic around them.

The killer continued speaking, turned away from his victim. The bearded man cast a wild look over the enclosure, yanking on the restraints again.

"It's all so astounding, this ass-backwards power structure in the human species." He spun toward his captive. "Did you know the default human being is a woman?"

The man stopped struggling. "What?"

"It's true. In the womb, gestation proceeds according to a female blueprint. Only the delivery of a proper cocktail of hormones and chemicals at the right developmental stages shunts the process toward a male embryo. Assuming the embryo expresses the right receptors and is otherwise receptive to the cocktail, or you get an XY female. Point is! Our species is *female* based. Men are only a hormonal tweak."

He chuckled and walked over to a table with medical tools and supplies, removing what looked like a futuristic plastic gun with clear tubes for barrels. A clear, cylindrical cartridge rested beside it.

"What's that for?" cried the man.

"Of course, how could it be any other way? Think of evolution. Men are not the basis of continuation of the species. All the key biological resources are invested in women. Women possess more endurance, resistance to infectious agents, and live longer. Women harbor the miracle of the womb, the organ creating the next generation. Women produce the offspring, self-contained but for a little genetic material sexual reproduction requires be kept separately for genetic recombination." He smiled through the distorting plastic. "Hence, men."

The cartridge popped as he fitted it into the jet injector. He adjusted elements on the device.

"But we're a bit of an afterthought. We carry genes for diversification but can do nothing with them, even if handed the complimentary genetic material. The species requires a woman to make humans. So Mother Nature neglected us, shorted us some gene copies so we are plagued with recessives in a chromosome that's been decaying since before we were a species."

The naked man glared at the injector with wide eyes. "What are you going to do with that?"

"I've told you. I have to sedate you to ensure the experiment can run. You are not behaving."

The man screamed. "Help! Somebody! Help me! He's killing us! Help!"

"No one can hear you down here." A loud, pneumatic click issued from the injector. "You're all examples of the genetic catastrophe that is the male sex. Extremes." He turned and stared at the panicking prisoner. "Where did I find you? Under an overpass? It doesn't matter." He turned back to the medical device. "Without the stability of gene copies, men are prone to extremes in phenotypes, diseases, skills, retardation. Genius. Psychopathy." He walked toward the man, who thrashed again on the gurney. Beside him, the near corpse began to hack.

The killer paused, injector in hand, staring forward through the clear plastic in the headpiece.

"I guess that's the delusion. For every genius, ten homeless madmen. Nine of ten inmates in prison, a man. Developmental problems. Nearly all violent crime committed by men. Wars, rapes, torture, cruelties, stupidities on international scales—men. Ha! We pulled one epic con-job convincing ourselves we're special. *Better.* Denying that our rare outliers in intelligence or skills were never paired with wisdom." He began gesturing with the jet injector. "Like crazed warlocks we created artifacts of power and ringed our little world with weapons of destruction." He shook his head. "Utter madness treated as a sign of superiority!"

"Please. You don't have to do this."

He killer sighed. "It's really awful what I'm doing. But, yes, I must." The prone figure moaned and pulled once more at the restraints. "As imperfect as it is, human intelligence is a special thing. This teeming globe has produced a seed with great potential. But evolution is messy. Millions of species now extinct. Entire genomes *lost.* The seed of intelligence is warped by male dominance. Fatally so. It's turned from something that could have reached out to the cosmos into a malignancy threatening to burn its own home-world to ash."

He approached the gurney again, the figure on it breathing in bursts, hyperventilating.

"We must go, we men. But good news! We *can.* Sperm banks the world over provide all women need to continue the species. Maybe they'll keep some of us around for playthings, I don't know, or to renew sperm banks. But we *must* go. Civilization cannot survive men much longer." He stopped behind his captive. "And nothing is more fitting than this—one more unbalanced man like myself will ultimately be our purposeful undoing!"

"No! You're insane! Help!" He screamed at the plastic ceiling. "Get me out of here!"

The killer plunged the injector into the captive's shoulder, triggering the device. The screams reached a crescendo with a pneumatic rush.

The figure on the gurney relaxed, his eyes swimming. The screams stopped. His breathing slowed and his eyelids dropped shut.

The man in the biohazard suit attached the monitor leads, checked the readings, and pressed the button on the nearby television. As the voice of a newsman filled the room, the killer exited the inner chamber through a thin opening. He zippered it shut. Water rained on plastic and a pungent chlorine reek filled the air.

"And there you have it. The candidates' final speeches before America goes to the polls tomorrow. Polling has swung widely, with many analysts for the first time speaking of a possible upset victory by Daniel Suite, the mercurial businessman who has promised to bring an angry revolution to DC."

Four naked men slept beside the television and its continuing political coverage. A fifth shook and coughed his insides into the air.

59

CASSANDRA BLUES

"We had to pull a helluva lot of strings today, Rebecca," said Savas, the car bouncing over the false construction zone outside the Holland Tunnel. "Call in a lot of favors."

He's right. And this one's on me.

Cohen bit her lower lip. It was *her* decision to put so much trust in this nobody PI. Whatever their Angel might have prophesied, however much trust the previous collaboration with Tyrell Sacker created, whatever his opinions of Gone, the weight of the decision landed on her shoulders.

Savas hadn't been there to make the call and INTEL 1 had looked to Cohen. That alone shocked her. All these years, Savas led. He led the group out of the ashes when the terrorists of Mjolnir had nearly burned them to the ground. But here, in this clandestine, underground labyrinth created by President York, her standing grew beside his, making them equals in the eyes of others. Part of that boosted her ego. But on days like today, when she made the critical calls in the middle of chaos, the weight of that responsibility crushed her.

"We ruffled a lot of feathers. Nothing like a forced exhumation to win friends and influence your uncle."

"Dylan," fired Savas. "Tombstone Blues."

In the backseat of the town car, Cohen laughed, grasping his hand. The muscles were tense. "Our credit's still good. Until we max it out."

"Don't get too cocky. The background check on this Grace Gone is littered with red flags."

"I know."

"Call me a coward, but this looks like a shaky horse to bet on. She is *not* who she pretends to be. The parents are ciphers. Documents forged. Maybe it's nothing worse than illegal immigration. But there's a coverup."

"I trust her. Gut feeling," said Cohen. "Besides, weren't you impressed?"

"She's impressive. But we've got impressive covered. Francisco is impressive."

"Like a prayer Hulk."

"Angel is impressive. *You're* pretty damn impressive. I'll never keep up with you when the data's coming in."

Cohen shook her head. "I've got nothing on Gone. Never seen anything like it. I'd swear she's cheating. No-one can think that fast. That sharp."

"And so what if Miss Smarty-Pants is right? What if there's some virus cooked up by a serial killer in the pocket of an international conspiracy? For God's sake, what would Nemesis want with this?"

Cohen shrugged. "Her money's here, used for these medical supplies. The link is clear."

"But what's her strategy? Bilderberg was about control. This would unleash, what?" He looked at her with wide eyes. "Chaos?"

"If Gone is right, fifty percent of the world's population dies. The CDC's simulations are very rough. They don't know how contagious it might be. But within months to years, barring unforeseen immunity or treatments, most of the men on the planet could be gone."

"Bad news for me."

"Bad news for the species. Civilization can't take a fifty-percent haircut and function. Maybe we could do without the politicians," she grinned, "but men are integral to society at every level. Skills, numbers. Women can't retrain in time. Automation is not extensive enough. *Catastrophe.*"

"So what's an ex-Bilderberger trying to destroy the world for? They want to run it!"

Cohen shrugged. "Nemesis was one part of Bilderberg. Maybe she was an outlier, changed her motivations when their whole system collapsed." Her mouth formed a thin line. "You remember the *Amazon* rumors about her?"

Savas scoffed. "What? That she surrounds herself only with women bodyguards and advisers, has beefcake models as sex-toys? Not very reliable. The sources were international criminals."

Cohen shrugged again. "Might fit. Maybe she thought they could ride out the chaos. Establish some gendered ruling class."

Savas stared at her. "Listen to us. This is crazy. It's like some episode of a sci-fi series."

"I'd have thought so too," she said as the car entered the passage along the side of the Holland Tunnel. "But an androcidal virus? That used to be crazy, too."

"Androcidal." Savas shook his head. "Now there's a word."

"Maybe Angel used it? Before she left. I don't remember." Cohen tapped his knee. "You've been quiet about Angel. You know something."

"You said it was about the Eunuch Maker."

"Yes, but there was more. Why would she go to ground because of the Eunuch Maker?"

Savas sighed. "I'm not sure. But I think it goes back to the beginning when Larry was putting INTEL 1 together. We've talked about this. How he got unstable people stabilized by the missions."

"Yes. A crazy working theory."

"Effective, as he implemented it," said Savas. "Each one of us had our *event*. He was such a genius finding ways channel it to something hyper-productive."

"And?"

"We know most of ours. Mine was Thanos. Mad John Savas and

all. Yours was the bombing, your family in Israel. Frank's, God rest his soul, was battlefield trauma. And on and on. We knew each of our traumas."

Cohen tensed. "Except for Angel."

"Except for Angel." He frowned. "Larry never talked. Angel never talked. After what happened with Anonymous, I think Francisco and Sara might know a little more. But *something* happened to her. Something dark. So dark Larry scrubbed it from the records, even. Fawkes made that clear."

"What then? You think it relates to the Eunuch Maker?"

"Somehow. That's my only guess."

"Another monster with cages."

"What?" asked Savas.

"One of the last things she said. She said *I can't face another monster with cages.* Something about *dissections.*"

"Jesus."

"God, poor Angel. I hope we're way off."

He looked at her. "You said there was more."

"She mentioned the election. Daniel Suite in particular. Said a darkness was coming."

"If he wins? I think she's right."

Cohen shivered. "I have to say—this election is the first time I've felt afraid for my country. Afraid *of* my country. I don't understand how so many people support such a monster."

"Fear's powerful. So is anger," said Savas. "Hell, after 9/11, I might have voted for him on the single issue of demonizing Islam and Muslims. You remember what Mjolnir wanted. *God!* I struggled. Husaam didn't just save millions in Mecca. He saved my damn soul."

Cohen gripped his arm. "I will always be grateful to him. You were wounded. Your hate came from terrible, terrible pain. Muslim terrorists killed your *son*. Why do people hate so much? What's their reason?"

"On the ground, hate is hate. Origin stories won't matter to those who get hurt."

"Well, Suite's supporters don't stop with Muslims. It's Mexicans and Jews, too. Death threats since Suite started retweeting white supremacists. Every week I hear from some friend or relative."

"You never said—"

"We'd enough on our plate. Nothing's happened. Some were bogus. Some weren't. But if he wins?"

"He can't win." Savas smiled. "We just voted against him. Got my sticker to prove it."

"God, I hope he doesn't. Because if he does, he and those white nationalists take over. And INTEL I, everyone in it, you and me—we'll belong to *them*."

60

Y-LINKED

Grace Gone hunched over her laptop screen, her office dark. A weak glow filtered through the foyer from outside. The blue from her screen overpowered the orange street lights, the room icy. She leaned forward, her hair creating a veil obscuring her features. The clacks of her fingers pounding the keyboard echoed in the room.

The Electoral College tally auto-refreshed in a small corner of the screen. Over the hours the numbers beside Daniel Suite increased. At this early hour in the morning, he'd netted three hundred and six, surpassing the two-hundred and seventy required. Suite was going to be the next President of the United States.

Gone focused elsewhere. Maps of DNA, annotated with restriction enzyme sites, promotors, coding regions, and distal regulators sat alongside raw sequencing results. Thousands of base-pairs flitted across the screen, computer aligned and highlighted by similarity and divergence.

She didn't know how INTEL 1 did it. She'd asked for the buried body, asked for sequencing from several tissues, ask for quality labs. They'd delivered. She rejoiced that despite handling and decomposition, the viral genome was still present in decayed tissues of the inmate who'd thrown herself off a roof.

She hadn't anticipated that the brave new world of gender identity would clash so potently with exploited genetic constraints in a case she was investigating. As she analyzed, part of her brain tried to imagine the struggle of an XY man to overcome societal and physiological barriers. She tried to empathize with the struggle of surgeries and hormone treatments, the family shaming and abandonment by friends. All to become the woman she was.

Confusing. But the complicated neural structures of gender identity were no match for the reality of physiology in some contexts. The case of a deadly synthetic virus designed to exploit the male genotype was just such a context. And the stakes were life and death.

Poor Dawn Lodmell who'd participated in a seemingly innocuous donation of blood to the science project of Dr. Linda Richards. A project others informed her would benefit women in the development of new contraceptives. A benign donation with no risk, simply the removal of a few milliliters of blood for testing purposes.

Except the researcher taking the blood was anything but benign. The researcher violated her trust, injecting a synthetic virus into the unsuspecting woman. He used all the inmates as lab rats to test his man-killer, to make sure that it had no significant effect on women.

But how do you define woman?

If by genotype, the killer's virus worked as designed. It didn't kill women. But Lodmell was not genetically a woman. Lodmell was a genetic male who'd resculpted her form toward a female biotype. But she couldn't change her chromosomes or stop Dyer's exploitation of them.

And so Lodmell died. Horrifically. In an experimental failure the killer couldn't anticipate and that he was lucky didn't reveal his plans.

The black veil of hair moved as she leaned into the chair, resting her head on the top of the backrest. She closed her eyes, exhausted. But her mind couldn't rest.

Y-linked genes. Male-specific genetic regulators. DNA elements occurring nowhere in the female genome. The virus could only activate its deadly plan, produce the proteins for replication and the horrific damage to the host organism, when it was inside cells with a Y-chromosome. A synthetic, deterministic, male plague.

Of man-made origin.

Man-made. The ironies sidelined by the monstrosity, and the fact that Gone knew exactly which man made them. The clues were written in the language of nucleic acid base-pairing, in the genome sequences of the deadly virus. In the common markers of modern molecular alchemy produced by genetic manipulation.

The killer could only be a trained molecular biologist, a skilled artist with genetic material, and an engineer of genomic structures. He'd taken elements of Richards patented contraceptive virus and created a Frankenstein chimera with some of the deadliest viral genomes in the world. He produced a virus capable of infecting both men and women, but that would only reproduce, that could only release the devastating armament of tissue liquifying factors, in a male genome.

And he'd tinkered far beyond an Ebola or Marburg-like man-plague. Those horrible viruses stumbled in the air, spread mostly by direct contact with bodily fluids. But as Gone sifted through the genes engineered into this androcidal bioweapon, she came across genes from other viruses associated with aerosolization and airborne transmission. The madman was building a hemorrhagic flu.

And this was an early version of the virus.

Lodmell died years before. This killer was patient. This killer kidnapped, experimented on, and murdered who knows how many men to develop and perfect his microscopic monster. What progress had he made since then?

But his strength was his undoing. He used the best tools at his disposal—Richards' viral backbone. The cloning vectors and genes in her freezers. Gone only had to take the sequencing information from the murder victims and compare it to the published research from the Richards lab.

Perfect matches.

The probability that the designer of the virus—the killer himself

—worked in her laboratory sky-rocketed. Only one member of that lab possessed the size and strength to hoist a dead man over his shoulder and cart him up a flight of steps. Or to place a ring of concrete around a dead priest's neck.

Thomas Dyer.

She opened her eyes, checking the monitor and seeing she'd dozed half an hour. She sat up, grabbed a water bottle, and splashed her face. *Time to move.* She had the proof. The data was only hours old, but she had her man.

She emailed her conclusions to Sacker. She texted and called him. But he didn't pick up.

Drunk again.

"Dammit, Tyrell!"

She couldn't move this case any further on her own. Dyer was as psychopathic as any serial killer, and far, far more dangerous with the virus he possessed. They couldn't just collar him with a swat team. They needed a biohazard-suited, combat ready swat team, and she doubted very much those were within easy reach.

But INTEL 1 had the resources. They could do the impossible. If anyone could get such a team together, they could.

"Sorry, Tyrell, but we have to move on this. With or without you."

She picked up her phone and dialed Rebecca Cohen's number.

61

ELECTION NIGHT

S acker threw a beer bottle at the wall-mounted flatscreen. The television shook, teased a moment like it might fall, but held on for dear life. Cheers erupted from the speakers and the bottle shattered on impact with the floor.

"We return to the headquarters of the Suite campaign here in Florida." More screams. "As you can see, a lot of jubilant supporters tonight as their candidate seems poised to pull off one of the greatest upsets in modern political history."

A man rushed in front of the reporter, brandishing a sign. The cartoon silhouette of a woman in a hijab filled the screen. A red line circled her head with a diagonal through it.

"Make America Christian again! Take our country back!"

Burley men moved the celebrant to the side. The reporter continued.

"As you can see, supporters are not backing away from some of Daniel Suite's more controversial positions. The question now becomes: just how will he govern? Will the firebrand who rose to national prominence on conspiracy theories and targeting religious and ethnic minorities temper his rhetoric? Will there be the predicted pivot to the middle as the campaign stage ends?"

People behind the reporter screamed "No!" into the camera.

"At least for his more ardent fans, they aren't in the mood for compromise."

Sacker hammered the remote with his fist and the screen went dark.

Fucking klansman's going to be our next president.

Staring forward, he reached over to the table beside his recliner. His hand swept the air over an empty six-pack carton.

"Great."

His eyes flicked to the kitchen cabinet. Through the glass in the doors, he could see the caramel color of the bourbon. His last bottle. But it was full.

Stop it, Tyrell. Not tonight. Don't let the bastard push you over the edge.

He pressed his hands to his eyes. *It's just too much.* The case snow-balling down a wild path. Gone was likely poring over data from research labs. Samples taken from an exhumed corpse, no less! INTEL 1 doing who knew what in the bowels of the earth. Getting hammered wasn't professional. Not right now. Not with so much on the line.

He leaned out of the recliner and stood, heading toward the kitchen.

Just a shot.

On the way he scooped his cell phone to check messages. Strange —Gone hadn't written anything all night.

Oh yeah. I turned it off. Why'd I do that?

He knew why. As he stopped in front of the cabinet, his pretense faltered. He'd been planning to get wasted for hours now, ever since it was clear that pompous bigot was going to be president. The beer had him pretty buzzed. But he aimed higher.

And I didn't want Gracie calling. Hearing me like that again.

He pressed the button, waiting for the phone to power up. The bourbon whispered, right at eye level, the caramel color rich and savory. He could taste the wood and the burn of ethanol in his throat.

Just one fucking shot!

The phone danced. Buzz, buzz, buzz as ten messages from Gone burped their way across his screen.

Damn!

He unlocked the device and opened the messaging app, scrolling through the texts. His eyebrows rose.

"Well, I'll be damned."

Dyer? That Nordic, uptight giant in a white lab coat? *Man-plague?* Now there's a phrase he'd not ever considered becoming part of his lexicon. But *Dyer?*

But the more his pickled neurons stumbled through the facts, the more sense it made. Sense? Nothing *made sense* in this nightmare. But consistent, yes. It fit the facts—the physical size of the killer, association with the Richards lab, the biological engineering.

Thomas fucking Dyer.

Well, if that didn't top it all for the night. A racist billionaire who promised to ethnically cleanse America ascends to the presidency. The Eunuch Maker turns out to be some Aryan whiz-kid in a lab coat with a damn man-plague virus. Captain America was due any minute to tell him it's all a Nazi plan from 1942.

Sacker grabbed a pack and flicked up a cigarette, clamping it between his lips. The whiff of kerosene from the lighter mixed deliciously with the burning tobacco. He pulled on the filter, the drag long and deep into his lungs. He took a final look at the bottle. It retreated, hiding inside the cabinet. It knew the winds had changed.

Not tonight, motherfucker.

Tonight. Gone had contacted INTEL 1, said she hoped tomorrow they'd organize some kind of response to apprehend Dyer.

He could be gone tomorrow or kill five more people.

Sacker liked Cohen. INTEL 1 was swell. But this was *his* goddamn case. He'd sweated out a half dozen dead bodies, risked his career to bring Gone in. All so the Feds could swoop in tomorrow?

He burped and tasted beer.

No way in hell.

Sacker shuffled to a closet by the front door, yanked the door open and grabbed his jacket, tossing it on a nearby table. He removed a lockbox and keyed in a code, the latch popping on the safe. The dull sheen of a nylon-based polymer welcomed his hand as he removed the firearm.

You're drunk, Tyrell. You need to back up. You need to follow the damn protocols.

He ignored the voice and suited up, strapping in the weapon, donning his jacket. He looked in the mirror by the door. His eyes were bloodshot. His skin flaked, the pores open. He could feel and see the effects of the alcohol.

Thomas Dyer.

The son-of-a-bitch had stood right in front of them at NYU, likely laughing behind those cool blue eyes. Drunk or not, the murderer was *not* going to get one more night to do his dark deeds. And whatever the hell he planned with that virus.

He opened the door and stepped into the cold morning air. It was dark, the dawn still two hours away. A short walk to his car and he pressed the key controller, the lights blinking, the door lock popping. He pulled the handle and swung it open, flopping into the seat heavily and slamming it shut. Fog left his lips as he fitted the key to the ignition.

Thomas Dyer.

The engine revved and the lights flashed on, revealing a thin dance of snowflakes. He pulled out into the road and gunned the accelerator.

62

DYER STRAITS

Thomas Dyer lived on Long Island, taking the train each day into New York City and NYU. Sacker followed a parallel course along the Long Island Expressway toward Old Westbury, exceeding the speed limit and getting away with it in the wee hours. The darkness surrendered to a soft glow on the eastern horizon in front of him. An hour later and he would have been blinded by the sun.

Once off 495, he relied on his smartphone GPS. The irritating voice chirped. The AI only botched the job once along some of the more podunk roads leading to the budding mass murderer's home behind a failing suburb.

He must rise early.

The commute to the rail station wasn't trivial. The train in took an hour, whatever the schedules promised. Home-to-work pushed two, adding to a grand total of four glorious hours simply getting from A to B and back. Sacker was very interested to see just what brewed at Point A.

If I can make it there.

Rushing out, he'd forgotten hangover prep. Dehydration threatened to sideline him the most. The headache built as his overworked liver burned through water to detoxify. His eyes squinted and burned. Turns brought nausea. Luckily, the menu was only beer. Things shouldn't get much worse. But he'd pulled over twice already for the volume ingested.

I'll make it there.

Damn the incessant text messages from Gone and Cohen at INTEL 1. The Feds could use the NSA super-spy-whatever to track his phone. He should've mapped the route, written it down, and left the phone at home. But that required far more brain function than he'd possessed in those moments.

So they knew his destination and they were screaming for him to pull over and wait. At least that's what they'd been screaming until he blocked their calls and texts.

He should've sobered up by now, recognized he was acting like a rookie. *Like a damn idiot.* Why indeed try to super-cop this collar? The Black-ops-in-America heroes of INTEL 1 could swoop in with Gone and save the day. Why not wait for backup?

Because the world is going to shit. Because Dyer could escape before they get here. Because I've had a few too many.

"Because of Gracie." In the end, pride might come before a fall.

Sacker shook his head. He pulled to the curb along a beaten-up road beside an abandoned development. Creeping into the woods, trees obscured a house on an overgrown patch of land. Less a lawn than a monument to the resilience of the indigenous grasslands.

He shut the engine off and exited the car, careful not to slam the door. A pebbled path led to a garage, while a rock and mortar pathway ran to the front door. He decided on the garage.

No warrant but all kinds of terrorism, national security, probable-cause bullshit.

He removed his Glock and eased up the moderate incline toward the garage. No sign of lights or movement in the house.

He can't have left already.

His luck couldn't be that bad. No, smoke rose from one of the chimneys. It would be dangerous to leave a fire burning and commute to work. No professional scientist would ever make such a mistake. Dyer was home.

As he approached the garage, his metal fillings vibrated to a deep hum. He paused, feeling the buzz extend down to his feet. The corner of his mouth twitched upward.

Personal generator, Thomas. Big one. Now, what might you be needing that for?

Breaking in was easier than Sacker expected. The garage had a small window in the back. There was no security system connected to it. He ripped part of a fingernail off trying to pry it open, but the blood and pain were worth the silence.

He squeezed through the frame and dropped hard to stained concrete pungent with grease. The impact rolled him into a rusted Ford pickup. Sacker stared up at the hulking flatbed. Hardly the wheels of a city-slicker and biomedical whiz-kid. But he was dealing with something very much else here.

Old days in bad neighborhoods returned to him. He removed a set of small tools, and walked around the truck to the door leading into the house. He picked the lock in seconds, pushing the creaking frame into a cramped kitchen space. Uncleared plates. A breakfast consumed. The smell of brewed coffee lingered. A white shirt hung on a chair. Dyer was home and awake.

Careful, Tyrell.

His eyes fell on a wall opposite the kitchen sink. Light from a window fell on a thick steel door, the kind Sacker had seen in industrial freezer rooms. His heart sank when he saw a keypad by the handle, barring the way. But today was his lucky day.

In a mad rush, huh Dyer?

The killer hadn't pulled the heavy door shut. The large latch had not engaged. Dr. Genius left the damn door unlocked.

Sacker placed his shoulder along the keypad and wall, his weapon raised. With his left hand he pushed the door, darting through the opening with his gun pointed down the stairway.

Nobody.

Empty stairs greeted him. Machinery hummed as he made his

way down the concrete steps to the cellar. It was unlike any cellar he had ever seen.

Walls of clear plastic subdivided the basement. Throbbing motors from hulking air filtration units decorated several points in the plastic maze. Their deep beats sent his developing headache into the red. Sacker squinted and moved toward an opening. A thick zipper split the plastic apart to allow entry.

Tyrell, what the fuck are you doing?

He stopped. He'd stumbled into a scene from Outbreak or some zombie apocalyptic television show. Alone in the home of a monstrous serial killer who mutilated his victims, posing them for public viewing in New York City. He stood in this maniac's underground hot zone laboratory. Behind the plastic wall lurked a deadly virus that made blood pour out of the eyes of men.

Sacker grabbed a biohazard mask on a nearby cart. He fitted it over his head, trying to make the thing snug around his neck. *Maybe good enough.* It would *have* to be enough, whatever the consequences.

Dyer was here. He knew it. The Eunuch Maker wasn't going to get away.

Sacker ducked under the zippered doorway and moved through a narrow plastic-walled corridor. The fogging mask reflected his ragged breathing back to him. The corridor opened to an inner room. His gun hand dropped to his side.

A reek unlike anything he'd known assaulted him. He gagged. The poisonous odor infiltrated and clogged his lungs, his stomach lurching.

Sweet Jesus God in heaven have mercy.

Blood-soaked bodies faced him in a semi-circle. Dyer had lashed the devastated forms to gurneys. Machines monitored them. Several had flatlined, the equipment beside others screaming about the dire state of the proto-corpses underneath. His stomach heaved again.

Dire. Dyer. Die or...what?

His head spun. The stink, the blood, the antiseptic walls.

Hangover. Dehydration. Water. I need water.

Neurobiology took over. Primitive tissues in his brain overruled higher cortical function. Sacker panicked.

Get out. Get water. Get help.

The doorway was behind him. Get out. *Run.* He spun, holding back the contents of his stomach, turning away from the hellscape he had stumbled into.

Thomas Dyer towered in the doorway with a two-by-four. He whipped the wood against the side of Sacker's head.

White lab coat. Brown wood. White light.

Black enveloped him as he hit the floor.

63

FRESH FROM THE JUICER

"A poor decision, Detective Sacker. Now that you've seen this, I can't let you live. Of course, you'd be dead soon anyway."

Squinting, Sacker woke to an agony of light. His head was a pincushion with ten thousand knives inserted. His left eye stuck shut and his mouth tasted copper.

Blood. *Where did I see...*

He yanked against the restraints.

"You can't escape. Stop trying. I should stitch your head. The plank gave you a good cut. But you won't bleed out. And it won't matter much now anyway."

He was still in the inner room. The nightmare forms were beside him, the stench overpowering. A man in a yellow spacesuit hovered above.

Stall. Feign confusion and ignorance. Hope Gone and the others would arrive soon.

"Dyer," he croaked. "What is this? It's beyond murder."

"Please don't insult my intelligence. You're here. You must be pretty close to the truth." He paused and looked off into the distance.

"You're working alone on this, aren't you? NYPD protocol is strict. You shouldn't have come here by yourself." Dyer laughed. "You're smarter than I thought. And more foolish. But I'm impressed detective. You figured this much out on your own. But they didn't believe you, did they? And so you decided to play hero."

Not exactly far from the truth, but the relief! Dyer didn't know about INTEL 1. He didn't suspect how much had been deduced. He wasn't rabbiting. They still had a chance!

Stall! Make him think you're defeated.

It wasn't a hard act.

"Go to hell," Sacker mumbled.

"Still, I've pushed my luck," said the space suit, hands clanking items on a metal tray out of sight. "It wasn't you or NYPD at the bank. That had Feds written all over it. Idiots shut down my account. Tipped me off." He sighed. "Yes, sooner or later all my breadcrumbs were going to lead someone here."

"What the hell is this? What did you do to these men?"

Dyer turned to him, peering through the plastic sheet of the suit, his blue eyes cold.

"It's a bit technical. The short version is that I'm not *really* a serial killer."

"My ass you aren't."

"I have *serially killed* many, it is true. But only as a byproduct."

Stall. "By-product of your psychosis."

"Perhaps. But not in the way you think. These unfortunate souls, and the evil men I killed before them, are part of an experiment, detective."

"An experiment." He dialed it to Full Sarcasm.

"Yes, indeed. An experiment in which I used my old lab's vectors as a springboard to design a most specific and terrible virus. A virus to wipe out mankind."

Sacker whistled. "Delusional and psychotic. You *fuck*."

"I don't expect you to believe me. Why would you? But the truth remains."

"Wipe out humanity?"

"No. Please pay careful attention to the vocabulary. I said *mankind*." Dyer chuckled. "Part of the problem, isn't it? So easily we assume humanity is covered by the word *man*. Part of our unconscious misogyny. But the truth is that my virus will kill *only men*. Like those victims you investigated. And it will spread across this earth soon. With it, I will remake intelligent life and civilization on the planet."

"*Jesus.* Please don't say you're going to kill me. I'm not going out at the hands of a total fruitcake. Help!"

"I'm so close, Detective Sacker. These men are my final experiment. Well, the last you and whoever else is chasing me will give me time for. If the infectivity is sufficient, I need only turn several like them loose at moderate stages of infection. The virus is highly contagious. It will only take weeks for the spread to get out of control." He exhaled. "World without men."

Meet him in his obsession. Delay. "You delusional psychopaths can't think out of your box. Kill all men? *Really?* Let's say you aren't just kidnapping and emasculating some poor bastards. Let's pretend for a minute that you've really got some Armageddon virus to wipe out every last man. How is your *world without men* going to function? It'll collapse in months."

Dyer drew his shoulders back. "Unusually thoughtful for a detective. Certainly for a man in your current position. You *surprise* me." Dyer moved several items from a table to the tray. "Yes, it's a significant danger. One I have of course considered. But our disease is too advanced. The patient, the entire biosphere perhaps, is threatened. The cancer must be cut out. But the tumor is very large indeed."

He came to a stop, gazing down on Sacker.

"If my virus succeeds, that may well be *it* for humanity. Not necessarily intelligent life—dolphins, other primates might get a shot when we're gone. And that's why the risk must be taken. Either we go extinct and save another chance for intelligence in this corner of the cosmos. Or *women* make it, and themselves become that force. This is my hope. My dream. The future of humanity is female. The only other option, the option with you and me, is extinction. And extinction, as it stands with our technologies, could be the death of most life. Certainly all intelligent life on earth."

Sacker shook his head. "You've *made* your point. You *killed* the rapists and other evil men. Turn yourself in. Let me go. End this."

"Now you disappoint me. I didn't figure you for a coward."

"I'm trying to save lives."

"You aren't listening. I *don't want* to save men's lives." He gestured to the dying bodies. "I want to take them. All of them. Millions. *Billions.*"

"You're insane. You're going to kill me and serve my dickless body to New York. That's all this is. More delusion."

Dyer pulled the tray beside the gurney. He lifted several crimson vials and held them over Sacker's head. It looked like blood.

"What's that?"

"Virus, Detective Sacker. Fresh from the juicer." He twirled the mixture inside. "I don't have time to verify the titers now, but it's been like clockwork for some time. This is as potent as it gets." He smiled from inside the suit. "And this one's for *you*."

Sacker's throat went dry.

"For me?"

"I've decided you'll make a perfect patient zero. Well, one of my several patient zeros. Seeding a virus artificially requires changes in terminology."

"Seeding?"

"Yes, you and several others I'll infect will spread this virus worldwide." He sighed. "As will I."

Dyer loaded the viral solution into a plastic cartridge, placing it into a giant injection gun.

"I will be the last to be infected. I'll travel with anti-virals to slow the progress, maintaining my contagiousness. My journey's planned in detail. Several key population centers and travel hubs."

He raised the injector and set it against Sacker's arm. Sacker squirmed and yelled, trying to free himself from the gurney. The restraints held.

"You're helping to make a better world."

There was a hiss and a sharp pain in his shoulder.

64

QUARANTINE

"We'll start with Frank Richard in the next room, dump him in a homeless shelter." Dyer replaced the injection gun on the tray with a rattle.

Stunned, violated, imagining a poison flowing through his body, a violent anger coursed with Sacker.

"You *motherfucker*."

The monster ignored him. "Greg Maynor we'll let get pretty sick and send to a hospital. Best place to start an outbreak, you know, a hospital. And you, detective, we'll get you good and producing viruses into the air, then return you to NYPD. Unconscious, of course. Then I've only to let myself wander the metros of New York, London, Tokyo, and Shanghai."

The cavalry arrived thirty seconds later. One moment the upbeat architect of an androcidic nightmare monologued about his ghastly plans. The next came a rush of air. Dyer spun toward the tent exit. Plastic ripped with the clank of metal canisters around them.

"No, no, *no*! Not *yet*!"

But it was too late for Dyer. Too late for his master plot of gendercide. The canisters erupted with a stunning sound and light. Sacker, his head trauma an agony, blacked out.

When he came to, an army of orange space suits surrounded him. They toted automatic weapons. Dazed, he watched in the third person, a bodiless viewpoint. They released his constraints, helped him sit up. The sounds around him came delayed, underwater and distorted. His eyes moved to a shape on the floor. A red circle, wet and reflective attracted his attention like a bullseye. A large body was sprawled over it.

Dyer.

His eyes focused. Dyer was dead. Shot, holes riddling the lab coat. Sacker scanned the room. Special forces in biohazard suits from some unknown agency buzzed like bees. They patched holes in the plastic, installed new equipment, and moved the corpses into protective bags. He marveled at the invasion force, military-grade skills and energy while imprisoned in BSL4 gear.

"Detective Sacker, can you hear me?"

"Yes. Sorry. I hear you." *Barely. What is wrong with me?*

"You're hurt. What's the nature of your injuries?"

A loaded question.

He stared into the plastic suit beside him. A young woman, black hair, deep-set brown eyes. *Indian?* A medic. A soldier. *Special forces. Special biological attack forces.*

"My head. Bad cut. Son-of-a-bitch hit me." He looked down to his left shoulder. His mind cleared. "And a doomsday injection." He gestured to the bleeding patch of skin from the injection gun. "That's what he said anyway. I'm patient fucking zero."

The young soldier's eyes narrowed. She turned away and to a microphone inside her suit. He couldn't catch her words. Sacker leaned back down on the gurney and closed his eyes. It wasn't hard to guess what was coming.

Quarantine.

"You know a Grace Gone?" The soldier again.

Sacker's lids flicked open. "Yeah. We work together." His head turned. "Is she okay?"

The soldier spoke again into her mic. Two broad men in suits moved past her to the zippered entrance. Moments later a small figure in an ill-fitting yellow suit limped into the room. He didn't need to see into the mask.

"Gracie," he said, smiling, turning his head toward the ceiling. "Glad you could make it." He coughed a laugh. "Old Sacker sure screwed the pooch this time. Should'a waited for back up."

Gone reached the gurney, joined by two other figures. They fumbled around in the suits as well.

Savas and Cohen.

"You've been infected," said Gone, looking at his shoulder.

"Yeah. How about that?"

"We don't know yet," said Cohen, her voiced raised. "You might not have caught it from the other victims."

"You don't understand, Agent Cohen," said Sacker, sighing. "He shot me up with the shit. See the gun on the tray? Full of virus."

Savas and Cohen locked eyes through their suits. Gone reached out and took his hand. The plastic felt cold.

"This won't do," she said and moved her other hand to her face.

"Gracie, what are you..."

"Shhh."

A soldier shouted across the room. "Ma'am! Stop! If you—"

She removed her face covering and dropped it to the ground. Gone took a deep breath of the air in the room and scowled. Activity in the room ceased. She removed her arm from the suit and touched his hand, flesh to flesh.

"God, it smells like festering death in here," she said, her other hand to her mouth.

Sacker shook his head. "You goddamned fool. Now you're stuck with me in quarantine." He squeezed her hand. "But, thanks."

"Could be worse." Tears filled her eyes.

Cohen put a gloved hand on Gone's shoulder. "You sure you want to be here for this? You know what's coming."

Gone smiled, drops falling from her face. "Susceptibility to illness varies across a population. Dyer hoped he'd decimate most of the male half of the species." She squeezed his hand. "But I believe detective Sacker will prove unusually resistant."

Sacker's eyes went wide. Cohen's mouth tightened, but she said nothing.

"Just a hunch," Gone said. "Maybe just a wild hope."

She smiled down at Sacker.

"Sometimes you have to hope."

FOUR MONTHS LATER

65

SCANDAL

C HAOS IN WASHINGTON AS INDEPENDENT COUNCIL REQUESTED: *Bipartisan Demands on Eunuch Maker Case Margareta Sorenson, Kelly Dwyer, and Anita Ramnarain reporting for the New York Times*

CONGRESSIONAL LEADERS *of both parties released a rare joint statement today demanding an investigation into last November's Election Night events that culminated in a still classified raid in Long Island. The House and Senate were unified in a rare show of bipartisanship seeking answers to the apprehending of the so-called Eunuch Maker, a serial killer of men who had left a trail of mutilated victims across New York City. In explosive revelations, several sources have leaked that the killer had plotted international terrorist actions with a biological agent.*

"Unacceptable," said the House Speaker. "The York administration lost the public trust with this cover up. Congress has been kept in the dark about far too much in a case of flagrant executive overreach. She shouldn't expect immunity from investigation. There's a new sheriff in town."

Confidential sources at the CDC and several academic institutions, including New York's Columbia University, have confirmed that they were involved in work to identify a novel virus of the Ebola family that was detected in the bodies of the Eunuch Maker's victims.

One researcher who has gone on the record is Professor Lapin I. Kin of Columbia's Center for Infection and Immunity. In an exclusive, Dr. Kin told the Times that he had been contacted by governmental agencies and had even taken a direct call from President Suite following the Inauguration.

"I'm not here to contribute to a scandal," Dr. Kin said, "but as a scientist I believe in complete transparency. For reasons of national security, the former administration leaned hard on us to keep everything confidential. But this goes beyond national security. Deadly microorganisms do not respect borders or ideologies. The world has to know."

Dr. Kin would not yet reveal more details, but confirmed that the Eunuch Maker victims had been infected with a deadly virus. "It's a relative of Ebola. And it's synthetic, engineered by man. Most likely by this killer, but this is currently only speculation."

When questioned by the press last night, Dr. Kin refused to deny or confirm that there were human DNA elements in the virus or that the illness was designed to strike only men, much like the Eunuch Maker himself.

"While I want everything to be made public, as a scientist I also believe in careful procedure. Researchers around the world are confirming our results, which will be peer reviewed, and published in reputable scientific journals. We're going to get this right."

In the meantime, Dr. Kin said that he was working with law enforcement and the federal government, as well as Congressional investigations into the matter.

"The truth of this will come out, and it's going to be much bigger than just one mad terrorist killer," said Senator Brian Young of Arizona. "We have it on very good sources that President York, in violation of numerous laws, was running a clandestine special forces and espionage agency, unknown to anyone in Congress or the federal government."

In what was supposed to be her lame-duck period, York has become the focal point of a national political crisis. Already a controversial figure for her leadership during the Anonymous Event, she has fought claims that she engineered a coup and then covered up its ensuing collapse.

"Finally, maybe people will start to believe what we've been saying about York," said Congressman Bob Child of Florida. "She is a dangerous figure, a budding tyrant who nearly brought down our democracy. Now she's trying to run a shadow government from the sidelines. That's not going to happen."

President Suite was quick to comment on Twitter in his famous confrontational style.

"York a tyrant! Secret police! Was there a coup? We need a trial for treason. Lock her up!"

Senate Majority Leader Williams took a more cautious tone while still calling for an independent investigation.

"And so, despite government claims, a lot of people are asking, what is the real story? What are they hiding? The American people want answers. And we're going to get them."

Meanwhile, as the smoke clears, a local girl has found her hour in the spotlight. Private investigator Grace Gone of New York was catapulted into the national scene when her name was found on leaked NYPD reports on the Eunuch Maker case. Lead detective Tyrell Sacker, injured and hospitalized after the Long Island raid on the home of Thomas Dyer, listed Gone as a consultant on the case, using unusually strong language to credit her with solving the mystery of the Eunuch Maker killings.

"Yes, he was very complimentary," said Ms. Gone as she was swarmed by reporters outside her small office in Queens. "It was an honor to serve this great city and stop a monster."

Since the report was leaked, Gone says that her phone won't stop buzzing.

"I've got a growing list of unread messages I'll never get through. Success is a double-edged sword," she said, waving off clamoring reporters in the doorway of her office. "But I'm thrilled for the new clients."

66

SACKED

Detective Rick Snyder beamed, standing at the front of a large conference table in the 12th Precinct, gesturing emphatically. Sweat beaded on his forehead. His tone was triumphant and he glared at Sacker like a trophy hunter would a downed kill. Detective Kathy Hill scowled and shook her head. At the other end of the table the hulk of Captain Lander slumped with exhaustion.

Sacker ground his molars.

You're welcome for the training, Snyder.

He touched his left temple and winced. The close encounter with Dyer's two-by-four still caused headaches months later. His left eye struggled to focus, the retina partially detached. Flashbacks from Dyer's basement horror show interrupted his daily routine without warning. Nightmares of claustrophobic spaces, plastic prisons, and bleeding bodies haunted him.

Thank God for Gracie staying with me.

Some *thank you* he'd given back. Avoiding her like the man-plague after their release, he kept trotting out a list of excuses. A mess at NYPD *did* need cleaning. The 24/7 infotainment machine tried to swallow her whole. She built her new business. He fought to keep his job. They'd been *busy*.

But that wasn't the whole story. Not even the main story. Police or new found fame, trauma, the need to decompress—they ran from something else.

No, I'm running from something else.

At least he was still breathing. Defying expectations, the virus spared him, producing not so much as a fever. Despite constant monitoring, his blood showed no signs of viremia. His immune system remained calm. Baffled researchers scratched their heads. Was Dyer's man-plague a dud after all?

He knew better. And Gone sure as hell knew better. Afterward, they both made sure the right people knew better, too. But that came later. Once he was out of government hands.

They'd have figured it out anyway.

He'd proven immune. Permission or no, ethics and statutes be damned, the government scientists were going to sequence his genome. In the face of a national security risk—a risk to the survival of *man*kind, anyway—such niceties as *rights* took a backseat. When they did, his secret was out.

Count your lucky stars you're out, Tyrell.

He should be happy. Joyful to be alive and free and not some long-term lab rat. Ecstatic to stop a killer and terrorist. Singing damned hymns to be out of quarantine and back at work.

The small matter of being sacked snuffed out the celebrations.

"Seven departmental regulations broken," clucked Snyder. "All in direct contradiction of *your* orders, captain." He glared at Lander, whose face flickered between an angry boar and a broken-hearted frat boy. "We still don't know which federal divisions he was working with. He won't say! They won't say! It's a *national* scandal. My mom sees it on the news. And that PI he put in the report, which he *leaked* —it's all over the papers!"

Choice criticism from the leaker-in-chief of the 12th Precinct, asshole. I didn't even get paid.

At least Gone got rewarded. Sacker honored their deal. As the PI had calculated, the publicity made her a rock star.

Careful, Gracie. This city can turn on you in an instant.

"You sound like a brown-nosing bureaucrat!" yelled Hill, snapping them all to attention. It was the first time Sacker had heard the young detective raise her voice.

"Insults won't change the truth," said Snyder.

Hill waved him off. "Everything you want to hang him with broke the case open. Solved it. Ended the murders. Stopped a dangerous terrorist. Or maybe you wanted to die from that virus?" She cocked her head so hard Sacker thought she'd pop a vertebrae. "You claim you're a man, after all."

"What did you say? Let me tell—"

"Enough!" boomed Ladner. For additional emphasis he slammed his fists on the table, spilling Sacker's coffee across the surface.

Was still hot. Sacker threw a stack of napkins on the steaming puddle.

"Just shut up, both of you," Ladner said. He sat up and straightened his tie, ovals of perspiration under his arms. "Tyrell's been here as long as I have. There isn't an officer who's served this precinct better. Hell, during the chaos Anonymous caused, he's earned enough respect for two careers."

He's not looking at me.

Ladner exhaled. "But there's more to being in the 12th than being a great cop. We're a family. There are bonds and rules. And loyalty's at the very top of my list."

Now he looks my way.

"Tyrell, you stopped the Eunuch Maker. But you were reckless. Dangerous. And more importantly, *disloyal.* Your actions made a fool of me and this precinct. Of the NYPD." He wrung his hands together. "You're famous now, along with that Chinese girlfriend of yours. I'm sure you'll have a lot of opportunities."

"So, you're going to fire me?"

"Goddammit, Tyrell!" The fist pounding again. His index finger hooked forward. "Don't you make me do that shit! Don't make me run you through the grinder. A formal investigation will make us all look bad." He licked his lips. "Don't think we don't know about your, ah, vices. Your *past*. We'll do what we have to."

You motherfucker.

"You'd go low?"

He caught Snyder glancing at him, a big, ugly grin on the brat's face.

"There's no reason to!" Ladner pushed a folder toward him. "Resign, dammit. Submit a letter. Tell the press whatever. You want to *expand* your horizons, chase other opportunities. This case was too much. Be creative." He tapped the folder. "Early retirement. Full benefits. Take it and get the hell out of here. Never come back."

I'll be damned.

For it to get to this point, Ladner had put in serious planning with powerful friends. *And the rat, Snyder.* But it was people over their heads who backed this play. No doubt they'd go full dirt on him. Snyder likely would provide some targeted lies to seal the deal. The *opportunities* Ladner mentioned were bullshit. They wouldn't exist. Not in law enforcement anyway. Those running him out of town would see to it.

Blacklisted. My life's work, shot to hell.

He tasted burnt ashes and bared his teeth.

"So that's it, then?" he said. "After everything."

Ladner growled like a pit bull. "That's it."

Snyder couldn't help himself. "You can take it, right? You claim you're a man, after all." He looked between Sacker and Hill with punchable self-satisfaction.

Sacker stood, staring them all down. He'd lost. He knew that. He'd expected to lose, but didn't know how dirty things would get until this moment.

Hill held back tears. Of anger, frustration, or sadness, he couldn't tell. His stomach knotted. She was great detective material. She was decent. *Too decent.* He wanted to say something to her, but didn't dare.

With Snyder as Ladner's new golden boy, it'd just make it worse for her.

Instead, he dropped his badge and firearm on the table, grabbed his coat, scooped up the manila folder, and left the room without saying another word.

67

UNDER NEW MANAGEMENT

Cohen dashed into Savas' office clutching a set of printouts.

"Virus results are back." Words rushed out as she caught her breath. "Confirmed from two different labs. Dyer didn't get the infectivity he needed. Order of magnitude less contagious. Docs say no pandemic spread possible."

"Didn't the quarantine shut this down?" asked Savas.

"Viruses don't respect police tape or even biosafety containment unless we're damned near perfect. One mistake and a highly contagious pathogen could be off to the races. We dodged a bullet. You dude-bros would be only myth."

"Couldn't they control it? Modern medicine and all?"

Cohen dropped into a chair and tossed the papers to Savas. "It's not like the digital viruses we fought before. Biology isn't brittle. Biology is messy. Dyer didn't have the time or numbers to work out the messiness. Not to meet his goals. He failed, thank God. Flip side is once you get a bad bug, it's damn near impossible to stop it. Few treatments besides palliative. Has to burn itself out."

"Big mistake parading his victims about."

"Sacker got that right. He's had some experience with bright criminals."

"So have we," said Savas. "Gunn and Fawkes nearly brought things down, too."

"They were more disciplined. And they were working with tools already in hand. Dyer was on the cutting edge, trying to engineer an organism to do his bidding. *That's* an ego beyond Gunn or Fawkes."

"Let's not forget Nemesis. It's confirmed then?"

"I wish Angel would get the hell back here to help analyze the digital trail. Took me days when she'd be done in hours. But *yes*. All the lines of funding trace back to her and her shell companies. What a mess."

"Why would she risk it? Bilderberg wasn't like that. Say what you want about them, they wanted order. Progress. As they understood progress, anyway."

"Bilderberg tried to kill millions to preserve their societal plans."

"But for a higher purpose, however misguided. But not like this. Not random."

"Maybe not so random," said Cohen. "Remove all the men, societies falter. Power vacuum. Men still run everything. Sir."

"Hitting low."

"Exactly. Crazy how so much power and injustice is centered on some dangling genitals. But maybe she thought the chaos would create opportunity. One her organization could exploit."

"Did she groom this guy? How did she find him?"

"Not clear. Not much in the data trail to reconstruct the history."

"Madness."

"For sure. Nemesis went over the edge. She's willing to burn the world to try and take control. And she's still out there."

The phone buzzed on his desk. Their eyes met and held a moment. Savas exhaled, picking up the receiver.

"Yes." He frowned. "I see. Of course. Send him right in."

"He's here. Just down the hallway."

Cohen's voice was flat. "Here we go."

They stood, moving toward his office door, left open from Cohen's rush inside. Before he reached it, a large figure appeared in the frame. A crowd of personal assistants and bodyguards escorted him.

Savas extended his hand.

"Secretary Brennem. I'm John Savas."

The unshaven and disheveled figure smiled. "Very pleased to meet you, Mr. Savas. It's not *agent* anymore, is it? Down here, I mean."

"No, sir."

"Something we'll talk about." He glared at Cohen. "Alone."

"Ms. Cohen is—"

"Your wife and someone I'm not interested in speaking with. I want the *man* in charge." He gestured to his accompanying staff. "Ms. Cohen please get some coffee for my team and wait for us down the hall. I saw a nice kitchen with lots of amenities."

Savas grimaced. Cohen's eyes burned.

"Of course, Mr. Secretary," she said. "Beginnings are important. And nothing is more important to the security of this country than INTEL 1. I can assure you." She cast Savas a pointed stare and left the room. The crowd followed her, and Brennem closed the office door.

"Let's have a chat." Brennem ambled to a seat at Savas' desk. "You got any whiskey?"

"No. I don't drink. Not for a long time."

"Shame. Hard to trust a man who doesn't drink." He grinned. His teeth were yellow.

Savas sighed. "I used to. Way too much. I need to function."

Brennem leaned forward, his tangled tie hanging at an angle. "Yes. *Function.* That's why I'm here. The *function* of INTEL 1. You've operated this, ah, organization, without oversight. With unapproved funds."

"Constitutional crises require extraordinary means. Agencies, FBI, CIA, NSA—after Anonymous, there was carnage. Disarray. The coup. York brought us together. We helped restore order, hunt down those who tried to control this nation."

The smile didn't lessen. "Yes, we understand that. Now. The briefings have been *fascinating.* Truly terrible times. But the crisis for this nation is just beginning."

"The forces of Bilderberg are on the run."

The smile became a smirk. "No, I'm not talking about this phantom you've been chasing."

Savas grit his teeth. "I can assure you, Mr. Secretary, Bilderberg was very real. The remnants of it still very dangerous."

"Possibly, but our analysts conclude the Bilderberg threat has passed. The Suite administration feels other, far more pressing dangers must be addressed."

"Which are these?"

"Something older and closer to your own heart, Mr. Savas."

"What do you mean?"

"The Islamic menace, of course. The established elites say you brought down our American bin Laden." He scowled. "God, I hate the label. False equivalency. Such an insult to the singular genius of William Gunn, wouldn't you say? A title the liberal press slandered him with. For truly he was a man of vision. He understood the threat we face."

"He was a madman."

Brennem frowned, his eyebrows rising. "The line between madness and genius is so thin, don't you think? We've read your files. Your work during that time was patriotic, but highly, well, *conflicted*. Muslims murdered your son."

Savas set his jaw. "A lot's changed."

"Has it?" He stared at Savas, the fierce blue eyes glowing behind heavy eyebrows. "The chaos of the last few years masks the long-term threat to our civilization. I take a long view of history, as does our new president. I appreciate what has come, the cycles, the purgings, the wars. It's all more predictable than you might think."

Savas leaned back in his chair, saying nothing.

"Bringing us back to INTEL 1. Your record is unusually productive. Great talent pool and leadership. Excepting the recent defections."

"Defections?"

"Agent Lightfoote, this cipher of a pair, code names of Gabriel and Mary." Brennem laughed. "So much cloak and dagger."

"Defection seems a loaded word, Mr. Secretary. They submitted their resignations."

"On Inauguration Day, if I am not mistaken." Savas remained silent. "Some would call this a betrayal. A defection from the new administration."

"Staff departures with administration changes are common. Just politics. Maybe they don't agree with Suite's positions."

Brennem's glance felt like a scalpel. "And do you?"

"I've worked in the NYPD, the FBI, and as part of York's covert INTEL 1. I believe in the power of good people to serve and protect this country."

"Ah, yes. York. The crowds are chanting for her imprisonment as we speak."

"It's absurd."

"Perhaps. But it's good to hear you will be staying on at INTEL 1. This asset *fascinates* me. A covert squad of talented people, hidden beneath the streets of one of our greatest cities, answering to no-one."

He stood, glancing around the room, a broad grin creeping over his face.

"In the trying times certain to come, I'm convinced such resources will be *most* useful."

68

FUGITIVES (AGAIN)

Houston hugged her knees in the chilly warehouse air, pushing herself deeper into a corner of the sofa. The make-shift hacker lair was a wreck. Dim lighting, the stink of unwashed basement dwelling computer nerds. But they'd be moving on soon.

Can't wait to leave.

Lightfoote set it up, of course. She'd reached out to them after the election. After the Eunuch Maker was brought down. A storm grew on the horizon, the future uncertain. Her bones rattled with it.

Lopez's deep voice pulled her mind back to the moment.

"They're creating a transport path," he said, an analytic tone failing to cover a suppressed rage. "See? *Here.*"

He gestured to a paper map of the United States spread over a stained table beside the sofa. She followed his index finger as it tapped several points along a major highway running north to south.

"It's a damned Latino funnel. They've had detention centers in several places along the route for years. But now—*billions* of dollars. Private companies salivating. With the new executive orders, those centers will become full-fledged camps."

"They won't call them that."

"Of course not. Just *humane* way-stations to get the rapists, drug dealers, and child molesters out of this once-pure nation. Only a coincidence all those terrible people are brown."

"You really think it's this planned out?"

"Sara, it's a logistics nightmare. How the hell do you evict nearly twelve million people? Move them across a country the size of the US to the border? It would be the largest ethnic cleansing in history."

"Ethnic cleansing in America."

"Wouldn't be the first time. The history books are written by the powerful. The nation was founded on genocide and slavery. Let's not act too shocked." He made a fist. "But it has to be stopped."

"It'll wreck state economies."

"For sure. White Americans won't flood the fields and work their fingers to a blistering mess. Or care for their own damned children. Clean their own bathrooms. But that's just the beginning. These spic loafers pay a hell of a lot in sales taxes, billions in Social Security to float current retirees."

"But they're undocumented. How do they pay Social Security?"

Lopez laughed. "Evil Mexicans got our ways, gringo! You need papers to work. So we fake them. Seen it many times. Heard it in confessionals from guilty mothers feeding their kids with those jobs. Employers are too dumb or don't care to check. They submit W2s and withholdings to Uncle Sam. Multiply by millions."

"Wow."

"Mmm-hmmm. We're a secret pillar of society!" He scowled. "So when they stuff us in boxcars, not only's the fruit going to rot, the houses not get built, yuppie mom's running around in a panic, but the bottom is going to fall out across the board."

"It's not going to be boxcars. Not in the twenty-first century. Not in America."

"Well, if Suite and his cronies hadn't lobbied for years to kill public transport, it might have been. As it is we don't have the rail system to do it in America." He gestured back to the map. "So, interstate. That's the patterning. ICE has it all planned."

"ICE?"

"Immigration and Customs Enforcement. Suite's black-shirts."

"Right."

"All the private detention centers—corporately owned but publicly funded—they sit along major highways." The index fingers of each of his hands moved along major highways from the east and west coasts, diving south. "And meet up at several key points. Sixty thousand people *per week* will need to go through these centers if Suite is going to do this in four years."

"My God."

"And they won't go willingly. They're going to hide. Run. Some will fight. How do you ethnically cleanse a nation? Hunt down the workers, their families, children? The thousands of legals who will be swept into this dragnet? How do you deal with those who exercise their second amendment rights?"

Houston set her jaw. "You militarize it."

"Bingo. And all the domestic terrorism laws are now in place for that." Lopez rose from his crouch and stretched his thick form.

Her eyes danced all over him. *He can fill a shirt.*

"My plan is massive disruption. Hit the bottleneck points. Give them no infrastructure for this logistical nightmare."

"The prisons?"

"*Camps.* Yes." He glared at the map.

Houston stood and angled her hips. "So you really want to do this?" He nodded. "Praise God. We'll finally be real terrorists."

"I have to do this."

She slinked beside him and flowed her body along his. "At least we'll *earn* our place at the top of the Most Wanted."

His muscled arm slid around her waist.

He recited. "One has a moral responsibility to disobey unjust laws. *King.*"

"Yeah?" She pressed her chest into his.

His voice lowered. "Disobedience is the true foundation of liberty. *Thoreau.*"

"Mmmmm," she purred, nuzzling his neck.

"Since governments take the right of death over their people, it is not astonishing if the people should sometimes take the right of death over governments."

"Oh," she gasped. "Who's that?"

"Guy de Maupassant."

"Sounds *French*."

"He was."

A delicious warmth spread through her. "I told you I like it when you talk dirty to me."

Lopez bent toward her.

A man's voice interrupted. "Hey—lovebirds!"

Goddammit. Houston scowled. *Hackers.*

She threw a dark glance over her shoulder. "Yeah, neckbeard. What?"

"*She's* here."

Houston locked eyes with Lopez. *She* could only be one person in this hacker underground. The coding legend that beat Fawkes. Bald ass-kicking punk girl who moonlighted with special government forces. A clop of combat boots on the cement floor announced her arrival. Houston slapped her hand on Lopez's chest, smiled, and turned around.

"Angel."

Lightfoote had looked better. She was dirty, her clothes a mess of stains. Her eyes were sunken. She hadn't taken a razor to her head for some time, sporting a bright orange fuzz glowing like a skull cap.

Let herself go.

But there was a spark in her eye matching the aggressive stance she took.

"Sara. Francisco. Angel has returned."

A mixture of emotions ran through Houston. The arousal with Lopez simmered, but extended to Lightfoote. Tension flowed between them. She tried to suppress it, but failed.

Why did you kiss me, you crazy girl?

"Thanks for the safe house," said Lopez. "Things are getting a bit dark."

"I hate always being right. "Different kinds of darkness. Different kinds of light." She eyed them both. "Sorry to bail. That fight wasn't for me."

"The Eunuch Maker?" asked Lopez.

Lightfoote shivered. "We don't say their names. But time to face a darkness I *can* fight."

Houston took a step toward her. "Suite."

"Yes." She frowned. "Poor John and Rebecca. Trapped in a castle with a mad king."

Lopez grunted. "The king is displeased with our actions. Our INTEL 1 accounts have been seized and frozen. All the alias resources. Bank, credit cards. You name it."

"You're enemies of the people now, big guy."

"So what else is new?"

Lightfoote darted past them, her gaze on Houston. "Lucky we have options they don't know about."

Lopez stared at the women. "For now. But they've got access to everything."

"Depends on how good their code breakers are," Lightfoote mused. "We've got resources. A little time. Let's generate new ones they can't find or touch."

"Wonderful," sighed Houston. "I'm afraid this is going to be worse than Bilderberg."

Lightfoote took a backpack from her shoulders and unzipped it, removing firearms and a laptop. "Maybe it's because of what we did to Bilderberg."

Houston arched an eyebrow. "John's theory?"

"Uh-huh." Lightfoote dropped on the couch, hackers forming a mulling crowd around her at a respectful distance. "Bilderberg was in the business of social engineering. Geeks in the basement ran models, thugs pushed and pulled nations and groups along some trajectory they fancied. We blew that up." She smiled. "Literally in some cases. Now there's nothing to hold back the old forces. Racism. Nationalism. Autocracy. The country tossed out York and embraced the Beautiful Leader."

Lopez shook his head. "So trying to free people we imprisoned them? Freedom is slavery?"

"No! We freed them to make their own choices." Lightfoote spread her arms out the length of the sofa. "Behold their choices."

Houston laughed. "Maybe Bilderberg had a point, then."

"Of course they did." Lightfoote opened her computer. "Every powerful ideology does, even when fundamentally flawed."

"And now we're back to the oldest flaws," said Lopez. "With little to stop them. They control the Executive, Congress. They're already weakening the courts. The checks and balances won't last."

"Now we need the Watchman back," said Houston.

"Watchmen?" scoffed Lightfoote. "Maybe they helped destroy Anonymous and Bilderberg. But no one's left. Only John. And I know they're squeezing him."

"I wish we had Fred Simon back.".

"It was a stupid name anyway." Lightfoot's fingers clacked on the keyboard. "Watchman. So gendered." She gazed up from the screen, a blue glow on her face. "We'll call it The Watch."

Houston crossed her arms over her chest. "What good is renaming a dead thing?"

"Because we need it more than ever. Our elders are dead. Only we stand. It's up to us." Green eyes sparkled. "Now we're The Watch. Resurrected."

A longhaired teen approached from behind, holding out a box.

"Hey, Angel? Delivery."

Lightfoote stared at the package like it would explode.

"Checked it," he sputtered. "We're not stupid. It's just a flower."

Houston's blood ran cold. "What kind of flower?"

Lightfoote turned back to the monitor, ignoring them. The boy reached in and removed a purple petaled blossom. He tilted the box. There was nothing else inside.

"Sonbol," said Lopez. "Nemesis."

"Jesus." Houston reached for her Browning. "She knows we're here. How the hell?"

"Doesn't matter." Lopez grabbed his coat. "We move. *Now.*"

"Hold your horses," said Lightfoote, punctuating the command with an emphatic clack. "It's a message. Just to fuck with us. Or there'd already be bodies."

"She had the advantage," said Houston, grabbing her bag and removing the gun. "Why didn't she strike?"

"Who knows?" said Lightfoote, nodding to the screen and closing it. "Low on long distance assets? Throwing down the gauntlet? Long game? She's a bitch, but she's not all-powerful."

"Not yet," said Houston.

"Still, we *move*," said Lopez.

Lightfoote drummed her fingers on the metallic surface of the laptop, a skull ring tapping out Morse code. "Definitely. *Tonight.* And we stop trusting the security of others." She cast a frown over the downcast crowd of hackers behind her, looping the straps of the pack over her shoulders.

Houston leaned into Lopez. "On the run again."

Lightfoote walked between them, placing a hand on each of their shoulders.

"Suite. Nemesis. There's more than one war we're fighting. Ready for a road trip?"

69

HELL AND GONE

"Pat, I said don't start."

Sacker tried to focus on the shot glass, push everything else away. The tap-dancing woman faded on the yellowed glass. Vintage, from the Harlem Renaissance. Like his hat. *Great grandmother Sacker, I think I want to go back to your time.* She must've been a force of nature at Connie's Inn.

The old bartender continued, unfazed. "I'm just sayin', you come in here, talk about this girl, and leave her out there. What's the point?"

Sacker sighed. "Why do you think I come here? To talk about her and drink. I don't want to go out there and deal with her. All these years and you still don't get how it works?"

"That don't make no sense, Tyrell."

No. No it doesn't. Except of course, it did.

"It's that case," he nodded. "Yup. That killer in the papers. I see it about you. Got you in a funk." Pat paused and tapped his finger to his temple. "She's the one in the papers, right? That Chinese girl?"

Sometimes he thought Pat moonlighted as a detective himself.

"Don't start."

"Well, she's cute. Kinda small. Those small ones aren't always so full figured. Chinese ones, I mean."

"Just stop, Pat."

"Hey, I'm only sayin'. Fella likes what he likes. Not judging." He bent over and whispered. "And I see you've got something for that little Shanghai sweetie."

Sacker threw some bills on the counter and grabbed his shot glass. "I'm calling it a night." He stood. "Too much talk."

The bartender frowned. "Alright, Tyrell. Don't take it out on me. You're gonna spin your wheels until you get out and see her. Might as well yank that tooth."

❧

THIRTY MINUTES later he pulled the car to a stop at Gone's office. Trash littered the sidewalk in front of the entrance, parting gifts from the flock of reporters camping out while the story simmered.

He approached, a smile breaking at the cheap sign: *Gone Investigating, LLC.* He stepped through the front door and into the waiting room, adjusting to the low lighting.

Ah, shit.

Her fame cooled, but Gone still held a full house. Eager clients buzzed, spanning all socio-economic strata from the indigent to yuppie divorcees. A rainbow of hues and cultures, ages and genders milled about the cramped space.

Big ole slice of humanity.

He'd made a big mistake. Seeing Gracie was scary enough. No way he was going to wait out that tension here.

"Another time," he whispered.

"Tyrell!"

His breath caught. Frowning faces turned in his direction, a force field of impatience and irritation assaulting him. But it was background. His gaze centered elsewhere. Gone stood in the doorway of her office, a client walking out. She beamed.

"Come in!" Her voice rose in pitch. "Please!"

An old man held up a piece of paper. "Hey! *I'm* next!"

Gone looked over. "Yes, after Detective Sacker. He's the one who brought me on the Eunuch Maker case." Eyes stared again. "I need to speak with him." She waved him in.

No choice now.

Maybe he didn't mind.

He navigated the furniture and the standing-room-only clients demanding access, avoiding eye contact with the simmering crowd. Gone closed the door behind him as he entered.

"You've been avoiding me!"

That pout. Always returning. Whatever she was doing, whatever mood or speech, her face gravitated to it. Not exactly bratty. Not sad. *Thoughtful.* Annoyed. Like the chaotic universe irritated her, challenged her to solve its mysteries.

"You get right to the point."

"I'm not good with games," she said, ambling to her desk.

He winced. Whatever was wrong, it was worse. She favored that weak side, her gait tilted and slower. She held a cane or crutch in her hand, stabilizing the wobble. Gone managed to circumscribe the desk and dropped into her chair, winded.

"Holstered gun next to you?" Sacker raised his eyebrows, staring beside her.

"Unloaded. For show. You'd be amazed how it gives a tiny woman instant respect."

"No games, huh?" He smirked, sitting across from her. The orientation caused flashbacks to the fall when they'd first peered across the desk at each other, the day she'd picked his life apart with her laser brain.

"I can use it, don't you worry," she said, tilting her chin down. "I can break it down, even. Monthly practice at the range." Her smiled faded. "So, Tyrell. Why are you here? Not to employ my investigative services again."

"You probably charge too much now. Your crazy public relations stunt paid off."

"Yeah, plan Z worked. Didn't realize I'd have to solve the Case of the Armageddon Virus to do it." Her eyes wouldn't leave his.

Damn this is hard.

Sacker cleared his throat. "I thought I ought to say goodbye at least."

"Goodbye?" One eyebrow arched. Her voiced dropped. "Why goodbye?"

"Well, my own investigating days are at an end, I'm afraid. Captain Ladner and the good people at the NYPD have shown me the door. Nice little goodie bag on the way out so I don't make a stink. But out the door for sure. I'll never work in law enforcement again."

"Okay. So?"

He leaned away from her. "*So?* Well, damn, Gracie, that's kinda a bullshit mid-life transition." He gaped at her poker face. "So, I guess it's goodbye. Detective work is done."

"Doesn't follow."

A headache stirred. "Doesn't follow? Gracie, *I'm done*. Blacklisted. The detective who made a mockery of his precinct. In front of the nation. Wouldn't matter if I cured cancer. That shit just doesn't fly."

Got to be a guilt thing.

"Look, none of this is on you. Okay? I knew the risks. I took them. Now we move on. We did good, yeah? Something positive we can take from—"

"Of course it's on me."

"No, that's wrong. There's—"

"Still doesn't follow."

Sacker sighed. Her eyes bored into his.

Get out of my soul, woman!

"One thing I need to know, Gracie."

She edged forward. He looked away.

"The day you took my blood. It wasn't for experimental controls like you said, was it?"

"No."

Stop looking at me!

"So, that's how you knew for sure," he exhaled. "That I was immune."

"Tyrell, I'm sorry, but I—I was worried. About what might happen."

Don't you fucking tear up, Tyrell. "Yeah, I see now. But it's no good."

His vision blurred. *Hopeless.* He jumped from his seat and grabbed his Bailey Ice Topper and coat, turning away from her.

"Tyrell, wait!"

He pulled the handle and swung the door open, ignoring her cry and pushing into the crowd of surprised faces. Gone struggle behind him, the cane clacking, the steps heavy and awkward.

"Tyrell!"

The tone sent a shiver through him. He stopped, ashamed. Forcing her to labor behind, cry out in front of a public crowd. But he still couldn't face her.

"Gracie, *please*," he said, his back to her. "This just makes it harder."

"You don't need to go."

Don't need to go? He heard her clumsy motion approaching. *Stop!*

"Yes, I do. It's over."

"No. Maybe you can't work for law enforcement. But you can still *solve crimes*. You don't have to stop being a detective!"

The cane rested from its noisy ticks. Sacker sensed her behind him. Still he didn't turn.

"How, Gracie?"

Her hand rested on his arm.

"Work for me."

"What would the people of the earth be without woman? They would be scarce, sir, almighty scarce."

— MARK TWAIN

"STEBBINS IS THE MASTER OF THE
THINKING READER'S TECHNO-THRILLER."
—Internet Review of Books

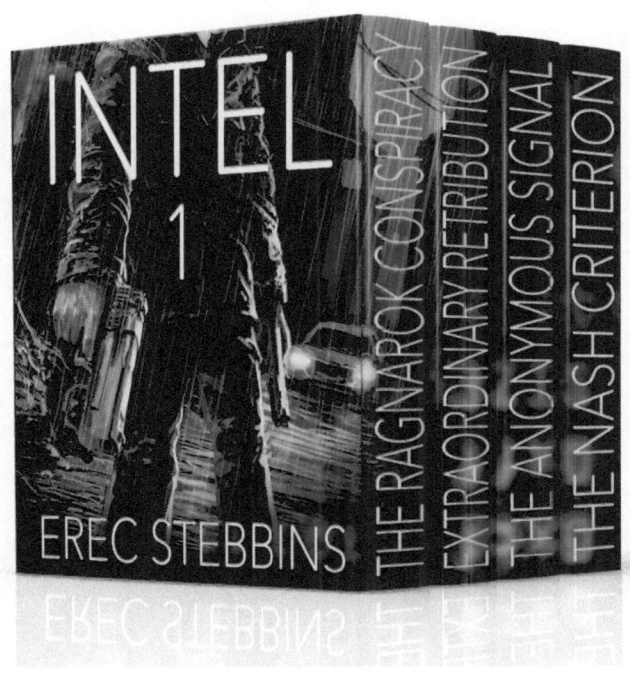

Four Action Packed Political Thrillers. Three
End of the World Scenarios. Two Unusual Love
Stories. One Secretive Intelligence Branch.

The *Intel 1* Global Thrillers

"A MONSTER NEW TALENT IN THE
THRILLER GENRE."
—Allan Leverone,
author of *Final Vector*

ABOUT THE AUTHOR

Erec Stebbins is a biomedical researcher who writes thrillers, science fiction, mysteries, and more.

He was born in the Midwest. His mother worked as a clinical psychologist, and his father was a professor of Romance languages at the University of Nebraska in Lincoln. In fact, his father's specialty, old Romance languages and their literature, is the source of the strange spelling of his middle name: "Erec." It is an Old French spelling, taken from an Arthurian romance by Chrétien de Troyes written around 1170: *Érec et Énide*.

He has pursued diverse interests over the course of his life, including science, music, drama, and writing. His academic path focused on science, and he received a degree in physics from Oberlin College in 1992, and a PhD in biochemistry from Cornell University in 1999. He completed postdoctoral studies at Yale University. He has worked for several decades studying the atomic structure of biological macromolecules involved in disease.

For more information:
www.erecstebbinsbooks.com
erecstebbinsbooks@gmail.com

DAUGHTER OF TIME

READER WRITER MAKER

A TIMELESS SCI-FI TRILOGY
BY EREC STEBBINS

From the future, a final plea. Out of the past, a last hope.

READER (Daughter of Time, Book 1): A young girl, born to die in freakish disregard. A doomed world, enslaved to forces unseen. A final hope beyond imagining. Become a Reader, because in the end, the most unbelievable step in the adventure - *will be your own.*

"Unique and altogether profound, reminiscent of Bradbury"
—San Francisco Book Reviews

From hatred, Love. From many, One.

WRITER (Daughter of Time, Book 2): A love story and sci-fi epic about the beautiful and terrible destiny of profoundly star-crossed lovers with a galaxy's fate in their hands.

*"A work of literary fiction that transcends its genre.
Read this novel. Immediately."* -Portland Book Review

Until all is lost, nothing is found.

MAKER (Daughter of Time, Book 3): The final element of a unique trilogy. A story in which the one that was lost will be found. Where the thief will guide against chaos and time. Where all that was held dear will perish. And in that final and utter destruction - there will be a *Creation.*

"Exploratory fiction at its most powerful and intelligent."
—ForeWord Reviews

www.ingramcontent.com/pod-product-compliance
Lightning Source LLC
Chambersburg PA
CBHW020354260626
47156CB00007B/2097